SAINT MATTHEW

IN

APPALACHIA

And Other Stories

JOSEPH MAIOLO

Overcoat **Books**

DULUTH, MINNESOTA

Overcoat Books
An imprint of X-Communication
118 Chester Parkway
Duluth, Minnesota 55805
218-310-6541

St. Matthew in appalachia and other stories

Author photo by Diana Phillips.

Cover and back cover photographs courtesy of Paul "Chicago" Kilgore.

Cover and interior design and layout by Tony Dierckins.

First Edition, 2012

12 13 14 15 16 • 5 4 3 2 1

Library of Congress Control Number: 2012953151

Softcover ISBN: 978-1-887317-95-5
Hardcvoer ISBN: 978-1-887317-96-2

Printed in the U.S.A.

For My Children,
Joshua Joseph, Ann Elise, Lotti Sun:
Triple Love from, and for,
Dad

∼

Also by Joseph Maiolo and Overcoat Books:

My Turkish Missile Crisis (a memoir)

Boy • *Youth* • *Man* (a triptych of novellas)

Three Frays from Mallorca and Four Stories

ACKNOWLEDGMENTS

"Saint Matthew in Appalachia" first appeared in *Great River Review*, Issue 57, Fall/Winter 2012.

"Playing Light," winner of a PEN/Syndicated Fiction Award, first appeared under the title "Flush" in a slightly different form in *The Texas Review*, Volume 5, Numbers 1 & 2, Spring/Summer 1984.

"Covering Home," winner of a PEN/Syndicated Fiction Award, first appeared in a slightly different form in *Ploughshares*, Volume 13, Numbers 2 & 3, 1987.

"For Some Desperate Glory," first appeared under the title "A Wry Sleep of Boys" in *The Sewanee Review*, issue 96, volume 4, 1988.

"The Tag Match" first appeared in a different form in *Ploughshares*, Volume 4, Number 4, 1978.

"Of the Cloth" first appeared in a substantially different form under the title "Brother, Father," in *The Greensboro Review*, Number 11, Winter 1972.

"Cumberland Spring," winner of a PEN/Syndicated Fiction Award, first appeared in a slightly different form in *Ploughshares*, Volume 9, Numbers 2 & 3, 1983.

"When Cassie Freemont Walked By" first appeared in a substantially different form in *New Virginia Review*, Volume 6, 1988.

"Death of an Elder" first appeared in *Great River Review*, Volume 2, Number 1, 1979.

"The Legend of the Happy Swimming Pool" first appeared in *The Greensboro Review*, Number 18, Spring 1975.

CONTENTS

SAINT MATTHEW
IN APPALACHIA

I MISS LISTENING TO THE RADIO WHEN THE PRESIDENT, whose name sounded like roses and velvet, spoke to us. He made me feel less afraid, and now it's pretty much the way he said it would be. If I am to believe it, the war is over, and I am sitting with Grandmother at the upstairs window in the house over the store on main street. We're watching the cars go by. Here comes a horse pulling a buckboard. I bet he'd be something on a racetrack.

In a while, we move from the window into our two easy chairs in the sitting area up front. Statues of the Holy Family stand on a table in the corner. Beside them are three candles Grandmother lights on special occasions, and when she wants to remember or help someone. She is teaching me how to crochet. I have hooked together a string of loops, a right puny buildup compared to the enormous lace bedspread covering the bed in the open room behind us, and I say so.

"The littl-a boords build-a their nest one twig-a at a time."

"Must take 'em forever," I say.

"*Pazienza.*"

I guess I don't have her patience, or that of the little birds. Even if I get to be pretty good at the finger moves with the needles, how can I take something so simple and make the grand patterns of her bedspreads and shawls? "Maybe I'll make a handkerchief," I say with a smile.

She laughs with me, then gets up and goes off through the long hall. Years back, she kept boarders up here, coal miners and railroad men, in three rooms off the hallway with numbers on the doors. The numbers are still on the doors, but the rooms are not rented. She sleeps in number 3. I have number 2.

After a while I go through the main hallway past the couch by the coal stove, through the kitchen and into the constricted back hall and its dark recesses to where it terminates at a small toilet-and-tub room, a sort of crossroads branching into what she calls the "apart-a-ments": a two-room to the left, a three-room to the right, small rooms in line, flower-linoleumed floors I rolled marbles down when nobody lived in them, and each with its own back entrance. She'd had me paint them with ten gallons of peach-colored paint she got on close-out at the hardware store. We had a gallon and a half left over, so she said to keep going, use it up on the bathroom ceiling, walls, floor, seat, and tub (outside only). It looks pretty good. We share this sinkless bathroom with whoever is living in the apartments. The tub serves for hand-washing.

I've never run into anyone back here, but I've heard sounds from time to time. Now, as I am leaving, I catch sight of the woman who lives in the two-room. Her door is cracked open, and she is sitting at the table in the small kitchen under a low-watt bulb, her lower lip pooched with snuff. Grandmother is talking to her in low tones, and every now and then the woman lifts a spotted rag to her mouth.

I go to the window up front and watch the cars and look at the mountains.

After a while I hear "*Poverella*. Poor thing," and turn to see Grandmother, wiping her eyes and lighting a candle at her shrine. She makes the Sign of the Cross, then tells me a story about the rich man who had everything he wanted except freedom from his fear of lightning. He bought all the land for miles around and built a fortress out of steel on a mountaintop. By that time, I can guess what happened to him. And it did.

In a week, Grandmother is upset with the woman. I can tell because when she comes back from visiting her she doesn't cry while she lights the candles. I understand that the woman is not able to pay her rent, but it can't be that because Grandmother keeps taking hot soup and clean clothes to her.

Time, being the slowpoke it is, creeps by; and in what seems like a month but is probably only another week, when I am in the little room at the crossroads, I hear men with big voices. They have come in the back way, and Grandmother is answering their questions, but none too pleasantly.

"I no know *niente*, nothing, about what you find-a up there. She's-a need-a *dottore*, doctor."

With my jackknife I scrape a peep hole in the painted-over window that once must have looked out on the hill bank before the apartments were added. They're all making so much noise, they can't hear my scraping.

Grandmother has an arm around the woman, bathing her face with a cloth. "Lucia," she says, "why noncha call-a me?"

One of the policemen goes to stand before Grandmother and the woman. "Now, Miz Francesca, we ain't got no quarrel with you." He looks at the woman, whose face I cannot see. "Lucy Stidham, we're going to have to take you now."

"You no take-a her. You getta ambulance."

I do not hear any more about Lucy Stidham, but I'm pretty sure that Grandmother visits her in the hospital, or jail. It's not something I can ask her about the way I can crocheting and people back in her village in the Sila Mountains of Italy. She often talks about them, so vividly they seem at times to be sitting at the kitchen table with us. My favorite villager is the little boy who sang the first words he ever spoke, then grew into a young man singing throughout the streets at Christmastime. When he was an old man, he was helped the rest of the way to the top of the mountain, where he sang to the entire village on Christmas Eve.

The final days of August, slow and lazy, seem bunched together into one hot, delicious little era. The radio's music is not so interrupted anymore. I cannot credit myself with a single good deed all summer, yet each day, as I go to Saint Veronica's, I scan the playground across the street for a boy to shoot marbles with. My only Bible-school classmate's daddy won't let him play before or after classes.

Today, Sister Rose Fabian, as always crisp and clean in her black habit, her face framed in white and with a blazing smile of teeth I see even when her mouth is closed, greets me as if this day, one of a continuum of days, holds the same promise as always, that no day is to be discounted as an opportunity for doing good and serving our Lord. Then she catches me looking out the window.

"Is it playin' you have your mind on already and not even the first page of Saint Matthew turned to?"

My inner voice responds: It is, Sister. The voice she hears merely clears its throat.

We have been reading and talking about the Sermon on the Mount; and, while I am curious about the difference between Mount and Mountain, it goes unquestioned as well by the boy in there with me. Everybody but Sister Rose Fabian calls him Jimbo. We are the only Catholic boys our age in town, and not a single girl, although he has a big sister who comes to Mass on Sundays, a beauty who lights up the little log church like the big paschal candle at Eastertime.

We turn to the pages printed in red letters.

"What's 'meek'?" Jimbo wants to know.

"Perhaps your classmate can tell us, James."

"Meek?" I say. "Meek? Whatever it is must be pretty tough to take over the whole world."

" 'Tis the opposite, boys. Gentle, it's meanin', and don't let's forget it. Not only that, but it says 'possess' not 'take over.' "

During the rest of the lesson, Jimbo and I go back and forth to the dictionary trying to find out the meaning of so many of the words Jesus used that day, but we can't really understand what he was trying to tell the people gathered around him so long ago, let alone us now. So much of what he said seems to be the reverse of the way things really are.

I say this, and Jimbo says he agrees.

Sister Rose Fabian tells us to read all of the Sermon at home, and to come back tomorrow prepared to talk about it.

➤ ➤ ➤

When regular school starts, the teacher, a portly woman with eyeglasses hanging around her neck and a manner like a mother in the movies, asks if anyone wants to be excused when the Our Father is said each morning, only she calls it "The Lord's Prayer." I tell her that we don't say "for thine is the kingdom..." and all that, so she lets me leave the room after the Pledge and sit in the auditorium until they are finished.

This three-story brick school building is all creaky wood inside and with a condemned spiral-chute fire escape we can't even practice going down. I wonder what we'll do if it catches fire up here and I am in one of the two little dressing rooms on either side of the stage where we're having classes. About that time, Saint Veronica's heaves into view through the slow-changing oaks and maples, and I figure that, as a Catholic, I might have a hedge against fires. Add Grandmother's mystic powers, and I might be safe from most calamities.

But I feel ashamed of myself thinking it. Before the Servants of the Mother of God came from Ireland, coal miners with black lung or mangled in cave-ins gasped in secular seclusion; now, some are in their final moments touched, smiled upon, and spoken to by the ladies in white, in bedside voices like Sister Rose Fabian's, a musical brogue trillin' r's and even droppin' g's, the way the rest of us do.

And then there is Father Bergson.

He has come bearing the simplest gifts. He is from Saint Paul, not the little coal town by that name twenty-four miles away, but the one up north, in the middle of the country. He says the long i funny and the short e right, even when it comes between two hard consonants in a three-letter word, like p-e-n. And his long o seems to come from out of a cave, it is so hollow-sounding. Vested for Mass, Father Bergson moves to the door in his usual stoop. He is a large man, bent as if to conceal his full presence—that is, a humble man. It is as if he is a moving tree, opening his branches for creatures to get beneath his shelter.

When at Benediction I stand below him in my cassock and surplice, holding the incense bowl like a small genie lamp, he takes the tiny brass spoon and sprinkles the exotic dust onto the smoldering charcoal in the thurible, then leads the singing of "Tantum Ergo," swirls of smoke playing around him as he swings the censer up at the tabernacle. I am transported by the sweet and holy smell.

Our southwest Virginia version of Holy Mother Church is, like the Trinity itself, many in one: Mother = Fathers + Brothers + Sisters. They have come from Minnesota and County Cork, from Galway and even Tipperary—a long way, I've always heard—to serve and save us. I am a parishioner in a home mission; I am also one of its missionaries, so to speak, for I sometimes assist Father when he says Mass and distributes the sacraments to people in isolated cabins in the mountains. I have never felt particularly close to the mountain people; we have too few things in common. Most of them have their own brand of religion, and some of it that I've seen at close range—Holy Rollers and Snake Handlers and speaking in tongues—I don't care for, much. That some of them ever became Catholic in the first place, while baffling, makes me proud.

On the Saturdays between Halloween and Thanksgiving I go with Father Bergson to say Mass for the Christmas Season at several cabins, finishing with the Daltons'. After we leave the main road and drive over a dirt switchback with big rocks sticking up out of it, we stop at a path and walk to the shack, all by itself on the low ridge of a hollow so bounded the sun might shine only a couple of hours a day upon it. Father sets down the black case and raps strong knuckles lightly on the door of gray spaced boards with words and pictures between them.

"Hit's the father, all right." The high, flat, whiny voice seems to be the cabin's itself, or a voice singing about it.

Until the door opens onto a little woman who looks like a little man. Her dress is a tan sack with arm and neck holes and writing on it. She is wearing high, black boots and a once-white bonnet. Snuff fills her lower lip.

"Hello, Mrs. Dalton."

"You can call me Minie, Father Bergum, like the Corporal does."

The Corporal is the man I know, secretly, as Granddaddy Scarecrow. He's been lying in the bed over there, I've heard, for seven years, probably in the same woman's nightgown he's wearing now. The stove is stoked up red, its flat top stacked with crusted pots, its potbelly coated with food magma. The walls of the cabin are papered over with layers of newspapers and magazine covers. A musket is propped in the corner by the bed beside a can serving, futilely, as a spittoon.

Making a quick Sign of the Cross, Father gives the old couple his blessing; then, like a doctor making a house call (I could be his nurse), he unlatches the black case and removes the stole, which he kisses and, praying to himself, puts around his neck. Onto the rim of the golden ciborium containing the Hosts he places the purificator and paten and completes the assembly, like a little altar of its own hidden away beneath the veil.

While Mrs. Dalton lights a candle stub, her mouth moves as if she is chewing a contemplative cud, Granddaddy Scarecrow wheezes from the uncovered pillow, and the stove belches out a cinder. Chilly as it is outside, I'm glad I don't have to wear a cassock in this pressure cooker. Father, his upper lip sweat-beaded, says the fastest Low Mass I've ever served, muttering the Latin so rapidly I can't hear the words I know so well. I can't imagine what the two stunned faces looking on might make of it even when it's slow, let alone now.

At Communion, as I approach the Corporal, the close-up of his face reveals little broken blue and red tributaries dotting the ancient skin stretched over high cheek bones, dark fissures in his chin carved by rivulets of tobacco juice. As I hold the paten under the whiskers, the mouth opens, showing a single yellow stump from out of otherwise denuded gums. The hundred-years-old tongue comes out, and Father places the consecrated Host, its circular edge turning brown before it is closed over.

> , , ,

And then it is a Saturday in December and cold, but no snow yet, so I skip down the steps and head for the 6' x 6' corner of rough earth where I hang around on my haunches like a bullfrog waiting to snare a boy to shoot marbles with. I've been playing at school all week, but I can't get enough of them, and I'm tired of playing against myself on the floor. As I crouch down, all set to send my steeley taw between an aggie and a cat's-eye, old lady Whitaker, in her droopy black dress and hat, her head shaking, her thin lips pressed into an evil smile, comes cutting the corner short and bumps me with her shopping bag, what everybody knows she uses to carry the heads she's always prowling for. I have no place to go, and so I close my eyes, giving my throat to her blade.

"Miss-a Whittaka, *veni qua* (come here). I give-a you somma pooty scarf-a." Grandmother puts her arm around the slumping shoulders, and carries the shopping bag for her!

Stand on that corner long enough and here comes Pegleg Collins, stumping for trouble; Puny Herndon, meanest little man in town; and poor old Yi-Yi, the man who can say only what he is called. They won't go up against Grandmother, except in arm-wrestling. Her reputation gives me an edge with the rough characters. But she doesn't appear tough with her lady-like posture, her flowered house-dresses tight at her corsetted waist, her shiny high heels and soft, gravelly voice.

She holds a continuous rummage sale in the store when it is empty, which it mostly is: dresses and shoes, scarves and towels, doodads for women and play-pretties for children.

In a few days the snow comes, not white floating flakes but hard little pellets that bounce when they hit. A raggedy woman comes in the store wearing holey shoes stuffed with paper. Grandmother gives her a pair of woolen socks and men's work shoes. She sees two children outside and takes some change out of her apron pocket and places it in the hand of the woman who seems to be standing there in a trance.

"You getta somethin' hot to eat for the littl-a keeds." She touches the woman's arm and leads her to the children, taking their faces in her large, swarthy hands as, astonished, they look up at her. It is clear that they have not before been so delicately touched.

A boy walks by, and when Grandmother tries to go to him he hurries away, but keeps his gaze on her as if something in her face holds him. Tears from his glistening eyes run into the streams flowing from his nose, somehow making his black face seem like a mask. Her own eyes are shining, but they never spill. She seems to know that tears at such a time might be taken as pity.

She keeps in touch, through a village scribe or a literate niece, with those she left in her village when she was nineteen. Having been taken out of school to work at an early age, she did not learn to read and write very well, but somehow has been teaching herself Calabrese through a process that combines a scrutiny of the Italian words and their English translation on the opposite pages of the Bible she has had Father Bergson order for her. As she somehow progresses to reading and writing cursive characters of an angled sameness, it all becomes mixed with the way we say English words around here.

She sews up clothes and dried foods in bed sheets to be sent to her younger brother in the old country. He was a soldier in the First War. He will open the bundles and distribute what is in them to relatives and a few others in the village. She tells me this like a story complete with characters, as if she is assigning the items to those she selects, complete with a little story about each one. She has me print the name and address on the sheet in black ink, a long vowel-laden name like my own, and an address that has become as familiar to me as the Latin Brother Charles drilled me in last summer until I could say the responses without looking at the card. I wonder if he still lives on goat's milk in a lean-to in the woods.

And then I am trudging up the street to the post office with the bundle slung over my shoulder and two two-dollar bills in my pocket. If any school kids see me, they will probably make fun of me for mailing off our laundry. But I don't usually see too many kids down at our end of town, and the post office is just two blocks away; besides, carrying the bundle makes me feel like a sailor on furlough.

Three weeks before Christmas, Saro, a dark, heavyset woman who sometimes comes from across the railroad tracks to do work for Grandmother, arrives at the top of the stairs and stands bent over and panting until we have to help her to the couch by the stove. She never says anything to me, and only responds to Grandmother with words I can't make out. She holds her fingers over her mouth when she does say anything, so I doubt that Grandmother understands her fully. And Saro can't know what Grandmother is saying, because Grandmother talks to her in Appalachian-Calabrese half the time, which even I can't always make sense out of. Maybe Grandmother wants the place to look good in case somebody comes to visit, but it's more likely that she hires Saro so she can pay her something in time for Christmas. Because all Saro does the first hour is to move to the kitchen table and eat what Grandmother fixes for her, before she says through her fingers, "I's feelin' mighty pore," and I can certainly make out those words. They mean that I'll still be mopping the hall and kitchen, and since she can barely walk up the steps, how can she scrub them?

What it comes down to is, instead of getting any help, which I consider relief for me, Grandmother puts Saro in the two-room apartment, gets her tucked up in bed, and puts me in charge of keeping a fire in the stove and coal in the bucket. Some relief. At least I don't have to wait on her. Grandmother's carrying bread and soup and this and that to her all day. But then, that takes time away from what Grandmother can do for us, and it is getting near to Christmas.

But there's no let-up.

The next night a knock sounds below, and the door opens. Grandmother goes to the top of the stairs. "*Chi nethi?* Who is it?"

"You have a room to let?" The voice is cracked, as if it has come from a great distance and has had trouble getting here.

"*Si.*" She gestures for him to come upstairs.

And so begins the first of the clumpings, a slow progression upward by twos, until, his hat in his hand, a man stands tall and dark-suited at the top, his feet a startling marvel of distortion. Grandmother leads him into the back hallway, each of his inwardly turned feet passing over the other with measured care. I watch him out of sight, then fool around at the dressing table across from the coal stove on the far side of number 3's door so I can keep watching till he comes back.

After a while, talking easily about the terms of rental, they emerge from the back hall's doorway. Since he cannot negotiate his way up and down the hill the back way to the apartment, he will be allowed to use the front-street entrance. His face is stretched with that thin, shiny skin so many old people have, soft lips protruding, cheeks blotched red, as if they have been lightly rouged.

He is heading for the top of the stairs, and there is a moment when I think he might fall. As he grasps the railing, Grandmother sends me down to get what he has left inside the door: a cigar box which feels light enough to be empty, except that I hear a muffled jingle as I take it up to him.

His name is Thomas Maynard. Since Saro has said that she's not up to moving, he has had to take the three-room apartment. When I come home from school the next day, I pass by him sitting in his suit, dangerously on a stool by the Smokehouse. He's holding the cigar box, open, on his lap. I make sure that he sees that I don't look in it.

"Hello, Mister Maynard."

"Son," he says, with a short nod.

I don't know if he knows me or not.

I do know that he's too big for that stool and that, later on, in his dark serge suit with a vest, he will come clumping through the main hall and our bright kitchen on his way into the back hallway. Carrying the cigar box, though it complicates his passage considerably, he always removes his hat indoors.

He comes and goes at odd times, even at night while I'm lying in number 2. When I hear the door open, I wait for the first of the pairings, then continue counting the fifty-two clumps.

Grandmother introduces him to food he has never tasted: spaghetti, frijoles, fried eggplant. What he says he loves best is the hot peppers fried in olive oil and tucked into a big hunk of fresh, hot bread. So she bakes an extra loaf for him on baking days.

A week before Christmas, I am dragging a pine tree-bush up the stairs, when Grandmother takes it from me and hands me a telegram. *"Anda, go. Find-a Signore Thomaso. Give-a heem."*

I find him a block up from his usual place and hand him the yellow envelope. While he opens it, I pretend not to but I look inside the cigar box to see several new pencils and a few nickels and dimes. As he reads the message, his face turns a shade sadder than it always is, and he rises with some effort, holding the box and picking up the stool.

"Can I take that someplace for you, Mister Maynard?"

"That'd be a help, son."

And so we begin our only walk together. At the Smokehouse he asks me to take the stool in to the owner.

Later, he is holding the cigar box and his hat at the top of the stairs. His sister has died over in Tennessee, and he must leave. "I'll have to stay over there," he tells Grandmother. "I thank you for your kindness, and I regret that I haven't been able to pay you. Soon as I get on my feet—."

Everything goes quiet. I cannot even hear the cars. Then I see in a blur that Grandmother has put her hand on his shoulder, and I know what her words are, even though I don't hear them.

That night, we decorate what we call the tree. It is not much more than a few fir branches grown out of a skinny trunk, and I'm not happy with it, but it's all I could find up on the hill that I could handle. It doesn't seem to bother Grandmother. She's hanging tin-foil icicles and placing cotton swabs carefully, but after a while we just fling them wherever we want to. She tries placing the new angel's hair delicately but loses patience and wraps the sparse boughs like a spider's catch. Then she stokes up the stove, I put chestnuts and tangerine peelings on top of it, and we sit on the couch. I am ready for the next part of the story she has been telling me for weeks about a rich prince who goes looking for the woman named by the title of the story "The Beauty of the World." But since it's almost Christmas, she tells me one instead about women who washed the feet of Jesus and dried them with their hair.

When it ends, I ask her to tell me a real story, but she impresses upon me that there was a time when people did such things, even for strangers. She then relates a couple of sad stories about a saint and some beggar in her home village, and before I know it I am washing her coarse and bony feet. But when I pull up my pantslegs to have her wash mine, she tells me that children did not take part in the washings.

"But I just did," I say, making my voice sound hurt and pitiable.

She tells me it was for practice, that now I'll be ready to carry on the tradition when I get older. But it comes to me that if Mister Maynard comes back, Grandmother might call on me to repeat such humiliating humility for him, and the spirit leaves me faster than it descended.

, , ,

Christmas Eve. Jimbo and I are in the church sacristy, putting on our black cassocks and white, lacy surplices, preparing to serve midnight Mass. Jimbo finishes first and gets to light the altar candles. I look out to see the dozen or so rows of oaken pews with a central aisle already full and with people ascending the stairs to the choir loft. When I turn back, Father Bergson comes in in his long black robe and ties the amice onto his shoulders, gathers the alb and places the opening on his head, inserts his arms, and lets it drape him. Adding the remaining odd garments, he stands with his hands beneath the ornate chasuble.

"Ah—"

I look up at him. As always, after he speaks my name with the o, a softly spoken request follows.

"Would you mind going to see if there are still people out front?"

I exit the outside sacristy door and go in my frilly vestments through the gravel pathway to the front of the church, where I come upon a small crowd of Protestants numbering even into the Baptists, and I wonder briefly what attracts them on this night, lined up to enter a church not large enough to contain them all. I know what has attracted me to theirs: All the boys and girls go there. In that brief encounter in the moonlight, with Latin carols coming from inside, I stand before the parents of my non-Catholic classmates and trace the sweet and haunting faces of their daughters reflected in their own.

Once on the altar with Jimbo and Father Bergson, I take up my tasks, go through the moves I have perfected, and say the Latin well. As Father reads the long Christmas story, the sisters bright with belief in the front pews, I sit in one of the altar chairs, fixed on the dancing candle flames in little red and green glasses at the side altar. One of them is guttering, and suddenly goes dark, its smoky wick sending curls of soot to the statue of Mary behind it. It must have been lighted by someone who came much earlier than the others.

When Mass is ended, and after Jimbo and I have kneeled in the sacristy to receive father's blessing, I start the walk home. There has been a small accumulation of snow, and it is cold enough for more. I pull the collar of my mackinaw up over my ears and push my hands deep into the pockets. The last of the cars leaving Saint Veronica's are moving out of sight. The town is ringed with mountains I cannot see but know are there because clusters of stars end where the sky stops in a jagged line all around. The back way home is soon too dark, so I cut over to main street. I have five straight, empty blocks ahead of me.

But something has been troubling me all week, and by the time I get to the third block, where Mister Maynard was sitting when I took the telegram to him, I know what it is. When I spoke up and offered to take the stool for him, and when he said, "That'd be a help," then called me "son" for the second time, I carried it to the Smokehouse while I walked beside him, pretty much making sure everybody saw what I was doing, I can now see, and, without meaning to, calling attention to his affliction. I'd only meant for us to keep each other company till we got home. I knew what news telegrams had brought during the war.

Now it comes to me that it was more than that. When we were studying the Sermon on the Mount at the end of summer and Sister Rose Fabian told us to read all of it at home and come prepared next time, and I did, I wondered what Jesus meant in chapter five when he said to shine your good works before men, but then in chapter six "not to do your good before men, in order to be seen by them." It bothered me some, but not enough to ask questions. That was the last class, and as soon as it was over I was going to shoot marbles with Jimbo, whose father had said he could play when Bible school was over for good.

What bothers me even more, now, is that, with the Christmas story so fresh in my head, and it 1,945 years since what Father Bergson called "the beautiful promise," I can't imagine anybody meeker than Mister Maynard, or Lucy Stidham, or poor old Saro, and so many of the people I see all the time and who come to Grandmother's store for something to wear, or some money for something to eat. It bothers me even more because, after I read the Sermon, I flipped ahead to The Last Judgment. (I couldn't resist a title like that.) But I don't know. Helping people who are hungry and thirsty or without clothes or in jail—why do so many of them need what so many others already have in the first place?

I thought about it some then, but I forgot about it until now, mainly, I suppose, because I pretty much eat and drink when I need to and I have enough to wear. But mainly I have Grandmother, who cooks what I like, shows me things and tell me stories, and who will come to visit me, I know, if I ever get put in jail.

By the time I arrive at the bottom of the stairs, my head is crammed with things I probably can't ever understand, and so I close the door with my backside and in the dark begin to make my way to the top. *Clump.* My first step hits the facing, and I push my other foot beside it deliberately. *Clump.* Onto the next stair step, I place each foot, turned inward as far as I can against the pain, and I begin again to move upward in clumping pairs. But my feet, not even fully turned, together on a stair step at the same time, do not fit easily. How then his big high-top shoes with rounded toes pointed directly at opposite walls? He could not have managed to go foot over foot, each onto a separate step; besides, I counted fifty-two clumps every time, not twenty-six. He must have had to spread his legs to get both feet on a step at the same time. I make the next step with my legs stretched outward, my feet turned inward, when my knees go weak and I can stand the pain no longer. I grab at each wall and push to keep from falling backward...but his hands were always carrying the box and his hat, *and I can see him going up the metal steps of the bus that would take him to his dead sister in Tennessee. Did he take his hat off? Did he reach inside the cigar box and find enough money to pay his fare?* If I can push off the wall and fall forward, catch myself in time to keep from hitting my face, then pull up to release my feet, I can maybe keep from toppling backward or breaking my ankles.

That's when it comes to me that time might not always creep by but pick up speed, and that the promise of the days that Sister Rose Fabian has cautioned me against wasting might come to trouble me more than contradictions in the Bible. Maybe time will put a shake to my head, or a stutter to my words; maybe time will even turn my feet. And I am shamed that I have tried to walk in such a way. It takes a certain man to reach the top of stairs with a burden, his hat in his hand, and then to make his way on through to small, back rooms for the night.

I have only to get out of this predicament I've put myself in, and in the morning Grandmother will wake me when she comes from early Mass, and we will see what the packages given by relatives contain.

PLAYING LIGHT

ONE DAY, WHEN HE WAS TEN YEARS OLD, Adam Ramey stood before his mother as she presented a jelly jar of change to him like a covenant, telling him to go to the light company and pay "Mister Honeycutt, and nobody else!"—and get a receipt with his name on it.

They both knew that she was testing him.

"Okay, Maw," he said, reaching out, grinning. "Okay," looking at her tight, line-thin mouth. And he gently tugged the jar the last short distance from her.

Adam's sister Nellie scrubbed at the washtub, head down, assaulting her father's shirt, salt-spotted now with the sweat of their older brother Jedediah, the new man of the house, who had been sleeping since he came home that morning from the midnight shift. Two weeks before, the father had been buried in the latest cave-in of the Bethel Mines, so complete a one, there was no digging for survivors.

Outside, Adam shook the jar like bells. As soon as he was clear of the house, he set it down, undid the brass-plated button of his overalls bib, and took out the makings for a cigarette. He found a wooden match in his good pants pocket and flicked it with his thumb nail. The paper almost burned up, but it worked. He picked up the jar and went on.

Turning the corner, he saw the magical sign: Pod's Pool. He peered through the fly-specked window, unscrewed the jar lid, and emptied the coins into his pocket. Then he set the jar against the wall and walked in.

Bowed black men sat in old movie seats. Blackened white men rubbed blue cubes of chalk onto the tips of the sticks they held, like spears, and shook from leather cups little numbered pills. Until that day he had been interruption; now there was deference, some nodding slightly, others stepping aside as they held their cigarettes and took the occasion to look down to flick their ashes.

He approached the racker of balls and asked about the action. One of the men standing nearby said to the racker, "It's okay, Trig. I'll take him back. It's the Ramey boy."

Trig rolled his eyes at the volunteer, but said nothing.

The man who wanted to be escort spat a glob of brown at the flared cup on the floor, and missed, though hitting had been done to the limit. Then he took the boy to the back room and stood gawking at the men at the round table there until the important one, without raising his head, turned his eyes upon the intrusion.

"Got you a visitor, Pod."

To which the only one in a suit and tie, whose head seemed screwed into a neck hole, looked lazily up again, this time letting his head come up with his eyes, and said, "What you doing here?"

"Hit's the Ramey—"

"I can see who the hell it is. Now you get on back."

The escort sidled out as the boy set his face to resolve, to pleading and more. He flashed his good smile and said, "I come to play," then set his brow beneath his horselike bangs.

His little show caused nothing much except that odd deference he was learning fast to play upon. Onto the thick lips of the one called Pod, the one who counted, the barest trace of a grin broke. "Well, sit," he said, looking away.

Lucky for the boy, it was nickel-dime-quarter draw, jacks or better, three-raise limit, can't check and bump. He had honed it with teenagers in penny-ante games in alleys. Anything beyond that might have been more than he could handle on his first time out with the likes of Podhead Mullins. He knew that this would be but practice for what would come when the shift whistle sounded and greenbacks and company scrip would become plentiful as play money.

The three not Pod were green as any boys worrying over a two-cent call, asking him to show first when he'd paid for the privilege. So in a single sitting he'd graduated from alley to his daddy's seat beside Pod. Against the soft-eyed suckers playing scared, already he was second in command.

With his quick-found status, Luck sat in his lap like a wanton, which made it all the more delicate because Pod, the boy was certain, divined already the magnitude of his—Adam Ramey's—talents. When the whistle blew, he'd maybe have a real claim on the chair where his daddy had been known.

"Let's go, Boatwright," one of the three said, and the lanky one, rose and sauntered out. The other two followed, one spitting at the corner cup, the other going for lonely pockets. The boy had half of what the three had lost—enough for a try at the real thing.

He had to occupy himself before Pod alone now, not daring to talk first or try to get the man to, for the man was sole ruler here and brooked no sentiment, which small talk might foster. When the man rose and shuffled to the brown trough behind hanging burlap and made water loud as any mine mule on flat slate, the boy took the occasion to count and set his stacks of change.

The whistle screamed a summons, up from the earth's innards for some, back down for others, and soon some would be coming with the brown envelopes.

"You aiming to stay?" Pod said.

"Yeah—"

The man was zipping up, coming through the sack curtain in a suit with knee impressions like growths.

"—aim to." Adam finished saying it with more firmness than he had intended.

And not another word until the miners began to enter, driven happy by payday, their eyes bright within blackened faces, nostril hairs sooted over, zinc pails and hard hats with carbide lamps all laid in a corner. Chance seemed their gay companion. For they came to play.

The five regulars looked first to Pod, then to the visitor, and excluded one of themselves as if by mime vote.

"Little Ramey," said Pod.

The nods said that they had either guilt for having escaped the cave-in or fear for the day when they would not.

"He's going to sit in," said Pod, "'least for a while."

So he had not yet ascended to the chair, but must win it. Like the first time in the field playing tin can, when he was hit by the big boys and could only then know that he was in the game—during the first hand (five-card stud, dollar ante, table stakes, pot limit, and the rest that went unquestioned as Pod announced it) he managed to fold a deuce without losing face or much coin, then stayed in the next hand till the second round, calling the first dollar bet in his life, then folded his jack-tray in the face of twin ladies and felt almost a winner as he saw the big money leave. Then he watched, inching his hand to his stacks until, at the barest tinkle, the one across from him doing his own fingering as if he had bought the right, and holding an ace-eight up to prove it, stared him to silence.

The third hand he won on the third round, an accumulation of what, in the lead all the way, he had bet and been called on. Bumps rose on his arms as he circled the pot and raked it in while the others looked on. Then almost nonchalantly he uncrumpled the pictures of Washington, Father of Our Country, he thought without meaning to, and smoothed the greenbacks with some deference of his own, then settled the small stack of them like a four-page book under the heavy metal tubes of silver he made. And all the while having passed the deal, tapping the proffered cut with a casual forefinger as if on only his command the game could proceed.

Now he became aware of the men hovering like dirty ghosts about the table, beyond the light. He felt the red of jack and king, the green and shine of bill and coin diminish the charcoal shadings of men gazing with black-rimmed eyes at the table that held the color, where he sat.

He did not want to come on strong too soon, but when they began to light up store-bought Camels and Spuds, in a moment of irrepressible well-being, he said, receiving his hole card, "Mind if I smoke, men?"

"Don't give a hog's pecker if you take dope, 'long as you play cards." This jokingly from the most sympathetic one, who had been on his daddy's last shift.

So he began to roll a smoke, delaying as he checked his hole and pondered a call while juggling the makings, until finally he just put everything back into the bib and Sympathy offered a Spud. Which he took, but had to light himself by digging for a match, and managed to do in time before, on the next bet, even though he had a shot at kings, he folded to Pod's ace-queen, in suit.

The cigarette pulled him in all the more so that Pod glanced his way, then looked over to the regular, waiting. Adam thought it was a signal, but he'd held his own, had a smooth shuffle and impressive deal next time at the deck. He'd offered Pod the cut, without looking, and felt something like disdain come from his right, then heard, "Couldn't stack shit with a pitchfork," followed by a laugh. He popped each up card with his middle finger and thumb, pitching it smoothly as he called out: "Tray. Niner. Bullet. Seb'm. Ten-spot. Home."

He thought he heard a sigh from his left, because of the tray or his fan-fare, and he caught a look from Sympathy. While they checked their holes, he scanned them up to Pod: to his left, Missing Fingers; next, Running Nose; then Sympathy; Black-rimmed Eyes, made dirtier because he alone of them had evidently tried to wash. Pod, he dared not scrutinize, though he saw the fingers going like sausages at the cards, riffling the silver.

"Ace bets," Adam said, and then did hear a sigh as Sympathy tossed in a wrinkled buck, Black Eyes folded and Adam took his cards too quickly and neatly to the side, Pod flattened the bill with two side-by-side halves, Adam dropped in dimes and quarters, saving his paper, and heard a new sigh. Fingers and Running Nose called with folding money, making the point and looking.

No raises, so he could see another, tapping with his middle finger in a silent little thump that said, Bets closed, cards coming.

"Your bullet," he said, nodding Sympathy's way as he tossed the first of the next round to Fingers, "and straight a-working. Cowboy, and hit'll stretch. Niner"—at which Sympathy immediately turned over and Adam called, "You're out"—then continued, "Ten and a pair. Home." It was the nine of clubs, and he worried the deck to order, squirming to free his stuck hind-end. "Pair bets."

Pod had already a two-dollar bill stretched between his vise-like hands. He popped it loud enough to cleave it, but it didn't dare, and he dropped it on top with his left hand, which went immediately to his stacks as he broke wind without so much as lifting.

The deuce bill looked good, though Adam was peering so cautiously at his hole, hiding it with his curved hand and pinching it with the other and the smoke from the butt curling into his eyes, that he wasn't sure what it was as it flipped back down with a little smack that must have sounded deliberate. He couldn't try again, but he'd seen black and thought he remembered from the first-round look, as he should have. He figured to have a three-card working flush which would look like a working straight flush outside, and nothing bet-ter than that. He put in eight quarters, knowing he shouldn't, but he felt it. If anybody bumped, he'd fold.

Fingers turned over with a grunt and got up, telling the waiting regular to take over, he might be back though, and Adam took up the discards. Nose dropped in his call. Sympathy was showing diamonds, and the boy was afraid of a raise, but when Sympathy added only two bills the boy thumped the official finger and announced: "Four players."

The gallery of men pulled in, snuffling. In the half-light from the bulb dan-gling bare over the main show, he could see the whites of their eyes. A pair of stanchions supported the beam of a ceiling so low that a miner not much taller than him was holding fast to it. The smell of carbide was heavy, and when they moved coal dust rose from what they wore. From a high window a shaft of late-afternoon sun lighted countless motes. He felt good under the large, dangling light bulb in a hand he had no business staying in, but he could not fold now. He flipped the cards, and the ring of eyes drew closer, one behind him labor-breathing above his head, others craning for a look-see.

"Pair still high," he said, checking his hole with care as he felt the wheezer see with him the hot-damn! king under his three other clubs. When Pod passed to him, he hesitated just long enough maybe to give them what they watched for, but he faked phony dumbness, saying, "Bet a dollar—no, make it two—and took from under what short tubes remained a couple of the four greenbacks. His hand quivered and he put it under the table, then brought it back quickly because he was dealer.

Running Nose with a likely straight put in two bills, then said, "And two," matching them.

Sympathy folded slow, throwing his cards to the boy.

"See it," said Pod, scooting in four.

He forgot to thump, and a murmur made him think that he had breached some unspoken rule of decorum.

Nose almost wiped at last with a sleeve, but didn't, saying, "How about my two?"

"Huh?"

"You see it?"

"Oh, yeah." He surrendered his two remaining bills.

"Deal 'em."

He did not flip the cards crisply and muffed the next one to Nose, who turned it over—the Queen of Diamonds—and said, "I'll sure keep it," with a chuckle. The one gripping the beam made it squeak, and the wheezer behind was close enough to be smelled even above the taint of dynamite. The room was now no more than the table, and they were all outside the puny light on the middle stack.

He tried to recall the discards for jacks, and none showing.

"Queen and possible," he said, weakly. Then he turned Pod's queen of hearts and managed to say gamely, "Two pair." Then his own deuce, and it was clubs too, and he owned the chair.

Again he scanned, for tens and queens, finding one each of Nose's and blanking out on the discards he should have remembered. Not a jack in sight, but he wasn't worried about Nose because Nose was beat both ways, probably. So he'd just have to see about Pod, who checked, and now he knew he had the whole thing.

Only he was almost out of money, no use to bet just a little. But if he checked, too, Nose wouldn't have no choice but to show at best a pair, or else bet his measly straight and sweeten the pot. So he was leader, had a sure lock. He counted out his scattered smaller coins and bet all but the two dollars he figured to take on to Mister Honeycutt, which was three-fifty.

Nose looked at him…then called!

Then raised five!

He sat up, studied Nose's cards again. Best there, a king-high straight; next best, pair of cowboys, and his own king-flush beat them both. But it wasn't his turn, and he had to erase everything from his face till it was all over.

Then Pod, who should have folded, said, "Call your three-fifty, your five, and bump"—he was thinking, counting—"seven more."

The boy's brow wrinkled like worms. Pod had his full boat and figured the three-fifty a bluff. Nose, a third-best straight. And he'd—.

"Just a minute," Adam blurted, then steadied because he knew now there'd been a mistake. All he had to do was correct it and the pot was his. "Can't check and raise." He smiled, looking around.

There was silence. He could feel heads shake in the darkened circle. Feet shuffled.

"Can in mule stud." It was Pod. He rubbed his big lips and yawned. "This ain't draw now."

Adam searched a face, and another, looking for…something. There was not much there. He could not act, nor fold. It had all come to this, and the empty jar outside. He looked again into eyes, thinking, What if he's testing? But still, test or not, he had to come up with twelve dollars just to call. And there was still a raise open.

"Can I play light?" He let his anger show. Why hadn't they told him before? He tried to recall the announced rules, and had to admit that maybe he was told, back when he was too anxious. But he did not recall. He saw himself with twelve dollars to repay later and all because he had to see Pod's hole card—ten or queen—to know for sure if Pod had suckered him, why Nose would raise into a possible full house and flush. But Pod couldn't have his filly with a ten and queen out. Still, he had to know for sure, or else live all his life without knowing.

"Well, can I?"

"Nope," Pod said. "Table stakes."

"You mean I got to fold?" He swallowed everything down. He'd rather lose than show them that weakness.

"Nope. Go in for what you got."

He looked once more to Nose's hand, shook his head slightly, then edged in Honeycutt's dollars and slumped. The fat bastard next to him would take it all, sure. That's why he owned the joint, why his daddy had to be coaxed home all those years.

Nose was looking at Pod's hand, not at all concerned about the four clubs—Adam Ramey's—staring him right in his ugly face. When Nose rubbed his chin, Adam thought, Why the hell don't you take a swipe at that nose, too? Then Nose put in a five and a deuce, topped it with an insulting quarter, and said, "Last raise."

Pod pushed the pot near the boy, and for a minute he thought he was being presented with it because Pod didn't have his full house and was saying so. But that wasn't it. From the pot Pod took twenty in bills and a quarter, placed that money in the middle, and clinked in his own quarter onto the new pot. "Call," Pod said. Adam looked to Nose, to near Pod, to the two pots. His head jerked in quick little chicken moves.

"You're in for that," Nose said, pointing to the bigger stack. Me and Pod's in for it all."

"Call," Pod said again, but folding his two pair and pushing his cards in.

He knew it! Jumped the gun and showed his hole. "King-high clubs," he announced through drool.

Pod was shaking his head. The watchers began to shuffle. Then Nose showed his jack—so what?—and reached for the pot before the boy.

"Flush beats!" the boy said, brow furrows moving the covering hair.

But the eyes around him were shaking their heads, too, whispering.

"Not in this here game," said Nose.

"What you mean? Flush beats!" Sweat, tears, a little piss—his waters were oozing as he saw the jar in his head. He hated the eyes, the hands of the one already counting, who could sit here today then go dig up his daddy for a company that'd sell him off for a potbelly at three dollar a ton.

Pod let out a sigh big enough to move air. "You was tole."

The boy did not see the big face, though he was looking for it now, but he sensed the look that passed between it and the counting man, and by then he could not see even the silver, going away.

"Split it, Maggard," Pod said. Then to the boy: "We're splitting only because you say you didn't know. Got that? You was tole. But next time, tole or not, ast."

Still, he wanted to scream, Flush beats! Still, he wanted it all, because he had won it all, faced Podhead Mullins and his fake filly and, goddamnit, won.

"Just remember: In mule stud, straight beats a flush around here," he heard Pod say. "Now"—and the last words were almost kind—"take it and go on."

Though he would not realize it until later, after he would become a regular, namesake to the hand he held this day, and laugh about the time of his knowledge, there were such coarse men who might have sweetened a pot, then thrown it. They would never have sent wasteful flowers or gifts to survivors, but they might, in a back room, when coal dust was heavy in the evening and no one could really tell for sure and those who could would not dare speak of it—they might drop a game to a boy bereft and send him on his way so that others would never know the truth and suspect charity and come running at every little calamity.

Nose raked the twenty-fifty into his stack, and still the boy objected with a look.

"You wasn't in for this here," Nose said. "Here's your half of this here one: twenty-two-seventy-five." He pushed it over, then said: "Better get on home now."

And he did, scooting the big scoop-seated chair of oak with arms big as his daddy's, where the man had left his sweat, so that his pantlegs came away with sound. They moved aside for him, looked after him, nodding something— so long or sorry or good luck or just good riddance, he did not know. He just stuffed his good pocket and hurried out through clicking balls to air.

There, he loaded the jar and dashed to Mister Honeycutt, who waited at his desk in the dusk. And when he paid with two bills, he was prideful to show that there was more. Then putting the receipt into the jar, he screwed on the lid, shook the music of money, and walked out.

He made a cigarette and all the way home re-ran the game in his mind. And when he arrived, she was sitting there, rigid as a store dummy. He didn't speak. He needed her to be first.

She looked at the jar, but said nothing. He rattled it at the room, then shift-ed to the bigger chair and sank into its covered springs. He waited for her to ac-cuse, flashed his teeth, waiting.

Suddenly, he jumped from the chair and ran to the back door. "Come on in!" he called to the girl climbing the slag heap to reach the end of the clothes-line.

And when she came, and when, from the outhouse, his older brother came, coated with coal dust, lined with sweat—when they all came, expecting tragedy, he knew that the woman he called Maw sat there already knowing, moaning in-side, wishing to God up in heaven above he'd lost and thanking the same God for the thirteen dollars he poured out on the floor for all of them to see.

COVERING HOME

COACH DISCOVERED DANNY'S ARM WHEN DANNY'S PARENTS were splitting up at the beginning of the season. For a while it didn't seem that Danny would be playing at all, but Coach called him at home where he was staying with his father and told him he needed his "natural curve and pretty good heat," said he'd been watching him warm up with Pye, their big catcher, before practice. Danny has always played second, though secretly he'd rather be at short even before the mound. The problem has always been that his arm isn't strong enough for short, but when Coach pointed out that the rubber is closer to home than the hole is to first—Danny could never throw from deep in the hole—it made sense even though the rubber was still farther to home than most of his plays at second were to first. After Coach talked to Danny's father and then they both talked to him, Danny was conJerryd he was a born hurler.

And after he popped Pye's mitt a couple of times hard enough to make Pye shake his hand, he was hooked. Each time he throws he imagines the big mitt to be the face of somebody he hates. But he doesn't dislike enough people that he can change with each pitch, so he uses movie and TV criminals and assorted villains from board games and videos. He has taught himself to do it over and over, treating Pye's mitt like a face in a hole in a wall at the carnival. Works pretty well, too. They're in the play-offs.

Danny knows he will not be pitching tomorrow; nobody will unless he wins today. So what he does now determines whether or not Ethan, the new kid, gets his chance. Danny and Ethan have been rotating between second and pitcher, but the guys don't work so good with Ethan on the mound. They say he thinks he's hot stuff. His father's always at practice, helping Coach and volunteering to drive the boys or take the equipment in his big van. Even mows the grass and fills in at the concession stand. No wonder Ethan plays every game. The only thing is, the guy's good. Danny has pointed this out, tactfully, on many occasions. Danny's glad to have good old Pye, big as a backstop, behind the plate; Rufus on third, who scoops them up like a vacuum cleaner; Jo-Jo at short, with an arm like a rifle; and at first Dingleberry, who can stretch five feet for the throw. But Ethan's pulled Danny out of a few tight ones: with a backhander in the seventh against the A's, a line-drive stab against the Yankees with two on, and a gorgeous double play against the Reds with Ethan doing two-thirds of it alone. But the guys still think Ethan's where he is just because of his old man.

Danny's parents haven't been coming to the games at the same time anymore the way they used to, back when he was on second without star status. After they split up they must have made it a rule to take turns because he has seen only one of them, if one, each game all season. He never talks about it with either one of them, but he can't see how they can work it out without talking to each other. All he knows is that there's never both of them congratulating him after he's won, not unless they are both there and just taking turns coming out on the field after it's all over, but then that would take some talking together, too. However they do it, it has worked out okay for them.

But today is different.

Earlier when Danny was getting ready in his room he heard his father, Jack Ferguson, come in, and then the tinkle of ice cubes in the kitchen. He didn't say anything, just kept putting on his uniform, and in a few minutes his father yelled through the hall, "That you, Dan?" Danny put his head out the door to show that it was, and Jack said he'd be at the game but probably a little late, he had to cancel a trip first.

Then in a little while Cora came in—she'd moved in with them a few weeks ago—and Danny heard the tinkle again. By now he was dressed, but he stayed in his room until he could get out without seeing Cora.

"I don't even like baseball," Cora said.

"Ssshhh," Jack said. "That's not the point and you know it. This is something we have to do."

"I am not ready to face a crowd of people yet, Jack. And you know as well as I do that she may be there today."

"That's just it," Jack said. He sighed loud enough for Danny to hear that too. "If she can be there, why can't we?"

"Because she may not be there with her boyfriend."

"Oh, he'll be with her."

"Your horns are starting to show."

"Knock that off."

In the end Cora agreed, if Jack would let her take the time she needed to get ready. When Cora went to Jack's bedroom and Jack went back to the ice cubes, Danny walked quickly through the hall and out the front door.

Now Danny is in the dugout, his pitching arm in his jacket sleeve. It is the top of the third, no score, Ethan at bat. Ethan's father, a large, imposing black man, sits inside with the score book; he is serious, energetic even when he is at rest. Danny is glad to have him there because Pye and Dingle and especially Rufus are not able to bad-mouth Ethan to Danny; Danny won't have to pretend to go along with it and even add something himself from time to time. When Ethan raps out a stand-up double, his father claps twice, enters it in the score book, and yells to Jo-Jo, coming up, to "Keep it goin'!"

Then Dingle moves on deck, Rufe in the hole, and Pye goes out for something at the concession stand. Danny takes the opportunity to say to Ethan's father, "Good hit, Mister Norris."

"Yeah," Ethan's father says. "Keep it goin'!" he yells out of the dugout.

Danny sees his father, followed by Cora, walking through the stands. Jack smiles at people he knows, turns to take Cora's hand, and sits with her at the bottom of the bleachers. The two of them stand out in the crowd of people mostly wearing jeans and short-sleeved shirts, sweat pants and tee shirts. Jack wears patent-leather shoes and a wide-lapeled suit; Cora, in a tight white blouse and tighter purple slacks, crosses her legs and sits straight, straining her breasts. Then Jack removes his jacket and places it across his lap, and in a moment he seeks out Danny and gives him a nod.

Jo-Jo then Dingle and Pye keep the rally going, scoring two, and then with two out Danny comes up. He feels self-conscious swinging two bats, knocking imagined mud from his rubber spikes, and after he swings at the first pitch and misses inches under it he hears from somewhere, "Sucker for a high one," and knows that he is. He just cannot help it: When they come in around his shoulders, it is as if somebody else's hands swing for him. He hopes the pitcher doesn't know, or that he won't be able to throw a high one whenever he wants to if he does. Danny crouches and that helps some; at least it helps the way he feels about being there in front of everybody in the first place. But still he strikes out.

As he heads for the mound he smells something in the air that reminds him of his father's new after-shave lotion; maybe it is his father's. It's like that disinfectant used in the boy's room at school, and he cannot help thinking that his old man dresses like a TV preacher and smells like a cleaned urinal. Between warm-up pitches he glances toward the bleachers without appearing to and sees Jack and Cora talking and laughing with people behind them. Cora is turned so that her breasts seem larger even than normal. Rufe has nicknamed her Unsinkable Cora. Pye and Jo-Jo call Danny's mother Barbie. They make it sound like a compliment, and he goes along with the joke because everybody in the infield except Ethan has split parents who are just plain plain. So he figures to get at least some status from his Ken-and-Barbie mom and dad and their "friends." They always call them that when introducing them. "Hey," Jo-Jo will say, referring to his mother, "I'd like you to meet my pal." "My chum," Pye will add. "My comrade," Rufe'll say. Jo-Jo will complete it lewdly: "My—oh, my!—my friend!" Then they all crack up. Pye says his old man's got so many friends he can't keep up with them. "Friendly Fred: That's my old man. Big problem, huh?" Danny's folks only have a friend apiece, and now they are both—they are now all four—at the game.

For while Danny waits in that awkward lull after the ump yells "Batter up!" and the infielders throw the ball around the horn, he sees Nikki, his mother, walking dangerously close to where Jack and Cora sit, her friend Cole beside her. After Danny gets the ball from Jo-Jo, he looks back to see Nikki see her mistake and veer off with Cole up the bleachers. Cole has on his running suit, and as usual Nikki is in impeccable black: slacks, blouse, ribbon around her throat. She is perfect: bleached-white hair, a mouth that seems always to be craving something, eyes that blink thick black lids slowly over violet contact lenses, and, as

Pye puts it, "legs all the way up to here." Pye once said, when he and Danny were comparing homeliness, "Frig, how'd you ever come out of somebody like her?"

Everything about her that really counts is delectably tapered; her legs, breasts, and fingers—like those of the doll which has set the standard—seem whittled into long, smooth cones. Her fingers count so much because she is so expressive with them. With long, deep-red nails she seems constantly to clutch at the air before her as she talks, as if the polish is never fully dry and she might as well use the occasion. Even her toenails are like a magazine ad. It has been some time since Danny has thought of her as Mother. She is Nikki Ferguson, who wears black so often she might in another time have been thought of as being in constant mourning.

Danny's imagination is virtually boundless this inning in replacing hated faces—all fictional—for Pye's big mitt. He and Pye have worked out a little system where Pye will squeeze the mitt several times, like a gulping mouth, and yell things like "Put it down his throat, Ferg!" Danny fans the first batter on strikes down the gullets of the decomposing faces of three ghouls from his old comic books. He dredges up faces of various movie villains for the second man, taking him after several foul balls with a pop-up to Rufe. Then conjuring mouths for the limitless electronic ogres from his video storehouse, he has a three-up-and-three-down inning going when he forgets on a pitch and sees the ball sail into the outfield, an in-the-park homer. He doesn't forget with the next batter, who grounds out to Ethan, and once again he is heading for the dugout, the warming jacket held out by Ethan's father. "Better keep this on, son," Mister Norris says. The man is too serious for the decent inning Danny has just had, and Danny suspects him of making too much of the gesture, deliberately showing Coach that Danny is tiring. Sure. He's hoping that Danny is, so Ethan can get a chance to show his stuff. Danny takes the jacket, then turns away, thinking the guys were right about those two.

At first Danny said he would divide his time between Jack and Nikki. He and his fifteen-year-old sister, Geraldine, were given their choice when Jack and Nikki sat with them at the dinner table and explained to them that they were splitting up, that Nikki was going to move out of the house into her own apartment. Jack and Nikki were very civil, very matter-of-fact, about it all. They didn't talk about not loving each other any more, nothing like that. They simply said what they were going to do and gave Danny and Geraldine their opportunity to say what they wanted to do. Nikki did add that her new apartment was small, that it might be better if only one of them at a time stayed with her, but she said that they could make out whenever both of them wanted to be together with her.

It was only after the family meeting, as Jack called it, that Jack and Nikki had a big argument and Geraldine left the house and Danny went to the family room and put on the headset. He sat listening to rock music for over an hour, and then Geraldine came back and they talked.

"I don't, like, have anything against him," Geraldine said, "but I'm going to stay with her full time. I think you'd be better off here."

"Why?"

"Well, like, you've got all your stuff here—you know, your computer and CDs and stuff. You've, like, got your room and everything."

"So do you."

"Yeah, but I can move easier than you can. Besides, I'm not, like, going to be around much longer."

"Where you going?"

"No place yet. But it won't be too long before I, you know, graduate and go off?

She went on to say that she didn't blame their father for anything; he was an okay guy in her book. It was just that, well, she hated to sound corny but a girl needed her mother. It was different with boys. Didn't he still want to do things with Dad?

"Like what?" Danny said.

"Fishing and, like, hunting and all that warrior stuff."

"Why, we don't do that much anymore."

"Well, just what do you, you know, want to do?"

He finally said he'd stay where he was for the time being.

He visited Geraldine and Nikki a few times, even stayed overnight on a weekend, but then everything changed when Nikki and Geraldine moved in with Cole. Cole had his son with him and Danny felt awkward going to an older boy's house to visit his own mother and sister. But then when Cora moved in with

Jack, it was awkward too. The best thing about it was that she didn't have any of her kids with her—that and the fact that Cora didn't try to act like a mother to Danny. She'd already had a bellyful of that.

Danny saw Geraldine only occasionally, since he was in junior high and she was a tenth-grader across town. But he heard about her from his friends who had older brothers and sisters who went to school with her. Pye said his oldest sister said Geraldine smoked dope at recess with a fast crowd; Jo-Jo said his big brother was bug-eyed over her. When Danny did see Geraldine the next time, she said everything was going pretty good. When Danny asked her if she wasn't—he couldn't think of the right word; he used crowded—if she wasn't crowded living with Cole's son Matthew, a senior, in the house, Geraldine said that she and Matt got along fine together; they just didn't get in each other's way. And when he pursued it further, asking her if she was ever going to come over to the house, she said she wasn't. "He's too strict," she said of their father, and she wasn't about to go back to that sort of stuff. Besides, Nikki and Cole were fun, she said. They let her and her friends watch whatever they wanted to on the VCR, and they had cable.

"With MTV?" Danny said.

She nodded. "STARZ, too." She bit at her fingernail and went on to tell him how they let her have parties without always being right there trying to get in on the act, though every now and then they might show her friends how to really dance. "You ought to see them," she said. "I mean, they're, like, awesome, Danny. I swear. They ought to give swing lessons."

Danny told her he didn't think Jack was so strict.

Her head jerked. "How about that woman who moved in?"

"Cora? Okay, I guess. She don't bother me none. She brought over her own VCR for their bedroom, so I as good as got my own now."

"You mean he lets you watch it without making you, like, feel like you're doing something wrong?"

"Sure does. And as for cable, that was the first thing Cora said she had to have, but that's in their bedroom too."

She raked her greasy hair with her fingers. "Guess they've hooked you up, huh?"

"Huh-uh. Think they will if I ask?"

"Well, like—." She seemed distracted, then came back to the question with an intensity beyond what it required. "I mean, I don't know, you know?" Then she braced up and told him that Cole had bought Nikki a new Grand Cherokee. Her face lit up, waiting for Danny to say something about that. When he didn't, she said, "And I get to drive it whenever Mommy isn't."

Then Danny began thinking about what he'd heard from his friends about her and he wanted to ask her about it, but didn't. Instead he asked her if she ever got to drive Cole's restored Corvette.

"Are you kidding me? Matt, like, had a fit when Mommy asked Cole if I could. He's such a jerk anyway."

"I thought you said you two got along okay."

"I said we just stay out of each other's way. He's one of these, like, new jocks. Super Sunday's bigger to him than Christmas. He thinks he's Michael Jordan or something." She laughed. "He even, like, started wearing an earring." She made a face. "You should've seen him when I lit up a cigarette in my room. I mean, like, Cole can't stand smoking but Matt's a fanatic."

"You mean you smoked in the house?"

"In my room. It's supposed to be my private space."

"Well, you never could at home."

"Yeah, I know."

They seemed for a moment to have nothing to say.

Then Geraldine said, "Funny, isn't it?"

"What?" said Danny.

She laughed. "Like, none of them smoke."

Danny didn't see Geraldine very much after that. Pye said his sister told their mother she knew guys were on the lookout for girls like Geraldine. Danny asked him what she meant by that, and Pye said he heard her tell their mother that there were guys who went after girls whose parents had just split up, that they were—. Pye couldn't think of the right word, something like vulnable.

"What's it mean?" Danny said.

Pye punched him in the arm and laughed. "Means hot stuff, Frig."

It is the bottom of the seventh, Danny's team leading by one. He has exhausted the hate faces from movies and games, and since he never uses one twice in a ball game, believing that if he does it's a sure hit, he must rely upon the real thing. He also believes that if he uses a real one that is not an object of hate, that too will be a hit, and so he must avoid all the marginal villains. Even Cora and Cole are not sure things.

In the time of his uncertainty and since the last inning will not wait for him to make up his mind, he walks the first batter. Pye calls time out and waddles out to the mound. "What's the matter, Frig?" he says, doing his best, Danny can tell, to act big-league and casual at the same time. "Just settle down and we got 'em." He puts the ball in Danny's glove with a little plop, whispers some hate names, and lumbers back to squat behind the plate.

After a strike down the gut to a woman he'd seen on the news who had killed her children, the next batter grounds out to first on an imagined sinker to Danny's dreamed-up version of the killer of a young girl so prominent in the newspapers. The base-runner advances to second. Dingle walks the ball over to Danny, pats him on the rump, and trots back.

"Put 'er in there, Dan old boy!" It is Jo-Jo. Rufe and Dingle chime in, Ethan mumbles something that sounds grudging, the outfielders come alive, and then Pye is squeezing the mitt open and shut as a collective cheer comes from the stands. With a sizzler between the dark, brooding eyes of the man recently convicted of killing twelve boys; followed by another through the teeth of a shrill woman he'd seen on a talk show; and then two straight balls to Ethan and his ass-kissing daddy, Danny gets two-and-two on the next man, who then flies deep to right on an unconvincing curve to that state-senator-who'd-just-won-the-election's genuine smile. The runner tags up and goes to third as Danny's right-fielder runs the ball in to Ethan, who looks the runner down and walks it to Dan.

"Time!" yells Coach, coming onto the field. He has his head down, his right hand slightly raised, his left in his back pocket—all sure signs from what Danny has seen of the majors that he will be jerked.

Ethan stays below the mound, surely licking his chops. The others complete the circle around Coach and Danny, and they stand there as if some solution to winning is about to descend.

"How's your arm?" Coach says.

Danny feels the blood in his face. He wants to give the ball to Ethan just to make this moment pass, for he cannot bear being the center of their attention and everybody else's. He is looking down, his glove crooked with the ball at his breast, when Pye slips a chunk of unwrapped gum into his right hand, limp at his side. Danny puts it in his mouth and begins to chew, glancing at Coach as if to say, Well, what are you going to do?

"What do you say, Danny?"

"Come on, ma-a-a-n." It is Ethan, the cocky little bastard with his big, fat father behind him all the way, letting Coach know that Danny's had it. Then Danny hears: "You can do it, Dan-the-man!" And this, too, is Ethan, now patting Danny's back.

The others follow his lead, and before he knows it he is buoyed by their words, his eyes beginning to mist. He takes off his cap and wipes his head with the same hand, looking his guilt and remorse at Ethan, smiling, saying through the juice of the gum, spit bubbles forming at his lips, "Let me just get this last guy, Coach."

"You got him," Coach says, then quickly alerts them to what might be coming: the boys'-league version of the old squeeze play. "Pye, go for the bunt. Rufus, move up at the first sign. Danny, you cover home. Same for a passed ball. If the ball's hit in the infield, make the sure play at first. Got it?"

They all say that they do. Then they pat Danny here and there, Pye caresses his head with his big mitt, and they break up and trot back to where they came from, frantic with chatter, pounding their gloves. "Give it your best shot," Coach says, and he too trots away.

Danny sees Mister Norris at the door of the dugout, scanning the infield with a Camcorder. He shoots Danny, removes the camera from his face, and says seriously: "C'mon, Dan-boy. Just one more." Then he turns and goes into the dugout.

Danny is hot with shame, and he forgets about the hate faces.

"Ball one!"

"'At's okay, Dan-boy. Shake it off!"

Before he can come up with anything, he throws again.

"Ball two!"

The batter has not yet squared off for a bunt, but Danny is ready to charge
the plate if he does. Only he has to pitch first. If he walks this man, he decides,
he will ask to be taken out. He fixes on the face of a terrorist from the morning
paper and throws.

"Strike one!"

The fans in the bleachers are clapping and yelling, the infield chatter constant. Pye too soon throws the ball back to Danny, who, still out of balance from
the pitch, misses it. With his side sight he sees the runner start for home, and
he is confused; but then Ethan is there just behind the mound, the ball firmly
in his right hand, daring the runner—who can't go home anyway; it's against
the rules—to take another step. Ethan smiles, clearly for Danny's pleasure, and
hands him the ball.

"C'mon, Fergie-baby. C'mon, babe," and Ethan is back at second.

Again, Danny forgets and pitches.

"Ball three!"

"Don't lose him, Fergie-baby!"

He puts the kindly televised face of a convicted priest onto Pye's mitt, and
throws.

"Strike two! Full count!" The umpire puts up both fists and rotates them.

Danny looks up, high above the backstop. There is a big sign there: RONALD
MASON MEMORIAL PARK. He thinks of the boy, drowned two summers back,
someone he knew. He holds up his hand for time out and gets it, bending to
tie his shoelace, squinting at the stands. But he can see nothing plainly, and the
blood is in his head. He takes the rosin bag and buys a little time with that. He
knows that if he wins, his parents will be out on the field, each one wanting to be
first. He knows that they will not bring their friends with them but will have to
come alone, together, that he will be embraced by each of them, between them.
The thought sickens him as he turns briefly to see the calm of the outfield, wishing he were there. He is aware of the clipped grass of the infield, the packed red
dirt of the baselines. The bags are hard and clean. He is conscious, for the first
time, of the true meaning of the word diamond, and he is the center of it.

But he is aware as well, for the first time, that he has nothing at all on the
ball without his own illusion. With it, he has gripped with his forefinger and

middle finger the space between the ball's seams and imagined its darting and breaking to the plate. That is now all gone, and he grips with all of his hand, all his fingers, as much of the ball as he can, pushing it tight into the weblike skin formed by his thumb and forefinger. Pye is squeezing the mitt and relaxing it; everybody—the other team, the other fans—everybody is yelling something— "'atta boy" and "little bingle" and "you can do it"—and he bends for his wind-up, begins the rhythm, looking at the mitt looking back at him like an oversized mouth. He tries but cannot stop the face it takes on, his own, mocking back, as he pumps and winds and rears back for everything he's worth, then lets go.

THE WHITE
UNIFORM

I

As a young girl I cut pictures out of catalogs and kept them in the pages of my schoolbooks. I liked anything with straight-line shapes mixed with curves, like a bed with posts and a round headboard. The stuff in the pictures didn't have to be pretty or cost a lot. I cut the pictures out of the catalogues in the outhouse when I had to go in there. Ever once in a while I cut out pictures of people, not just because the models were good-looking but because of a woman's or girl's face or the smiling eyes of a man. I got so good with the scissors that the outline of the person cut out remained whole in the page. More and more, I got tired of the figures themselves and made up new ones for their blank outlines. After while I threw the cutouts in the other hole and kept the pages with the human holes.

About then I got to dreaming about getting out of the coal fields some day. I found books in the trailer that started coming around about places not like those mountains where dirt roads only led to coal and to towns like the mean place filled with drunken men we had to call home. It was started with war over coal, and that's what they called it, just with another word meaning the same thing.

Carbo.

When the place you call home is a slave to what's been piling up under the ground for all time, and when you are little, you smell it for a while in the air, in a coal shed, in a coal bucket, and it makes you gag till one day it don't. Even the narrow yellow-sheen that sluices down from the mountain like it's a creek loses its stink. You want to see a flower, you got to go to coves ain't been dug yet. Everwhere you walk, it's black. Ever time you breathe, you're only taking in, and with your daddy it's just a matter of time what will kill him first, the coal dust a breath at a time or the whole mountain all at once. By the time you get old enough to take over some house duties, you don't smell much of anything, not even the one reminding you you can be a mother. Living there like that, you are coal.

But there wasn't much time for dreaming. Now that my mother was carrying Lon, I had to take over the clothes-washing and have the tub ready for when the men came home. With Daddy's water hot and waiting on the stove, I emptied the pots and filled them back up for my brother, Zack, who threw Daddy's old water out so I could wash the tub between times. Virgie was two then. If she needed looking after, Zack washed the tub out when he was finished with it.

The closer Lon got to being born the more I had to do, but there was something about my daddy made me want to do extra for him. Something about him made my chin wrinkle up when I studied his face. It seemed like he'd wandered into the coal mines from a clean and safe place. "Nosiree, Delmar Alford's not about to join no union," I'd heard a man say once. "But he'll wish he had someday when it's too late." Another one had said: "It's that little girl of his. He ain't going to risk missing ary a shift."

By the time Lon was about to come into the world, my daddy'd turned into shadows, all black and gray with white streaks, like bones, where his skin showed. He didn't even seem as plain as the human outlines in the catalogue pages, because he'd already been filled in and no matter how hard I tried I couldn't make new pictures of him from what might have been in my head.

The day Lon was born Virgie was asleep on the floor with a piece of cheesecloth over her, and I was alone with my mother. When I heard her and went to the bedroom, she was twisting on the mattress and biting down on her lip. Tiny toes were wiggling out of her.

"Hit's a-starting," she said around the ugly sounds she was making. "Pull it on through."

I didn't move.

"Just grab aholt." She grunted. "Get over here. Then go get somebody."

The second order gave me courage to do the first, and I took hold of the feet. When I got the legs through to the knees, they kicked out of my hand.

Good thing he was so little, and slick. Once I got him started out again, he came fast.

, , ,

We'd been in there with him all night. Those sisters came in ever now and then and took his pulse like they just wanted to see if it'd stopped yet so they could take him away and change the bed. All the time he was wheezing and her sitting over there never saying a thing, just sucking in her mouth from time to time. All she ever did for him anyway was tolerate him, and him the one going down there ever day. When he choked out a couple of words last night, I was the one figured his time had come.

Back before her time had come with Lon, one day when I was alone with my daddy, I fixed him something to eat before it was time to. While he was chewing real slow the way he always did, he smiled at me and said he'd clean up after hisself. Then he gave me a piece of scrip and told me to go to the commissary and buy myself something just for me. "Don't even tell nobody what you get. Eat it all up. I'll take care of her."

I sat there all night looking at his face. It was always set against calamity, and this was the last one. How many times since he passed on I'd been told mine was set, too, like I was always fixing to cry. I didn't know about that, but I usually had to think on it before I'd let out a smile. By then his eyes were so dried out and all that coal dust in them sores had started inside. One of the sisters came in and put some drops in them, and it made me think of back when he was strong and they were always so teary. "Is my pappy a-crying?" I used to ask him. "No," he'd say, "your pappy's just a-laughing tears." Probably his eyes washing out the dust on their own, back when they could. Sunshine used to sparkle in the water in them, and ever now and then, when he smiled, he did look kind of happy. He'd maybe hunch over and light a cigarette and come up from his cupped hands blowing smoke with a serious look on his face, then see me and give out a grin.

When I was setting his plate on the table, I'd catch that look of his with those black-rimmed eyes he could never get clean, none of them could. That look said don't go into the mines for work, look what it done to me. *"We don't get a nickel before the coal's loaded, Delmar, and that ain't right. And, by durn, you know it ain't right."* Not a nickel for setting timbers and track, not for dynamiting, not even for digging. Two hours or two days—whatever it took to dig a ton of coal, they got paid for one ton, and he knew how much that was, if they were lucky to get the full amount even then. "Some pay's better than no pay," was what he'd answer them. And there he was now, streaked black in that clean white hospital bed, drawing his last breaths and nobody could do a thing for him, not even me.

But maybe I could make him smile one last time.

When she said she was going home for a while, she needed to rest, I knew it was for her snuff and I let her go. That's when I got the idea. That and the look in his eyes. He jerked his head a little toward where his clothes were hanging, and I knew we had the same notion. I took a cigarette from a wrinkled pack in his shirt and struck a wooden match I found in there with it. "I knew what it was you wanted, Pappy," I told him. I used my old little-girl name for him to take him back to our earlier time together. He gave me a smile but it was too sad to really be one. I puffed on the cigarette to get it going, then held it to his cracked lips. He drew in and blew out the smoke and I took it away but he weak-slapped his hand on the bed and I put it back to his mouth. He drew on it and moved his mouth away from it so he could inhale the smoke. When he did, he went into a fit of coughing, so bad I looked out in the hallway for help. I thought he was going to die right then, and I didn't want to leave him alone so I went back to the bed and tried to talk him out of choking.

"What is it, child?"

I turned to the clear voice and rustle of cloth and saw for the first time the tall sister in the white habit blazing in the morning light. She looked like a playing-card queen all blanched out.

"Smoking at your age?" She said it with a stern look. She was moving to the bed all the time and made the connection. "The last thing he'll be needin' is smoke in his lungs. Discard it, and be quick."

I hurried out through the hallway and the smells of liniments and bedpans. Near the entrance a man sat on a wooden chair. His face was bent over into one hand. His other hand was resting on top of his head. It was missing fingers but holding a burning cigarette with what was left. I had to get close to the man to drop my daddy's cigarette in the can, and I was worried the man would spook, but he didn't move.

When I went back to the room, the sister and a big, slow girl everbody called Lulu were cleaning up my daddy and changing the sheets. I saw the black blotches on the ones on the floor.

"Is it a kindness you're wantin' to give him? Then come help, child."

I went over and helped prop my daddy up while they got one sheet under him and another on top.

"Now take up the dirty ones, that's a girl, Loretta," she said to Lulu all in one breath, "and put them in the laundry."

While the sister was fussing with the sheet, she started to say something. "Now—"

My daddy grabbed her wrist and gave her that hurt smile, and I could tell she knew what he meant, too. She took his hand off her wrist and placed it on top of the covers. "Now, there's a good man," she said. She had light in her eyes. Her mouth smiled even when she didn't seem to mean it to. "Don't be worryin' about your daughter, Mister Alford. It's only talkin' to her I'll be doin'." She gave me a look so warm I forgot how bad off my daddy was. "Only talkin'," she went on. "She's a good daughter who loves her father. Our Savior loves her and her father as well. He loves us all." She put her hand on his forehead, patted his hand, then left us alone.

He died later that day.

Only Sister Jillian's hands and framed face showed outside the uniform she told me was her habit. She wore eyeglasses, the kind called spectacles by older folks. She'd come from Ireland all the way to the Catholic missions in our area and was assigned to Carbo along with other nuns to set up a hospital. She told me just a little about herself, like she didn't think her own life was worth so much. She was always busy at the hospital and going to church. She couldn't even come to my daddy's funeral. There'd been a cave-in.

Later, I agreed to meet with Sister Jillian at the sisters' house next to the hospital. At first we talked a little after they had their church service they called Mass in the house. She'd worked night duty, and her white habit was dirty. I wondered if a miner had spit up on her like my daddy about the same time I saw her see me looking at the spots.

"Another one die?" I said.

"Oh, no, child," she said. "Silicosis, bad as it is, is not always fatal."

It seemed to me it always would be, eventually, but I just said, "The black lung or what you call it—why'd it have to kill my daddy?"

"The fathers of many children throughout the world die every day from it."

I found a red spot on the sister's habit. It seemed to me I was being told what I felt was nothing special.

Sister Jillian must have seen some look on my face, and she said, "We are made to know, love, and serve God in this world and to be happy with Him in the next."

I wondered why we couldn't be happy in *this* world, too, and I told her so.

"We are not to seek worldly happiness, but to do good works and love Jesus."

It didn't make good sense.

I quit meeting with the sister after three times. Even if I'd wanted to keep seeing her, it would of had to be in secret. My mother had a fit when she found out. "Quit messing around with them Cathlicks," she yelled at me. "They'll put a cast in your eye not ary a Hardshell preacher'll ever be able to pray outen you."

And I did.

One late afternoon when the sun was slanting over the far ridge, I was walking the dirt road that led out of Carbo on the up side. I picked up a stick and ran it on the top strand of the barbed-wire fence near the ditch line. The fence ended with a post stuck part way in a hole and leaning beside a roll of rusty wire. I poked the stick through the roll till it touched a bird's nest tucked into the middle of it, empty and dry now, but it must have been some protection.

I was wearing the pink dress my mother had got me at the Salvation Army with some of the money the coal company paid out when Daddy died. "But I ain't a-wasting none of it on no more shoes when you already got yourself a good pair," she'd told me. "The ones I got don't fit no more," I said, but they did. "Oh, yes, they do. I got 'em plenty big. Your foot ain't growed that much in just a little over a year."

I heard something, but I couldn't see through the bushes, so I climbed up some rocks and saw a clearing beyond. It wasn't an animal, and it wasn't a man. It was just Jimmy Dell Ellis.

"I seen you over there, a-looking," I sang out, and he duck-walked behind a
big oak tree. I went to the clearing, sashaying in my brogans like a huzzy on the
streets of Carbo on payday.

"Opal Alford!" Jimmy Dell said while he was moving out from behind the
tree like he was surprised to see me. He wasn't as big as me, and I was just a slip
of a girl then. "You look right—"

"Well? Right what?"

"Your hair's red as blazes and all tangled up like a tumbleweed. And that
there dress—you're prettier'n a grown-up woman."

I tugged at my dress top and my bosom moved, which I wanted it to.

He blinked and rubbed his cheeks with his fists.

"What in tarnation happened to your face?" I said. "You get yourself tore
up in that last cave-in?"

"Nah, just got my puss scratched when that durn mule I was tending knocked
me against the coal wall. They was all a-running out a there like a stampede."

I saw the poke laying there beside him, and I went over and squatted down
in front of him, holding my hands together and dropping my arms between my
legs. The dress tucked down almost to the ground. My shins and knees showed,
and my socks were sucked down into my unlaced brogans, and Jimmy Dell was
gazing away, just dying to see up my dress. I reached up and began turning the
necklace my daddy left me around my throat. Ever time the sun caught it just
right a shine line came on Jimmy Dell's cheek. I stopped turning it, and when it
dangled down he gawked at it, or maybe pretended to see what he could of my
bosom, which I was bending over so he could.

"What's that doodad hanging on it like a little plumb bob?" he said.

"Here," I said, "go head and touch it. Hit won't bite."

He flipped it with a finger. "Why, look's like coal."

Jimmy Dell wasn't too bright, and I felt like having a little fun with him.
"Huh-uh," I said. "This here's coal so hard hit ain't even coal. This here's anther-
cite. Harder'n any there is, 'cept diamond. You let this little bitty piece grow in
the ground a couple a hundred centuries, you'd have me a wedding ring."

"Heck fire," little Jimmy Dell said but like a joke, "I ain't got to marry you,
do I?"

"No, but you do got to tell me what's in that poke there."

He opened it and pulled out a Mason jar of clear liquid, and said, "Why, I bet you already knowed."

Course I did. Why else let a little runt like him get worked up over me? "Where you going with it?"

"I got to take it to a feller."

I stood up, prizing my brogans off with my toes. "Tell you what—give me a pull on that there jar, and I'll show you if you want."

He sat where he was under the oak, and I moved over and sat beside him. He handed the jar to me with both hands, and I drank. It burned hard, but I swallowed it down harder.

Then he turned the jar up, and when it touched his lips he lowered it and said, "Now, let me see."

I reached for the jar. "Give me another'n first."

He did and after another drink I smacked my lips and wiped my mouth with the back of my hand, then got tired as all get-out and just laid back. I scratched at my leg and looked up all dreamy. "Well, come on ahead."

He kneeled below me, and when I lifted the pink dress a breeze took to that area of me under it like a bellows.

"Can't see nothing," he said.

"Pull 'em down a tad," I told him. The last of the sun was hot on my face, and I was drowsing but I felt like singing.

"'I will twine with my mingles of raven black hair.'"

I couldn't have been out but just a few seconds when a commotion woke me up all the way and I opened my eyes. A fully growed man, but not tall, was standing below me wearing a shirt and socks but nothing else. All his lower muscles were showing big.

"Now, you git on out of here," he told Jimmy Dell. "Git, you little piss ant, or I'll—." He raised his arm, and Jimmy Dell ran off. "I ain't a-going to hurt you none," he said to me.

"You bet you ain't," I told him. "Get away now or you're going to be sorry."

"You're real sweet, honey," he said, "a-letting that little feller stoke your fire. How'd you like a nice, red-hot poker?"

And I did. I wanted it shoved way up inside me to fill up a hollow that
hurt so much it felt like a growth. But I didn't want him doing the shoving. His
nekkid half was so white it seemed lit from inside, highlighting flecks of coal
dust. About that time the oak's branches lifted above me like taking in their
breath. I listened to hear it coming back out but it never did, and I couldn't
wait anyway.

I rolled over twice and got up holding a stick. When he came at me, I
whacked down hard on the thick rod angled out from the middle of him. He
turned, squealing, and I whacked him on his bony rump. He went running off
through the bushes, and I yelled at him: "My daddy's Delmar Alford. You better
go back in the hole you come from."

Then I picked me some wildflowers, put on my brogans, and went on back
down the road.

꙳ ꙳ ꙳

Over the next year, I went off in the woods with the Collins boy and let him do
it. When we were supposed to meet the next time, his cousin showed up instead.
I asked the dark, good-looking boy just what did they take me for. He said he
didn't take me for nothing bad. It was just that he'd always had a yen for me and
he'd begged his cousin to let him go in his place.

"What'd you give him?"

He was good-looking but mighty shy.

Then it came to me. "You pay him?"

He didn't answer for a long time, and I waited him out till he finally said,
"I give him a quart jar of my daddy's shine." He turned to go like a little boy's
been scolded.

"If you'd of brought me some, I might could be drawn to you," I said to his
back, but I already was, without a drink.

Three months later, when I was walking by the sisters' house on my way
from school, Sister Jillian called to me from the porch. I walked on. I knew she'd
seen my belly, and I didn't want to talk to her that way.

Two more weeks and I went to the porch on my own and asked one of the
sisters who came to the door to get Sister Jillian.

"What have you been through, child?" Sister Jillian said when she came outside. "You didn't do something dangerous and sinful, did you?"

"It just come out its own self."

"Where did it happen?"

"I was sitting on the hole."

"O, my dear girl. Perhaps Father should—"

"Not there. Besides, we ain't even Catholic."

Sister Jillian seemed to swallow what she really wanted to say and came out with: "You must not cheapen yourself, Opal. When a good man comes into your life, it's the best of yourself you'll be wantin' to give him."

"I had to have something, too," I said, at the same time I was glad not to be getting fat no more.

"There is so much more besides that, and surely for a girl as bright and pretty as you. Now, promise me you'll think more of yourself and begin taking instructions for becoming a good Catholic young lady."

⟡ ⟡ ⟡

When I was sixteen and still little and sort of pretty, I started working at the Carbo Cafe. There was a sign hanging over the entrance with the word Eats on it, but everybody just called it the cafe. I swept the floor, cleaned the windows, and washed the dishes. I was so short then that I stood on a crate to reach the sink better. It was such drudgery I kept some cutout pictures propped nearby to pick me up.

I was all the time looking at my pictures back then and thinking about the Catholic lessons and some of my talks with Father Shivsky, who was tall and red-headed like me and acted like what a saint must be and talked so soft I liked hearing from him even what I didn't understand. "A daily examination of conscience is a good way to keep up with our natures, huh?" He often added that soft "huh" at the end like he wanted you to have a stake in what he said. "You are such a kind and loving daughter." He had to of meant to the memory of my daddy. My mother found fault with everthing I did, and I told her that now I was sixteen and working and giving her money and had stopped going to school I'd do what I wanted about religion. I even tried to tell her about Sister Jillian and Father Shivsky. "If you'd just meet them, Mama."

"Hmp," was all she said, which was better than usual.

"They're so good, Mama. Why, the father talks so soft you just have to listen."

"Why can't he speak up? And what you mean a-callin' that man that. He ain't your daddy?"

I learned why I was really born and how I was expected to live, and I learned some of the prayers I liked saying. They settled me down, especially the rosary. Saying the Hail Mary over so many times made its own peace, like a drum I once heard a Cherokee Indian beating while he was singing something that could've been a kind of rosary. If I could turn how bad I felt about being trapped in Carbo into what it took for Sister Jillian and Father Shivsky to come here on their own, I aimed to go all the way and become one of them.

One day when the cafe was empty, I was on my crate at the sink listening to two crazy flies chasing each other. They'd bang into the window and everthing would go quiet, but they'd take up again. I turned around ever now and then to watch, and I saw they were fighting over room to light on the Tanglefoot flypaper hanging in the middle of the ceiling like a big clump of black wool. Ever time one got near, the other one would scare it off and come back its own self like there was only one spot left, but the other one would circle back, drive it away, and it went on like that for some time.

I was washing dishes and wouldn't normally have heard the screen door spring open and slam, I'd heard it so much. But this time it just sprang open quieter than usual and didn't slam shut. I could feel it, like hearing just one chug of a coal train when they mostly came in pairs, or when the wind upswayed that oak's branches like breathing in but nothing after. It was somebody standing out there looking in who wasn't a regular. I never heard the door close, just footsteps on their way to the kitchen.

I shut the spickit off and turned around about the time those flies were coming fast at the flypaper from different sides and disappeared into it. I looked at the doorway like I already knew what was there. Smoke, looked like little clouds, was all around his head from the cigarette in his mouth. He raised his face out of the smoke and took off his hat and sort of bowed. "Hello, pretty." He told me I was sure something standing on that crate, like it was some platform just for a few special girls. I knew he was lying, but he was sure something to look at his own self. I couldn't hardly stand it, and partly because I would have sworn to God that while he was looking at me from that doorway he was crying! That was something I'd never seen before in any man except from coal dust and sure to the Lord not in a face like that.

Anybody else might have come in just sat down on a stool and the waitress took care of him. But the waitress had gone over to the commissary to get some light bread when he was coming in, he said, to get a piece of pie and a cup of coffee. "If you'll serve it to me, I'll have me some real dessert, later."

His name was Emory Necessary.

The crying wasn't real. "Just smoke got in my eyes, and the sight of you," he told me later on one of our meetings in the car he borrowed from a man. Emory Necessary didn't live in Carbo and at first came to town just twice a month. He always brought along some clear whiskey made by the owner of the car, and after a couple of meetings I took a little swig even though I knew by then I shouldn't since I was putting myself into what Father Shivsky called the occasion of sin. But that passed and it wasn't long till I took a drink automatically and even asked for it when Em didn't reach under the car seat and bring it out. I got to where I looked forward to the man and to the whiskey.

With all the work I was doing at the house and cafe, I felt grown-up enough to do what I wanted, even go out with a twenty-two-year-old man looked thirty. After a few months he came to Carbo ever Saturday night and took me to a dance hall over near Pound Gap. At first I held on to him while he led me around the dance floor. I would have followed that man anywheres. I even took puffs off his cigarettes to let him know I was regular, with him all the way.

I loved the dancing and must've had a natural way with it. It felt so good bouncing around in the pink dress that still fit and keeping a straight-up rhythm along with the other.

"I ain't never seen spring in a girl's legs like yourn," he said. "Like dancing with two girls."

That was back when it didn't mean what it came to mean later.

At the end of a song I twirled and he led me with some pride, I could tell, back to our table. We always sat by ourselves. I felt the music all the way to the table and couldn't wait for it to start up again.

I said I'd marry him but he'd have to swear not to go back to selling whiskey.
I was already carrying Lettie but not showing yet enough to have to tell him. I
didn't ask him to quit drinking yet, and we still had some good times even after
we married. I guess I was still new to him, or new enough, but then I really began
to show. "We can't keep going out now," I tried to tell him, "and there shouldn't
be any drinking in the house."

"All the fun's gone out of you," he said. "All you ever wanted out of me was
a baby anyways."

"Why, that ain't so," I said. I'd just heated and poured his water in the zinc
tub same as I'd done for my daddy and brother. But now I was washing the
strong back of my own man. I knew that now he was working in the mines
again and not selling whiskey he felt bad ever now and then and had to let it
out. Whatever I said I watched how I said it. Even when he was drinking mean I
played like when I'd first seen him in the doorway that day he'd been crying over
the sight of me and it was just his nature not to want to admit something like
that. It kept me going through the hard times after the baby came.

We left Carbo to get married and stayed away. Emory took us from one
place to the next, even over into West Virginia and Kentucky a few times. He
didn't like coal-mining, but it was all he could do. I wrote a letter to Sister Jillian
and one to my mother, but I didn't go to Carbo to see her. I didn't want Emory
coming face to face with her again. The one time he went back with me wasn't
any too pretty, and if I went back without him there'd be even more trouble.
Mainly though, I was carrying my second, or third, baby then, and I lost it, only
this time in a real bathroom. I hadn't felt like even going outdoors, let alone to a
place like Carbo, where I'd lost the other one Emory didn't know about.

I wasn't supposed to have any more nor to be able to. "I'm a-cautioning you
not to even try," the granny woman told me.

How do you not try with him? He was always back then wanting me even
when he was sometimes hurting me and yelling at me to get out. I wasn't superstitious, but I felt strong signs that the poor little baby boy born to me the next
year shouldn't have been. During the time I was carrying him the second lost
baby before him stayed like an empty place in me. Like one of my old human
cutouts and the haint of my daddy, what wasn't inside me no more kept me apart

from what was. Ever day my time neared, the granny woman's warning set up in my head like one of the commandments.

I craved different food that summer. "Me, too," Emory said. I ached and my bosoms swelled. "Why, mine do, too." He couldn't even let me have that. I suffered my time alone and my poor little boy's, too, then produced him just easy as all that.

We'd just left Vansant and were living in Haysi, where Emory got on at the mines as graveyard-shift boss. The tiny little woman looked like a witch who'd helped with the birthing handed him to me and said straight off, "He's right puny. Soon as you can, better get him on goat's milk."

I took the closed-up little heap of him. I couldn't hardly feel his weight, but I could feel his heat and I opened up the blanket flaps. I wished I'd left them closed. I had to hold him so careful I was afraid he'd get hurt just being alive. Then I thought about how Lon was born but almost not, coming into the world backwards but it seemed forward, and hurting his mother, who might of died and was spiting him for it ever since.

I let his little mouth find its mark and tried to settle myself. But my mind brought up my daddy's haint in torture telling me he needed something. How could I put him to rest? I looked at the busy head pulling at me and thought of the pappaw he would never see and who I'd got Emory to let me name him after. I owed him that for what I'd done for him that day that made him die too early.

II

The snows came, and melted, and people were still celebrating the end of the war. But I wasn't celebrating anything unless being free from my man was equal cause and, whenever I thought of it, maybe it was. I'd left the battles that had become my life with him and come to the city where my older brother who'd left the coal mines as soon as he could and had come and found me and Virgie and the children a little, unpainted house with cheap rent. It wasn't much, but it wasn't Carbo.

I could almost hear myself remembering it all while I was off someplace where I couldn't do nothing but remember. One minute I'd been looking at my cutouts and saying my prayers and going over my Catholic instructions. The

next I was getting myself tied to a man who walked in off the street and wanted some pie. Now I was always telling my inside self the way you do when you
think-speak how things were not how they were going to be and sure not how
they should be no more. Mama'd told me a lot of things not to do, and I didn't
do them, mostly, but that's one I sure wished I'd of listened to her about, and to
Sister Jillian to be a "good Catholic young lady."

I knew what they'd said about me even before he came into the cafe that
day, and I hadn't cared till Sister Jillian said I had to live better. But even now,
the good times with him came back as the good drinking times, and I craved it
sometimes something awful. If things had been right from the beginning with
him, I wouldn't of changed so much, got so big and plain. If he'd still felt the
way he did when he'd met me and during that first year, he could've kept me like
he met me. And then when Lettie was born, he'd blamed me, so I let myself go.
But no matter what, I wouldn't of stayed around there to raise poor little Delmar
to be a mule tender, and he might not never be able to be even that.

Father Shivsky told me to examine my conscience, and that was what I
aimed to do even if it was too late. I was carrying hate and guilt, too, around
on my bones which didn't need anything extra. In the looking glass I saw in my
own face the bad side of the only man I had ever known. I might of went off in
the woods with those boys, but boys didn't count even if one of them was nice,
good-looking, and quiet and almost daddy to my first baby. It might've been better if he had been. Now I was too ruined after Emory Necessary to take up with
another man. It was like I'd sucked in the hate part of him in one side of my face
and my daddy's sorrow in the other. I'd heard that mean Honeycutt boy worked
in the mines with my brother said it was Emory Necessary's fertilizer made me
grow big and ugly. I'd been so mad I almost told Emory on him.

But more and more I came to make some sense out of it. Sister Jillian told
me that my body was a temple of the Lord and I should not let anyone defile it.
Father Shivsky told me to avoid the occasion of sin. I told myself over and over,
Just think, Opal, if you'd of listened. And look at the two of them, going all their lives
without what causes so much trouble.

And her in that white habit and me in mine, getting ready to go to work in
the city at The Columbia Restaurant.

The brand new white uniform made me think of Sister Jillian, and I felt clean and proud until I went out into the light of day. I kept walking because I had to, but I didn't look to either side, just boarded the bus and made my transfers to the streetcar, all the time think-saying the rosary I fingered in my uniform pocket. When I got off at my stop and stepped down into the street, there weren't too many people out yet. But what there were, I felt a few look at me like I was the center of a big cone of light. When I stumbled a little on a sidewalk crack, I might as well have been on a stage with a carnival man calling out: *Look at her!*

I'd taken the job requiring the white uniform for the better tips and steady day shift. The Columbia Restaurant. It was called by that fancy name, but it was really just a bigger, cleaner version of my last cafe, where Virgie still worked. And when I compared kitchens, it was worse. The cook was meaner than any I'd ever worked with. Or *for.* He gave out orders like he owned the place, when he wasn't any better than the rest of us who'd come up here looking for work. Only what he said, went.

I'd had to buy the uniform just to get started making the better money. The salary was only five dollars a week at just about all the cafes and even higher-classed restaurants. Tips were what counted, and they could count up in a place like The Columbia if you knew how to manage yourself. I was hard-enough-working, but I had a tough time managing my body that had gotten too big faster than I could get used to it. As soon as I got established here at The Columbia, I was going to try to get Virgie on, too, late shift, so we could keep taking turns with the children. I wished Virgie had gotten on first. She was little and pretty, and she knew how to smile at the customers. If we just didn't have to pay rent. But the only way out of it was living back there in Carbo with our mother.

This morning was the beginning of my second week. I went into The Columbia and said hello to the woman who opened up and sat in the little office in the back, going over the books all day, scheduling, keeeping time on everyone. I didn't know how to take her. The radio was always playing low, and the goose-neck lamp on the desk was bent close down. The woman didn't seem any too happy to be there, but being in charge went a long way with her. I thought of her as Miz Boss, seeing as how I took her to be the manager's wife. I didn't really call either of them by any name. I'd never been told what it was.

Mornings, opening girl had counter duty, which meant peanuts for tips, but then moved at noon to the good tables in front. The further away, the more walking, the better tips. At slack times, the manager had all the girls cleaning windows, washing booths and tables, filling sugar bowls and shakers. Always getting ready for the next meal or next shift.

"Opal." The woman had come to the door of her office.

I was bent over getting napkins from under the counter, and I looked up.

"Can you take the counter again tomorrow morning? Velma needs a day off but can't take it unless you cover."

I wondered why the new girl who'd just started couldn't cover, but I didn't ask.

"The new girl quit," Miz Boss said, just like she'd read my mind.

I'd been counting on a good day tomorrow, enough to make a payment on the uniform and start taking home some clear money. While I fixed the coffee and cut the butter squares and filled the jelly bowls for the singles who would line the counter for breakfast or coffee and doughnuts or just coffee and leave a nickel or dime or nothing, I looked at the picture calendar hanging over the table I was working on and thought back to how I used to make time pass when I was a girl working in Carbo's cafe. It was quite a ways from Eats to The Columbia.

In a little while it started. A customer rose and left, and I took up the plate, cup, and utensils, found a dime under the rim of the dish, and swept it into my side pocket. It went in little and quiet. I wiped the counter in quick circles until all traces of the customer were gone, hurried the dirties to the back, put them in the rinse sink, and returned to the front as another man sat down.

"Ham and eggs." He looked me in the eye, like waitresses never got right the first time what he told them he wanted, then said slow and louder than he needed to, "Up and easy, coffee," then stuck his face in his newspaper.

When they raised the paper you didn't ask any more questions, because they'd flap it down a little with a jerk and look over the top of it like they were already busy with the news of the day and I was interrupting world events, and then they sure weren't going to leave anything bigger than a dime. So I brought medium toast, cream, and sugar. Ever now and then, one would say his egg was runny or didn't I have some strawberry jam instead of apple jelly. I had to remind myself that Sister Jillian would have shaken her finger at me for how I felt about them being so particular, but when the war was just barely over and so many people at least where I came from still didn't have enough to eat—well, I had all I could do to keep keeping my mouth shut.

I talked little as I could. Just shook or nodded my head and went and got what they wanted or took back what they didn't, but snappy as I could and with a fixed look I'd learned to wear on my face. If it was to somebody with the sound of the mountains in their voice (and there were plenty of us up here), I'd talk a little to him. If it was somebody else, I'd see that little crease of a grin and more often than not hear, "Where are you from?" It was bad enough in the cafes where I'd had to talk more, but in those places most of them were from the mountains and I'd at least worn a dark skirt and sweater over a dark blouse. But in other ones, with more people without mountain voices, while I stood there in a uniform, what always came next was: "I thought I detected an accent." When I had to ask a woman from Brooklyn, New York, to repeat herself, twice, I still could not understand what she ordered, let alone the comment she made after she asked me where I was from, except for that one word: accent. I served her the closest thing to what I thought she'd said, and must have got it right because she didn't complain.

Later that morning the coins I dropped into the uniform pocket began to make a lively jingle, then little thuds, until a fairly good weight of them rode safe on my thigh. I ate a quick sandwich in the back booth and was hoping to have a pretty good day at the front, only I was already tired. My back ached like it always did that time of month, but after I met Sister Jillian I'd trained myself not to pay it any mind. My mother'd always been superstitious enough about it for both of us and Virgie, too.

So I got up, poured two glasses of water, and went to the front. That time of day the window turned into a looking glass, and while my big self was heading for it it was filling up with more white. It already brightened the room there so much it made me want to squint, but I held my look. It was just like I was a part of the people passing by outside.

I came to the table where two men sat holding closed menus and talking like they hadn't seen each other in a long time. I stood there a minute with the water glasses, then caught closer sight of myself above them, between their own reflections and two fedoras hanging on the racks on each side. The picture we made reminded me of one of my cutouts when I was a girl. I placed the water glasses, took my pad and pencil out of the single pocket with the change, and looked somewhere above the men's heads but nowhere really.

"Good afternoon."

I glanced over the pad, then back, but not so fast I didn't get an impression of the face of the one who'd spoken. I held the pad up to hide more of my face. I could feel the blood rising there and had all I could do to answer the other one's questions about the special of the day, the meat loaf and vegetable choices, as I looked at what his finger pointed out on the menu and fixed my lips before each answer, all the time writing on the pad in made-up shorthand what the cook could not read. I'd have to fix it before I gave it to him or he'd have a fit.

I sneaked looks to see their smiles and heard in the words they used not a whine or a slur but the clearest sounds. I hadn't heard such voices in men since Father Shivsky. And wouldn't you know? One was a father in a black suit and white collar. Sun spots danced on and off the table as the people outside passed by. I reached to point out something on the menu, when the one raised his hand and we touched. It was really just a brush; I'm sure he hadn't noticed it. I took the menus and was about to make the long reach across the middle of the men to replace them in the little rack, when the priest asked me: "Are you new here?"

"I've been here two weeks, Father," I said, surprised at myself for answering it so easy.

The one who made me weak when I looked at his face said, "We'll be seeing a lot of you." He smiled. "If my friend here orders dessert, just ignore him."

I saw in the window that I was holding a smile like it belonged there all the time. I was holding the menus, too, and was ready to reach when the father took them and replaced them for me.

"Why, thank you," I said.

"Thank you." They both said it like one voice.

When I turned to go, I heard the gentle men who would be seeing a lot of me say, "Now tell me all about what Glenmary Home Missions is doing down there. How's the new church coming along?" The father laughed. "A log at a time. Quaint and inspiring." "Now that the war is over——."

I was out of hearing range by then, and the noises took over. My body was not just taking up too much space now but beginning to sag. I pulled it up straight and even felt a little graceful as I made the long walk to the kitchen.

I started through the right swing door, and it slammed into me. Things came down on me, and I fell, my head thumping the floor. A hot stickiness oozed through the uniform to my skin. I tried but couldn't get up. The bright colors in my head, behind my eyes, were changing.

Hands were wiping me and feeling of my wrist. A cool rag was put on my forehead. But they were raising my legs, and my tips were falling out. I couldn't tell them not to. It felt so peaceful being helpless.

"Don't you know your right from your left?" It was the voice of the boss woman.

"I just wasn't thinking." Velma's voice had hate in it.

"What are you so fired up for? She was going to cover for you tomorrow."

"Please, ladies."

When I heard that voice, I shut my eyes tighter.

Then he spoke lower, but I heard. "Is she pregnant? I'm a doctor."

"Not that I know of," the office woman whispered, but I heard that, too.

I turned my head from them like I was still out and didn't know what I was doing.

Off to the side Velma's hard whisper came through the soothing voices: "One side's not enough for her."

"Sssssshhh! You knocked her down. You ought to be ashamed."

"Better put her legs down."

"And gather up her change. What's that?"

"Give it to me, please," the doctor said, "Do you have a place where she will be more comfortable? And go get Father Cresman in the booth, will you?"

"Take her back there. There's a couch, but it's pretty small."

Nobody said anything, and I felt them all wondering if she'd fit on the small couch. It made me want to come around. "I'm okay," I said and felt my chin dimple up into dozens of little craters the way it did when I was hurting inside. "Just help me up, will you?" I let them guide me to the couch and asked if I

could have a few minutes on it. When I laid down, he came over and by then the
father was there, too. He gave me my rosary.

"Are you Catholic?"

"Not yet, Father, but I been meaning to again."

"My," he said, "that's a pretty crucifix. Is it onyx?"

"I don't know," I said. "A man carved it out of a piece of hard coal my daddy left me when he died." I left out that the man who carved it was my husband.
I also left out what I'd told Jimmy Dell that day I was being so mean.

"Anthracite," he said. "How interesting."

"Excuse me, Brad." The doctor bent over me. His nose was sharp, and his
eyes made me want to smile at him. He'd come from the barber's, sure. Dots
where whiskers had been showed through the talcum I smelled, and I thought
of my babies.

Pregnant? It was enough being reminded that I still could be. But unless
heaven wanted to make a double miracle, it wasn't likely. I looked the doctor in
the blue eye. "No, I ain't—I'm not," I said.

He looked a question at me.

"What you asked before," I said. "Just...heavy," and I could hear the old taunt
I'd given out as a girl about poor Hazel Bolt coming back now before him, about
myself and from myself. *Fatty, Fatty...can't get through the kitchen door.* When I turned
away, I smelled the gravy on my uniform somebody had tried to wipe away.

I couldn't get over all the attention I was getting now that I'd fallen when I
didn't get much at all while standing on my own two feet. It made me want to get
home to Lettie and let her know how much she counted. Little Delmar, too, if I
could get through to him. Things hadn't gone easy on them. I just wished they'd
had the daddy I'd had, but then in reverse we parted ways on mothers, too, if I
could allow myself a little praise.

The office woman commenced fussing over me, giving me a cool drink
from a glass. The doctor told her to "See that she doesn't go out until she comes
around fully, but she should not work anymore today." He walked across the
small room with the woman, talking so low I couldn't hear. I wasn't really listening anyway. I was worrying about losing time.

"Is she all right? I mean, should we call an ambulance?"

"No, no," the doctor said. "She's just fatigued. After she rests a day or so, I'd suggest you have her work tables closer to the kitchen. The counter might be better."

I shifted my eyes away from him when he came back over. He drew back my eyelids one at a time and looked in. "You need more iron," he said, "especially this time of month."

My face went hot.

"Eat plenty of spinach and kale, and get more rest." He smiled. "Will you do that for me?"

After he left, the office woman gave me a sweater to wear, but it was too little. The more she tried to help, the worse it became. She finally gave me a scarf to carry. At least I could hide the big spot until I got home. Everything was going to be all right, she told me. Then she gave me my tip money and three dollars the doctor and priest had left, and she walked me to the front door.

"I'll be back tomorrow," I told her. "I need the work."

Leaving the house in the bright, clean uniform for the outside world was embarrassing enough. Returning early from work in a dirty one made me want to disappear. On the streetcar I took a seat by a window and had trouble banking myself on the lurches. Over the seats across from me was a picture of a man with a white see-through cross over his mouth and throat and a pack of cigarettes near him. Printed beneath it was

More Doctors Smoke Camels

Good for the T-zone

My eyes fuzzed over, and I turned my head to the window and kept it there until I got off for my first bus transfer.

I had to wait along with two Salvation army soldiers, an old woman, and a man so dirty and drunk it was like I was back on the streets of Carbo. When the old woman looked over, I spread the scarf over the spot. The bus came, and when the dirty man didn't get on, I saw that he was there to panhandle the ones waiting. But he hadn't asked me.

Buses felt tighter than streetcars. People were too close to you and there was less sitting room for what I needed. I looked at the long back seat the way I always did and headed back there. I gripped the seat backs along the way with one hand and held the scarf over the spot with the other. When I was almost there, the bus speeded up, causing me to run in quick, little steps the last few feet to keep from hitting the rear window. I managed to pull up short and, with a turn, plop down and scoot over, where I sat on the ridge between two spaces, giving each half of me a little comfort.

I sneaked a look at the brown gravy spot and planned my attack: cold-water soak, overnight ice block, tooth brush and concentrated Ivory flakes with some Bon Ami, a bleach rinse. I'd put my uniform up against anybody's, even a nun nurse's, and Sister Jillian seemed to walk back there and sit beside me in her black-and red-spotted uniform, and I commenced talking in my head for the both of us.

You scrubbin' your habit at night, starchin' and ironin' it like me? I bet you have two good ones.

If it's comparin' you're after, it makes no difference, you see? I'm washin' one every night as well.

Why we have to look so spotless? We're sure not that way now.

I doubted I could come up to Sister Jillian's white. There'd be Lettie and little Delmar to see to, and the housework Virgie wouldn't have done. She'd be surprised by me coming home so early and her listening to the radio and playing with the children but not doing extra for them. Good thing I have the spare that the new-and-used store threw in for three dollars extra. Secondhand, but it'll do till I can clean up the new one. Give me time so I can rest some today...he'd said to get more...with a nose like the handle on a delicate tea cup I saw at that auction when I was working at the cafe and would have bought with my own fifteen cents if it hadn't been for her.

I got off at the stop and waited twenty minutes for the next bus that would take me where I lived now. I couldn't call it home since I couldn't do much to it and didn't feel anything for it. It was just one of a few dozen wooden army barracks made over into houses after the war. I was thankful to have it, but if being happy is for when it's all over, I had a lot to look forward to. In the meantime, I had to be somewhere. That kind of thinking made me want a drink, and if I'd had one I'd of taken it right then and there. Without thinking, I reached in my pocket to finger my tips, felt the rosary, and it passed.

I boarded the bus, and seeing it was almost empty I just took a seat near the front. It made only two stops between here and the block before the house. That time of day I wouldn't have to worry about a crowd. I looked across and down a few seats and was surprised I hadn't seen the man who lived up the hill when I first got on. We'd said a few things to each other when we'd come from work on the bus and got off together, but nothing ever much. We kind of knew each other without ever saying so, but he was so shy I didn't want to embarrass him. I did wonder why he was going home early today, too. He worked in the city hauling trash. I looked back at him again, and when he looked I smiled at him. He had a face it was hard not to look at. Bones showed through the sickly skin of his face. His eyes were tucked way up under his forehead and were shining water. I knew without asking that he'd worked underground so long with his face set against disaster it'd become fixed that way.

So like my long-ago daddy.

When we got off at our stop, I said hello and asked him if he'd had a shift change. I'd been rotated myself between shifts at the cafes before The Columbia, and when they clashed with Virgie's hours we had a hard time working things out.

"Had a change all right. They let me go."

He looked so bad and sounded so pitiful I didn't want to say anything back, but I couldn't not. "I'm so sorry. You been looking for something else?"

He wheezed. Turning his head, he wiped his mouth and nose with a blackened handkerchief, and I saw the shame on his face. "They ain't nothing much else for me up here," he said. "I just can't work no more at nothing."

I looked off and said in our way of talking, not the one in my head: "Well, guess I'd better be getting on home. Good luck to you." I started to go to my side of the street.

"We're a-going back," he said. "I'd a whole lot rather die back there in the hills."

I couldn't leave him without at least asking his name. "I'm Opal Necessary," I said. Then I looked away so he could use the handkerchief if he had to before telling me his.

He said it so low, I never heard it. He coughed. "I knowed you when you was little. Knowed your daddy."

We looked at the ground.

"I hope you get better, sir."

I couldn't tell if he was crying or not. The sunshine was sparkling in his eye waters, and he looked a little better even showing only gums where teeth should be.

He tipped his hat and set it back atilt in the mountain way and went on up the hill. I started across the yard, around the wood pile, to the house. When I looked back at him, he was hunched lighting a cigarette, and water came to my eyes. But Sister Jillian had told me more than once to remember: "It's not to be feelin' guilt you're goin' to live your life from now on. You gave your father what you thought he wanted most, and nothing could have kept him alive any longer." Just like Mama's time had come with Lon and my time had come twice and almost twice more, his time had come, and I had to fix it in my head that he died getting something he wanted. At least he had that.

By the time I reached the door, I knew I'd pulled the wool over my own eyes in a moment of plain foolishness. That spare uniform never did fit, except in my head when I saw the doctor smile. I got it little on purpose to make me fit it. It had to be let out all the way and, Lord, I'd be working on the big, dirty one for hours. Brilliant white for the Lord and a dying miner dirty for good and laid out in a white bed, starched white for serving the counter and tables and falling on your big hind end, blood- or gravy-spotted—what was the difference? You worked or paid or both to get that way. Work clothes, pickaxe, lamp, carbide. Shining white or crow black. A body might just as well go back where they came from. You couldn't escape it anyway. Your voice and ways marked you for what you were and always would be, even if you do forget yourself for a little.

But it was just because I had been able to forget myself, even for a minute, that I had felt new and alive like never before. A little like what I imagined Sister Jillian must feel like, being so sure of things and of herself.

The two men had spoken to me like I was just a normal woman they always spoke to that way. And because they had, I had said back to them, just as normal as ever, "I've been here two weeks." Such a simple thing to say to strange men.

And the one had asked me about the spinach and kale, *"Will you do that for me?"* I couldn't help wondering if collards and mustard greens would do. Or those pocked sprigs mean enough to battle through the black blanket in spring we used to eat.

"I will try," I whispered.

I fought off the chin crinkles that wanted to put my face into misery, and I made it smile when I opened the door and reached into the little imitation font with regular water in it I kept tacked on the inside doorframe. Father Shivsky gave it to me back when it looked like I was going to be baptized. Virgie, pretty and little as ever, was sitting on the rug playing with the children, just like one of them. They all stopped and looked up at me at the same time I was making the Sign of the Cross with my wet fingers.

FOR SOME
DESPERATE GLORY

"Of boys that slept wry sleep
And men writhing for air."

— Wilfred Owen, "Miners"

When Flush arrived at the mine that morning, there was a new boy there, a dago. Flush stood at the mine mouth with Goff, who was rolling a cigarette. Flush watched the new boy, tall and cocky, and when he lit the cigarette, it almost burned up.

"That the new wop?" Flush said. Goff took his cigarette out of his mouth and looked at it as if it had the answer. There were only two fingers on that hand, but he managed to hold the butt and flip its ash. He put it back in the corner of his mouth and nodded.

"Man and his boy. Just come yesterday. Don't you go causing no trouble."

Beelcy the mule came out of the mine pulling a coal car. She had on an old hat with ear holes. One of the boys led her over to the tipple, where she was maneuvered so that the coal car was readied for dumping.

"Don't you go talking to me like no kid, Goff."

"Yeah, I won't. Almost forgot: You ain't no kid no more."

"That's right. I go into pick-and-shovel today."

"Why, you could of done that a long time ago, ever since your daddy—."

Goff made a face and tapped Flush on the shoulder; but when Goff's hand stayed there, Flush pulled away.

Beelcy dropped her own load coming back around to the side track, and somebody yelled out: "Dang, Beelcy! What you been eating, rats?" Somebody else said, "I wish she would. By damn, if she liked them she'd sure never go hungry working for the Black Diamond Coal Company."

By now the men and boys of the day shift had assembled. They stood or squatted around the mine mouth, some smoking, some chewing tobacco; all of them were dressed essentially the same: brogans and denim overalls, collared shirts buttoned to the top, miner hats with carbide lamps attached. Some wore gloves. They all carried lunch buckets. Most of them were already, or still, dirty. The night workers came from out of the hole in the side of the mountain.

A boy walked a pony behind them. The pony stopped, snorted once, and put his head down. "Get on, Muley," the boy said. The pony did not move, and so the boy hit it on the head with a wooden club.

The pony looked at the boy, Flush saw, as he and the others took up their picks and shovels and went into the mine. "Hit him in the hind-end," Flush said, pointing. "You want him to go thataway."

"When'd you get to be so smart?" the boy said to Flush.

"Yesterday, when he turned fourteen," Goff said beside him. "Now get that pony on out of here. We got to have that car."

"They's one already back there with Beelcy," the boy said.

"Yeah, but we got Flush here with us today. Heck fire, we might load us two at a time."

Salyers came up to Goff and Flush, saying, "You two want to work together?"

They said they did.

"Okay," Salyers said, raising his voice. The others were coming up behind them, and Salyers held them all there together. "Listen here, you men."

Maggard hawked and spat. There was still light, but it would be gone a few more feet in.

Salyers continued. "Maggard, you and Triplett work together setting timbers further on back where me and Triplett was digging yesterday. Dye? I want you and Hensley up ahead of Goff and Flush." He looked beyond the group. "Who're you back there?"

The men parted, turning their heads.

"This here's Pisa," a man named Tatum said, using a long i.

"Angelo Pisa," the man himself said, correcting the name.

"That your boy there beside you?" Salyers pointed.

"*Mio figlio*—"

"Name's Frank," the boy himself said. He was as tall as any of the men, far taller than Flush.

"You speak English?"

"Yes, sir. Understand it, too." There was an enthusiasm in his voice that could have been feigned. A couple of men laughed.

"You sure you just a boy?"

"Be fourteen in just a couple of weeks." Frank glanced at Flush. Beyond Frank was a boy smaller than Flush.

"And who're you back there?"

"'At there's Crede Potter's boy," Maggard said. "Little Crede."

"All right, then. Little Crede, you tend to Muley. Frank—"

"Yes, sir!"

"—uh, you take Beelcy. You boys got a club?"

"Yes, sir!" said Frank.

"What for?" said Little Crede.

"To col'cock that animal when he won't move," said Triplett.

"All right," said Salyers. "Let's get going now. Ain't nobody going to make a cent till we load us some coal."

Flush felt good going in on the day shift with Maggard, Salyers, Tatum, Goff, and Dye. They were old hands who always came back. Which made him think of one in the last accident who hadn't—Ike Absher, better known as Spider because of his arms and legs and the way he creeped instead of walked.

Triplett had told the story many times at the commissary, sitting around the stove. He had been with Spider, cleaning up a small side room after a shoot. The other men were working a new vein. Both men were ankle-deep in water, crouched with picks under a shelf. Triplett said that Spider told him he was getting stiff and moved out to stand up. Triplett said he heard the blower about the time he saw Spider rise and that he yelled for Spider to duck at the same time it blew. He knew right away what had happened, he said, and threw himself on the floor so that his face was under water. He stood it as long as he could, took a quick breath, and then went under again. He kept doing it until he couldn't feel the heat anymore. Then he ran like hell out of there. There wasn't any use to try to help Spider. As Spider had stood up, the blower—a gush of methane gas, what the miners called firedamp—came out of a crack in the coal wall like a quick wind. Triplett knew that Spider would meet it with his burning carbide lamp, and that's what he did. The gas blew, taking Spider's head off. But it was a small blower, just enough of a pocket to cause a blast at all. Triplett knew that too as he buried his face, and he knew that as soon as the lighter-than-air firedamp burned itself off at the top, he had to get out of there because after the methane would come the afterdamp, which gathered at the floor, and there wasn't anyone could tell in advance just how high it would rise. One whiff of afterdamp was all it took for sure death. So when he heard the rats, then saw them running, he'd yelled to the others to get on out, and only poor old Spider got caught because he was too tall. But then if he hadn't, up high, the methane might have gathered lower down for when Triplett stood.

Now Flush was thinking about his daddy over at the old Bethel mine. The cave-in had been so massive they'd never even looked for him and the others. But now Flush was one of them, and he felt a thrill as Little Crede passed around the water to pour into the carbide chambers, as Flush popped the heel of his hand over the flared lamp and struck the flint, turning the dial for the right amount of gas to flame, and especially so since the dago had to ask Little Crede to help him. Flush felt like one of the men as he made his way into the rocky cave shored by timbers, the lamps causing what was left of the coal to glisten. As many times as he'd led a mule in and out of there, it had never looked like this.

It was the summer of 1939. School was out for good for Flush. He had told his mother, as soon as his older brother left for work in Portsmouth that spring, that he was through with school. He didn't care what the law was. He had finished seventh grade and was the only man left to work. It wasn't sacrifice on his part either; it was just necessity. Ever since his father was killed he had been anxious to draw his own paycheck, even if the bulk of it went to his mother. With what he had made just driving the mule he had had enough left over to be his own man, and that was what he meant to be. Now, even if he had to make his way a shovelful at a time, he'd have more.

After work that first day he went to the company commissary, the social hub of the town. It was almost dark, the sun having disappeared over the western ridge. His ten-hour shift, including lunch inside the mine, had taken up the day.

He had gone home, rinsed his face of coal dust, and left, telling his mother just to save something for him to eat when he returned. He arrived at the commissary and swaggered inside. It was the time he had waited for above all others: a pick-and-shovel coal miner walking dirty to the potbelly stove where the men sat, the stove burning warm to knock the chill off the cool mountain air. He stood around awhile, not quite bold enough yet to take the one empty seat.

In a few minutes Goff said to him, "Sore?"

"'Bout what?" Flush thought that Goff was asking him if he was mad because except for some sporadic talking after the first hour in the mine that day Flush had become sullenly quiet. He'd hated those ten hours almost more than school. Goff made gestures to show that it could get a man in the back and shoulders, that kind of work, and Flush said, "Nah, I feel okay."

"Well, set a spell," Salyers said, pushing the chair at him. Flush sat and took a bite off a tobacco plug being passed around. The men talked and rubbed at their hands. Flush pushed himself to the edge of the chair so his feet would touch the floor. Then Mister Kincaid, who ran the commissary for the coal company, brought over a jar of pickled pig's feet and some crackers, and the men paid a nickel apiece and a few even ate around their tobacco quids. Flush couldn't do that, yet.

"A cold beer'd sure taste good," said Maggard.

"Yeah, or some of that home brew you had last week," said Goff.

They settled for Grapettes and Doctor Peppers, other men came in after a while, and soon the place was crowded with eating, talking men. Even though he had to take a leak, Flush kept his seat.

After a while Angelo and Frank Pisa were the center of attention. Angelo was telling his listeners in broken English how he had come to West Virginia in the first place; when he stalled on a phrase Frank filled in.

"I coom-a C. O. D.," Angelo said.

The men laughed but didn't seem to know what was really funny about it.

"I sign-a on with a labor agents inna New York." He went on to explain how immigrants were contracted for and sent out to coal companies, tickets paid for by agents who were paid back by the company, with a commission for every man they sent.

"Sounds kind of like slaving to me," said Triplett. They all laughed except the Pisas. Angelo didn't seem to understand what to laugh at; Frank seemed irked at the comment.

After a brief silence Dye asked Frank, "How'd Little Crede get along to-day?"

Frank grinned. "Still little enough to be ascared of the dark."

At the word little Flush shot a glance at Frank. "You mean too young."

"I mean too little," Frank said, then added with a chuckle while he pulled the chair from under Flush, "Have a seat, Pop." Flush fell forward but caught himself in time to keep from going down.

"It's-a okay," Angelo said. "Noncha make-a trouble, Frank."

The men looked at Flush, bare smiles on their faces. It would have been better if they had laughed outright. Flush glared while Frank set the chair for his father, who took it reluctantly, gesturing to Frank with his face to take it easy, now.

As the men began to talk about the coal and how, Maggard was sure, they were being cheated at the weighing station, Flush wandered among the aisles of canned meat and bread and work clothes. He was hungry and thinking of going home to eat, but he bided his time until the talk stopped and several of the men got up to leave. Then he walked out without being seen, and he waited by the door in the dark. The men came out in single file, a few of them looking at Flush. Frank was last, gangly, dragging his feet, then at the door hurrying to catch up. Flush put his foot out and caught him just right. He went over and Flush jumped on him and began pounding him in the ribs. Frank rolled and came up on top, pinning Flush by the shoulders.

"I'm going to whip your ass good, you little showoff."

Flush kicked his legs up and out. The more he kicked, the tighter Frank held him. Just when Frank drew back to hit him, the men were there, grabbing Frank and pulling him off. Flush got in a light blow before the others grabbed him. Angelo slapped Frank on the shoulder and, talking heatedly in Italian, took him away.

They stayed away from each other after that night. When their eyes met on those mornings as they gathered at the mine, Flush clamped his teeth at the tall boy's leering. He burned to get back at him but knew that, face to face, he'd have no chance. He'd just watch and wait for the right time. As the days passed, the miners cleaning up what was left of the vein, Flush languished in the dark and damp cubicles of the mine. He had taken to raking with his shovel at the mine floor, rocks and all, restless to fill up a coal car with anything with weight.

"Can't do it," said Goff. "They'll reject this one."

"Let the coal-sorters worry about it," said Flush.

"Now, you listen to me," said Goff, rubbing at his finger stubs. "You ever been a sorter?"

"Not long. And don't plan on being one again no time soon."

"Well, I was when I was no bigger than Little Crede. It ain't no easy job. But besides that, I'm telling you, you fill that car up with junk and we all pay for it."

Frank came up with Beelcy pulling a car. "Load 'er up," he said. Then he shined his lamp at the small pile and shook his head. Flush and Goff paid him no attention, and he stood there, biding time. Then suddenly he grabbed a shovel and pinned a big rat to the wall crease, cutting off its head.

"Don't you go killing no rats, boy," Goff said.

"Why not?" Frank said, scoffingly.

Flush laughed.

"They're the only other thing alive in here besides us," Goff said. "You see a bunch of rats running, you better follow them. Now, get on by. We'll let you know when we're ready."

"But I need some more for this load."

"I said get on by," Goff said. "And I meant it."

As Frank clicked his tongue and moved Beelcy along, Flush said to Goff, "I'm going to get that wop one of these days."

"Well, in the meanwhile let's get the rest of this blue jim. No rocks. You hear?"

Later that day when the miners were eating their lunch in the glow of their lamps—some went outside, but most of them were in so far they didn't want to use any of the thirty minutes walking in and out—Salyers came by. "After you

eat, we're going to start tearing down. I want all of you in the far back, all working together." To close it up they would pull down the support timbers and col-
lapse the roof, with dynamite if necessary, working from rear to front. "I want
Frank and Little Crede in line up front of you. Whatever coal you find that's
handy and big enough, throw in the car."

There was a general murmur as the men got up, blackened and weary.

"All I know's what I been told," Salyers said.

"Maybe when we finish this here one, we might ought to talk to the union
people."

"I'm-a no for union," Angelo said.

"I ain't neither," said Triplett, "but I ain't in favor of no slave wages."

Angelo looked at Triplett. "I'm-a no slave."

"We all are," said Dye. "I say we talk union after we close this mine up."

"Okay, knock it off, men," said Salyers. "We got work to do."

They went to the end of the tunnel and took up positions. Several of them
stood by while the others began to take down the timbers. As the last support of
that section was knocked out, the roof collapsed, sending dust throughout the
mine. Flush realized sorrowfully what he should have known before: The timbers were actually holding up the roof; without them the mountain above would
fall. But that did not happen in the next section. There, the men switched places,
and when the supports were knocked out nothing happened. They all stood in
front of the section, looking back and up, waiting.

"Knock that overhang down," Salyers told Dye. "It ought to fall in then."
Dye took a long steel pole with a spear tip and chipped beneath the overhang-
ing slate. In a few minutes there was a sound as of something rushing, muted,
and the wall gave way. The roof followed. Several men moved in to gather up
the largest chunks of coal and carried them where Little Crede, like a soldier on
guard, held Muley harnessed to the front car. Goff and Maggard strained at a
black boulder and carried it to the car. There they called for Dye and Flush to
help them, and the four of them hoisted it and let it fall in. Maggard and Dye
turned to go, but Flush looked at Little Crede and stopped Goff. Goff and
Flush went over to him. Little Crede, like a dark, overdressed pigmy, was snif-
fling, tear tracks running through the caked dust on his face.

"Hey, what's the matter, boy?" said Goff.

Muley balked, whinnied, and Little Crede jerked his head down. "N-Nothing." He sucked at his nose. Holding Muley's halter with one hand, he wiped with the other.

"Ascared?" Flush said.

Muley began to drill a loud hole with his water, and the boys watched.

"I ain't a-sayin'," Little Crede said.

"Hold on there, now." Goff said it to Little Crede, but it seemed for Flush too. "They ain't nothing wrong with being scared. I tell you what: You go on out and get yourself a drink of water and take a rest, and Flush here'll tend Muley."

Flush didn't like it. He'd served his time tending. But he didn't say anything as Goff walked Little Crede ahead several feet, then urged him on.

Coming back, Goff said, "Just watch that pony kind of close. Hit's spooked."

Flush turned to look behind him where Frank was standing with Beelcy. Frank hawked and spat, then grinned, it seemed. Flush couldn't see him too well, but he knew that wop bastard.

They worked the next section and the one after that, filling up both cars. Flush took the first out to the tipple and dumped it, then found Little Crede and told him to come on back in with him. They waited at the circled-back track junction in front of the mine opening until Frank came by with Beelcy. When he passed the junction, Flush and Little Crede, who now led Muley, went in. Nobody spoke. As Little Crede was unharnessing Muley to re-harness him in front, Frank arrived with Beelcy and his car.

"Here," Frank said to Little Crede. "Harness him on the front car." Frank and Little Crede passed on opposite sides of the track, and Frank said, "I wonder if old Muley ever gets to hankering after Beelcy. You see him just look over at her twat?" Then Frank hitched Beelcy to the front of the rear car, and they exchanged.

Flush understood what Frank had done, but there was probably another reason, too. He still didn't like the dago. After the next section, they came to a side room, large and shiny, irregularly dug. There seemed to be plenty of coal still there, but of course there was a limit to how far up or in they could dig. It was without timbers and would have to be blown shut. "I don't get it," Flush said to Goff: "Blow something shut and something else's got to open up someplace."

"Yeah, but that'd be above the mine. Hell, let it fall up there where nobody could ever get."

"Yeah, but how about when we have to go back to open up Bethel?"

"We never shut it like this." Then Goff's voice went solemn. "The whole mountain fell in. Hit's solid as new."

Which made Flush think of the empty casket at his daddy's token funeral and how someday he might come up on him again.

Salyers had taken a couple of men out and come back with blasting material. "Goff, you and Dye set the charge. You other men see what you can salvage over there." He pointed to another side room farther up.

"Leave Flush here to help," Goff said.

"Okay. Flush, get them what they need. And, Goff? When you're ready to blow, let me know."

Goff nodded, took up the auger, and went with Dye, carrying his pick and shovel, into the large side room.

Flush stayed in the main haulage tunnel with the blasting material. Then he moved to the entrance and watched as Goff and Dye started a hole chest-high in the far wall. They turned the auger, which slipped in easier than it ought to, several feet to the turning crook. When Goff called for dynamite, Flush glanced ahead to see Frank looking back at him above the coal car and mule. The meeting of the glows of their lamps made an eerie spot between Flush and the rear of the car.

As Flush took up a stick of dynamite in each hand and began to carry them gingerly into the room, he heard the pony whinny. Dye called for the tamper, too, but Flush could not manage that with the dynamite, and so Goff and Dye started out to get the tamper, a squib, and some fuse.

"Just hold them a second," Dye said, as they were passing in the middle of the room.

Flush had stopped briefly, holding out the dynamite, when something like the rush of air sounded above.

"Just—." Dye's face went strange.

Flush looked quickly at Goff, who looked at Dye. The three were frozen in the moment. Then suddenly Flush was propelled across the cave, still mindful of what he held, and he heard something like a woman's scream as, in the last moment, he managed to wrench himself around and hit the far wall with his back. In a roar of dust the room came down before him as he backed under a ledge, not knowing it was there. He was conscious of a sharp pain in his back and, closing his eyes, he waited to be crushed.

But only his back and, now, his feet hurt. He opened his eyes to darkness, feeling the pieces of rock dust hitting his head, smelling the ancient, rotted insides of the mountain. Spreading his arms, he gripped the sticks of dynamite, then carefully laid them aside. He tried to move but his feet were covered, his hat and lamp gone, and so he bent forward and felt a slab of rock. Reaching up as high as he could, he put his face on what he felt, and then he screamed. He could hear sounds, far away, and he stopped screaming and listened.

"Help! Somebody there?" he yelled to the sounds, but he choked on the fouled air and began to cry. But crying could not be done, he was gasping so, and then he became aware that he was praying. After what seemed like too short a time he heard a voice, somewhere above him, call, "Hey! Anybody down there?" He looked up and saw a faint light outlined in dust, aslant toward the top.

"Hey!" he screamed. "Yeah. Here. Oh, God, here!" He wiped the dirt from his eyes. The light turned downward then in a shimmering wall of motes curved upward, then down again and disappeared.

"Who is it down there?"

"Adam," he screamed.

"Who?"

"Flush! God, hurry!"

"Get on up here, then!" the voice yelled. "Damnit! Get!"

Flush was too weak, and choking, to answer.

"Can't you move?"

"N-No, can't." He heard the slide of stones hitting against what was in front of him. He reached up again and felt the slab. "I can't get up."

Then the light was only several feet above him, atop the slab, the voice a spectral booming. "Okay. Take it easy. Grab aholt. But don't jerk or this thing's going to fall." Now there were voices on the other side, someone yelling, and the light above him turned away, yelling, "Get up the goddamn top and help!" Then back to Flush: "Grab aholt!"

Flush reached up, high as he could, feeling for the hand but missing or not far enough, he couldn't know. The light showed him and he touched fingers, hooked his own into them, but still he couldn't move. They tried to pull like that, with hooked fingers, but it wouldn't work, and he felt alone as the hand withdrew.

"Don't leave me!" He bent down, removing some of what held his feet, and gained precious inches of his reach. "Here!" He reached again, connecting solid.

The voice garbled, then came out again: "How stuck?"

"I—I can make it...here." And suddenly he was free. The hand pulled him up the face of the slab, and as he reached the top the slab slid to where he had been. The hand held and the two of them were scrambling up, over sharp rocks, through dirt, until Flush fell into a little gulley and had to stop.

"Come on, quick!" The hand jerked at him. "We're almost home."

Then Flush knew who it was.

At the top were other lights, other hands, and Angelo Pisa, who took Frank's hand from Flush's and took his son down. The others followed, sliding, rolling, and Flush was on the other side, cut and bleeding at the bottom of the heaped mass of stone.

"These boys is killed."

In the commotion—men and lights moving, the sound of terrified braying far up the tunnel—Flush saw that it was Maggard who had said it, and Flush was stricken, wanting to say, No, we ain't, when he looked beside him. It was Dye, bent ugly beneath the rock, a piece of his skull busted out the back of his head. Flush turned away, closing his eyes, then heard in his head these boys and searched, finding a pair of hips, a nearly fingerless hand beside them. He just looked, trying to swallow without moisture; and then he saw, as if they belonged to something else, white ankle bones shot out through the shoes. There was another rumble then, and what was left above in the room gave way as Flush was dragged to the main tunnel.

The mad braying continued until somebody yelled for somebody to "Cut that damn mule aloose!"

Salyers said, "You men go on and get a crew and jacks and get them two out. You two! Get the Ramey boy on out." His voice changed. "They ain't no use in doing anything about the little Potter boy yet. I'll send somebody in to get somebody from the company."

"Better get the undertaker," somebody said.

"The company'll have to get the sheriff too," Salyers said.

Whichever two picked Flush up, one of them said to the other, "Ain't this a terrible way to die?"

The other said, horribly, "Sure is." He paused, then added, "Let's get this boy on out of here."

As they picked him up—Triplett on one side side, Hensley on the other—Flush looked at the general area of what had been Goff. Then he remembered that he had been pushed across the room. They carried him down the middle of the track, toward the braying, as he watched the walls in the bobbing lamps.

"My God Almighty," Triplett said, walking around something on the track.

"They ain't no durn God'd let a thing like that happen," said Hensley.

They moved ahead, slowly, and then Triplett yelled to "Clear the way up there."

Beelcy was backing up and kicking the coal car, then trying to run ahead, but the car in front of the mule would not let her pass. The mule butted the front car, backed up, and kicked out. Finally Tatum got close enough to cut the harness, and the mule ran around the front car and out the mine. Her braying sounded like screams. The men had to walk sideways with Flush around the two cars. When they reached the front of the forward car, its pony gone, Tatum pointed.

"Jesus," Triplett said, slow and soft.

The men had turned with Flush, and now he could see something jamming the car from underneath. "What is it?" he said, smelling the foul odor of human shit.

Triplett looked at Tatum and Hensley and shook his head, and they carried Flush the rest of the way outside.

"Let me down," Flush said. "I can walk okay." He went to Frank, who was sobbing, his hands covering his face. Frank's father sat beside him, comforting him. Flush felt tears rise to his eyes, and he rubbed them away and sat down quietly beside the Pisas.

"Your face, is-a hurt you?" said Angelo.

"Nah, it's okay," said Flush. "Is he—?" Flush nodded toward Frank.

Then suddenly Frank sat up straight, turning his head away. "Ain't nothing wrong with me," he said.

Triplett came over, stood a moment, then spoke: "Floyd Gilliam's down at the foot of the tipple, waiting to take you two boys in to town to get you fixed up."

Angelo and Triplett helped the boys to their feet and walked with them down the side of the mountain. When they reached the waiting truck and Frank and Flush began to get in the cab, Triplett asked them if they'd rather ride in the back. "Why don't you dump your load, Floyd? Let these boys have some room in the bed."

Floyd dumped the half load of coal, and when Angelo began to get in the back with the boys Triplett asked him if he would stay to help.

"It's okay, Pop," Frank said.

"We're going to need every man we can get," said Triplett. "You sure you boys is okay?" They said they were, and Triplett told Floyd to take them straight in to the doctor and then bring the doctor back with him out to the mine.

"Salyers said he was going to take care of that," Floyd said.

"Well, you come on back with the truck then, Floyd."

Flush and Frank settled into the back, and Floyd drove off down the mountain road. They sat with their backs against the cab, their legs laid out straight, and they looked at the road.

"I want you to know I appreciate what you done," said Flush.

"Skip it," Frank said.

"I'm just...did you see Goff and Dye?"

"Yeah, I seen 'em. They looked awful...didn't you?"

"Soon as I got off that pile Pop took me outside. But I saw—. God. Did you see what happened to Little Crede?"

"That him under the car?"

"What was left of him. I had to close my eyes coming out through the mine. He...broke up."

"What you mean?"

"When the cave-in started I ran back to see what was happening, and I only saw Goff and Dye running for it and all hell breaking loose in there. I had to jump back out of the way. About the same time, I heard Little Crede scream, and I started to run after him. But the men was up that way, so I figured they'd take care of him and I'd better see if you was still alive. Goff and Dye had disappeared. Well, you know what happened with you and me after that. But what happened to Little Crede was—." He stopped and shifted his legs, looking off to the side of the truck.

Flush by now pretty well knew, but he said, "What?"

"That pony he was holding—you know how spooked it was. It was like it knowed what was going to happen and was trying to warn us all. Well, I guess Little Crede was holding him by the halter, standing on the track in front of him. The pony reared up and knocked Little Crede down and then run over him. Little Crede stayed on the track, and then the car hit him and drug him a hundred feet. His arms and legs come off while he was tumbling, and then the car jammed him so bad the pony couldn't move the car no further. That pony broke out of the halter and ain't been seen since." He hung his head. "They ever catch that bastard, they ought to hang it."

Flush bowed his head, and they sat there without saying anything for a while. Then Flush spoke. "If I hadn't made Little Crede come back in the mine with me, he wouldn't of been killed."

"But you might of if you'd of been holding Muley. Only you wouldn't of been standing in front of him." Frank paused. "If I hadn't changed places with Little Crede, he would still be alive."

"You would of been able to hold that pony back. You wouldn't of been standing in front of the track either." Flush paused, trying to let his praise sink in; when he saw that it confirmed Frank's point, he said: "I seen what you done 'cause he was scared." It didn't seem enough, and he added: "It was mighty good of you."

They were silent for a while. Then Frank said, "They said Little Crede shit in his pants while he was dying." He began to cough, saying, "Pore little guy."

Flush touched his face where it hurt the most. "Yeah. And pore Dye, too, with a name like that."

"And those black rings always around his eyes, even on Sunday."

Flush sighed, and a shudder caused it to sound like a sob. "Just think: three of them dead." He was thinking about Goff and all the tricks he could do with his finger stubs.

"Yeah, and we're still alive."

"Well, I sure wouldn't be if it wasn't for you." He reached over to shake Frank's hand. "I want to apologize for ambushing you at the commissary that night."

Frank tried to smile, but he sobbed instead. Tears began to sluice through the black caking on his face.

It made Flush think again of Little Crede, caught being afraid.

"That was different," Frank managed to say, and then he did smile.

Flush looked off into the mountains. He felt his own tears coming, and he hated them. "What you mean?"

Frank's voice cleared. "That was fun," he said, as the truck lurched, throwing them together into the corner.

THE TAG MATCH

THE TWO BOYS STOOD MUTE WITH THE ANTICIPATION OF COMMERCE. Talmidge was giving them last-minute instructions.

"Now, your business is to *sell*. Stay out from in front of the spectators. And don't ever just stand still watching the matches. Keep moving."

"When do we get our nuts?" Jake asked.

Talmidge ignored the question. He was looking at Kelly. "I don't know what we're going to do about your apron there." And he hurried off to the other side of the hall.

Jake and Kelly were left in their uneasiness to watch the first few people coming in. Kelly was embarrassed because he had rendered his apron useless by taking it home the night before and sewing it up in sections so that the pouch could accommodate half-dollars, nickels, dimes, quarters—even pennies. He had not reckoned with where the peanuts themselves were to be carried.

"Always got to over-plan, don't you?" Jake said.

Kelly was too ashamed, too mad, to answer. He'd had to go through some difficulties just to get the apron in the first place. And the sewing had taken him a good while. Now it was all useless. Besides, it wouldn't do any good to answer. They'd been having frequent quarrels lately. The apron, he thought, was Jake's way of making him feel lower than he felt already.

He adjusted the apron and looked around, as if he were expecting someone. It was the only way to avoid Jake's questions: look busy, preoccupied.

Talmidge was running back towards them now, wielding a butcher knife. Kelly cowered quickly behind Jake. God, how he wished he'd never sewn those sections!

Talmidge had him by the shoulder. It was the end. "Turn around here. What are you doing? Can't you get him to turn around?"

Together, they prepared him for the knife's plunge. But first, they were going to strip him of the apron.

"There!"

Oh, my God! he thought.

"Now both of you get on over to the concession stand and draw your first nuts."

Kelly picked out the red threads on the way over, skulking behind Jake.

, , ,

Arno had got it into its collective head that what it needed that year was a wrestling "arena." The sport was catching on fast; it was the coming thing. Just why the semi-professional baseball team the town had sponsored had failed last year was still a mystery. It, too, had had its promise, and for a time there it seemed that the entire town had awaited the home games with almost rabid anticipation. It had been a great curiosity to see the giant players strutting around town in slick suits, taking meals in the restaurants, the little Cubans making a quick sign of the cross at home plate.

And the softball league had done well, too, before the baseball. Every night of the week at the field by the swimming pool the townspeople swarmed the bleachers to watch their favorite teams: the Lions, the Boosters, the Kiwanians, and the like. But now many of those same players were coming to watch wrestling, some of them had moved away, and some had even become major-league baseball players.

After the wrestling, there would be bowling leagues and, after the bowling, little league. And for a while after these, there would be talk of a skiing resort—talk, that is, of the technicalities involved in making and preserving artificial snow in the Cumberland Mountains of Southwest Virginia, where the strip-mining of coal would render the idea of such a resort into nothing but a tarnished dream.

But that year—1949—it was the wrestling.

The so-called arena was in fact the old basketball gym housed in the decaying town hall. In the center of the hardwood court now stood a regulation commercial wrestling ring—that is, a boxing ring. Folding chairs were set up on all sides. There were two entrances: one through the courthouse, a small wooden room where justice was meted out; the other through barnlike doors leading in directly from the street. The better-dressed people of Arno—the "people with money," as those without it called them—entered through the "legal" side, through Judge Bandy's courtroom; most of the Arnonians used the barn doors.

✽ ✽ ✽

At the concession stand Jake already had filled his apron with bags of peanuts and had obtained the necessary operating change. Kelly continued to pull sullenly at the threads dangling from the denim apron. The girl in charge of the stand said that she had hot dogs to fix and a thousand other things to do, and so she piled up stacks of peanut bags on the counter and handed Kelly five dollars in change. He wanted to count it, to be sure it was all there. He had bought a little note pad for such entries, to tabulate his sales, to tally his bags. But there just wasn't time for that. Besides, he was already out of favor with Talmidge (who was anxious for them to get going), the girl (he could see) really wanted to talk with two big boys lurking at the other side of the counter, and Jake had started for ringside.

So he had to content himself with separating the quarters and fifty-cent pieces and putting them into his left pocket, the nickels and dimes into his right. But when he began to stack up his bags by 3's, that did it. The girl told him flatly to get on with it, that the bags would soon become disarranged in the apron anyway, and that the idea was to sell the things, not inventory them.

He stuffed them in in silent anger, but as he walked to his side of the ring he arranged them as best he could into secret stacks inside the apron. The hell with her, he thought. The hell with Talmidge. The hell with even Jake.

Kelly was to cover the two sides near the courthouse entrance. An old stage once used for live shows sat like a cave to the left and up from the legal entrance. Rest rooms and dressing rooms for basketball players constituted the wings of the stage. Tonight, the rest rooms would be used by the spectators—they would have to ascend stairs on either side of the stage to get to them—and the dressing rooms would be used by the wrestlers. There would be four matches: first, a woman's singles match; then a tag match between two pairs of men; then a woman's tag match; and last, as the main event, The Brahman against the Masked Wonderman.

It was near starting time; the seats were filling fast. The men with money were at ringside, some with women but mostly in groups of their own kind; the older men of Arno, almost all without women or male companions, sat in the back. Kelly analyzed the seating arrangements: Business would be good up front, scanty in the back—which was good. He would get to see the action at close range. It must be, he thought, that the older men—miners or disabled miners, for the most part—sat in the rear because they chewed tobacco and needed to be back there to to spit and go to the bathroom more easily, as they were beginning already to do. Soon they were making a steady stream to the stage. The men with money who sat up front mostly smoked cigars and cigarettes, and they seldom got up once they were in their seats (except to go over to one of their own kind and chat for a few minutes).

As the first match began, Kelly had sold already an apronful of nuts and had to return for a refill. But he didn't give the girl any reason, this time, to get mad at him. He merely stuffed everything into the apron pocket and returned to his section, barking out now with some enthusiasm as he went, "Peanuts! Peanuts! Get your hot peanuts!" (They weren't hot at all, but rather hot-in-demand items, or so he hoped.)

The two women up in the ring were engaged in heated combat, as he saw on his return. Except for some of Georgie Lee Gibson's fights on main street, he had never seen two women do battle in public, squared off like men. Those in the ring were both husky ladies—one was actually fat—and they were dressed in what appeared to be one-piece swim suits with but a single shoulder strap. The fat one's suit was imitation leopard skin. She looked like something from *Alley Oop*. Both wore black leather boxing shoes. They were pulling each other's hair and slapping each other (all apparently against the rules, as the referee called repeated infractions) and bouncing off the ropes, ramming into the other's stomach with their heads.

The match ended with the men with money booing the women wrestlers as they left the ring and went up the stairs to the stage and their dressing room.

The older men in the back scratched their heads skeptically. Then four men came on, one of them brushing against Kelly in the aisle. The wrestler smelled like something cooped up too long. The wrestlers pranced as they walked, like great draft horses that think they are being shown. No, Kelly thought, the one there in the red-and-gold cape looks like a bullfighter in the news reels, the others like the bulls.

The men with money began to go to the bathroom more and more now. The peanuts must have been making them thirsty. But they were taking their Cokes with them, and on each return they became louder and more insulting to the wrestlers and began paying more attention to Kelly. "Hey, Peanut! How 'bout some peanuts?" They were beside themselves with laughter. With the booing and the joking and laughing, Kelly wondered of they were really paying any attention to the match. He thought it was good one.

It was the men's tag match, two against two, except that only one on each side was supposed to fight at any one time. The other two waited outside the ropes on the platform. The object was to wrestle your opponent near the ropes, then to tag your partner. When the tag was made, your partner could enter the ring, take your place, and finish off your mutual opponent. Your partner would be fresh and strong and would be able to make the pin quickly. But of course both sides would try to do the same thing, and so there was as much excitement outside the ropes on the landing between the partners who waited and staged their own match, of sorts, as there was inside the ring. It was as if you and your partner fought equally hard for the pin and for the opportunity to touch your partner, to let him in on the victory.

The men standing outside the ropes were dancing around on the platform, running to the corners and back to be as near their partners as they could get, reaching out their hands to be touched. But even when the tag was made and a partner entered the ring, fresh with power, something always seemed to happen to prevent the new one from making the pin. And the match wore on for quite a while.

He was at ringside, selling his nuts to the owner of the Appalachian Appliance Store, when he saw a man enter through the barn doors and circle around behind Jake's section. Kelly had never seen a man like him before.

The attraction was immediate, though for what reason, except for the man's appearance, Kelly did not know. He quickly made change for a sale and, without hawking, maneuvered through the crowd to get a better view as the man moved around the back of the hall.

The man brushed lightly with his right hand at his long black hair, swept to the back of his head, overlapping and falling around oversized ears that seemed added on like earphones. It bunched in little curls around his collar. Except for his father's, Kelly had never seen a man with hair that long in Arno. The man was tall and broad, and he wore a shiny suit that looked newly cut from light metal. It glistened like mail.

Kelly had by now made his way to the back of the seats. There he pretended to be looking for something. He moved quickly, glancing to take in all of the man he could without appearing to. He was now following him, to the left and just behind him, as the man strode on. Kelly was prepared, in case the man should turn, to look as if he were searching the spectators for a customer.

He had learned from his father, when he had lived with him, to put great stock in the quality and appearance of a man's shoes, and when he looked down at the man's feet he saw a pair of black-and-white wing-tips, clean and sleek as two birds, better even than some his father had made and worn. The man had a good stride, too: He walked with confidence, with grace, his little duffel bag swinging effortlessly in his hand like a bear's paw having taken a clump of berries from a bush.

He felt out of sorts with himself for having slouched so much in the aisles. So he cinched his apron tightly, set his shoulders straight, and picked up his feet clearly and distinctly with each step.

He had followed the man as far as he could. They were approaching the stage. As the man ascended the stage stairs, Kelly halted, turned back. But when he looked again at the shape of the man going into darkness, he saw the large head turn once, quickly, and he knew that the man was aware that he had been watched.

> , , ,

The tag match ended with boos and cheers, and some of the men in the rear got up and left for good. Then as intermission was announced, most of the spectators rose, milled around at ringside, went to the rest rooms, crushed in on the cranky girl at the concession stand (Kelly hoped she'd try to get smart with one of the men with money, just once), and generally visited one another. Kelly made his way through the crowd and met Jake at the aisle that divided their sections.

"How're *you* doing?" Kelly asked.

"I guess I must've sold fifty bags." Then Jake added, with a smirk, "You keeping track of every little thing?"

Kelly felt the old hurt surge up. The apron mistake would follow him now until the next excuse came along. Only this time he couldn't let it pass. "Why didn't you keep track? Then you'd know." It was a dangerous rejoinder and he knew it, but the crowd, the battle before him so thrillingly staged, the lingering tingle from the strange, big man spurred him on. "Two more and I *will* be at fifty. And that's no *guess*."

As the crowd settled down for the women's tag match, he had to go to the bathroom. But business was too good and he did not want Talmidge to see him leaving his post, so he stayed on until the rest rooms would be clear, the match loud and exciting. Then he slipped out the back of the section and up the stage stairs. He approached stealthily, glancing at the match, until he found the door. He opened it slowly, still looking out through the stage over his shoulder, letting the door close quietly, and he turned into one of the ladies who had wrestled in the first match. (He recognized her by her yellow hair. Nobody in Arno had hair that color, except maybe the widow Mays.) She was fully clothed, he was relieved to see, and apparently just leaving.

She stopped him with her hand. "Hey, sonny, just a minute. This here's a place for men." She and another husky-voiced lady behind her laughed, and he ran out the door for the other side.

As he made his way across the stage in semi-darkness—there were lighted only a couple of low-hanging lights over the ring in the entire hall—he saw the Collins boys, Emory and Lionel. They were smoking cigarettes in the corner. He wanted one himself, in the worst way, but they were not good friends and he knew they wouldn't give him even a drag. So as he passed them, he said before he knew it, "Stunt your growth."

He realized his mistake soon enough. Emory pulled him behind a partition downstage and held him while Lionel began to untie his apron. Kelly was smaller by far and couldn't keep them from taking it, though he tried . Neither could he yell: That would bring the house—Talmidge and all—down on him. So he held on to Emory's leg and locked his legs around Lionel's ankle, hoping Jake would come by, as a trickle started.

The Collinses broke free easily enough and began throwing the apron over his head, back and forth to each other behind the partition.

Emory pointed, laughing. "Look! He's pissed in his pants."

He tried, in vain each time the apron sailed over him, to catch it, never getting more than a few fingers on the strings. The peanut bags were falling out; the boys—all three—were crushing them with each step. His pockets, bulged with coins, were like clubs to his meager thighs. When Lionel missed the apron and it fell to the floor, they all made a dive for it. And when they got to it, a big black-and-white shoe held it by a string.

He looked up slowly from the floor and followed the black socks stretched taut over thinning calves, up to the bare, almost hairless legs, up still past thick, scarred knees and over a pair of white, shape-defying thighs, to the colored shorts similar to that of military issue. From the superior position the crotch revealed itself like a stallion's. Where the shorts met the failing stomach there were line traces like an odd assortment of scars, and these ran still higher into a smoothly white, even sickly chest symmetrically bounded by aging pectoral muscles that must once have been of some magnificence. Out of the top protruded a thick, veined neck supporting dazzlingly white teeth, then the ears like vegetables on a snowman, and a beaten nose. It was all capped off by a deep brow over eyes with heat in them and a large crown of black hair, made wild as when one pulls a shirt over the head.

The Collinses were picked up by the hands that swept in unseen, their heads were knocked together, and they were set down. They disappeared through the proscenium arch and off the lip of the stage like a pair of lemmings over the cliff. Then hands helped him to his feet, set the apron string around his neck, tied the waist-strings in the back. He looked at the eyes, now cooled, but only once, as the figure crouched before him, putting what was left of the peanut bags into the apron pocket; and as he started back across the stage, having forgotten the original purpose of his journey, the big, gentle hand ruffled his hair.

⟩ ⟩ ⟩

He crackled through the aisles. The sound commingled with the jingle in his pockets, and he felt like a one-boy tin-pan-alley band, catching the side-sway of his hips, moving like Cagney. Pulling the apron lower over the wet spot, he fairly danced through the lanes. He fancied that he sported himself gaily through the paths of the foe. Working his way back to ringside, he hustled off, first, the bags that rattled most. He felt a keen elation as he sold Buck Little, the used car salesman, a poke of ruined nuts.

But nothing seemed to make any difference to the crowd. By now it was angry, evidently bored with the ladies' tag match. Men were yelling to get this one over with and "Come on with the other bums!"

The women's tag match came to a merciful end with all four women in the ring—against the rules—the two from one side pinning the others at the same time. The referee did not call the infraction. It must have pleased the crowd too much. The appliance-store owner and Buck Little called Kelly over: "Hey, Peanut! Give us all your nuts!" They roared at their joke and bought every bag he had. He went back for more, and it was not long before he sold those as well. By then, the main event was being announced.

The Brahman was introduced first. He galloped down the aisle and leaped into the ring, a fairly short, squat man with a hump on his back and a long, curling, black mustache above a curiously gray goat-like beard. He wore a western hat and doffed it to the crowd repeatedly as he bounced into center-ring and pranced around the sides, inserting his thumbs into his trunks and pulling at the elastic band from front to back, back to front, all the time snorting like a bull. The men with money cheered him, the first time they had shown real favor all night.

When the Masked Wonderman was introduced, he did not immediately appear. "He's scared! Scared to show his big ugly mug!" The Brahman yelled to the pleasure of the crowd. They loved the double meaning, and the noise was peak when a man dressed somehow hesitantly in black tights, a black sleeveless undershirt, and a black mask with ear-, mouth-, and eye-holes edged almost shyly at first to the brow of the crowd. Kelly stood briefly on the ring's outer platform, craning to see. The crowd booed and, now in direct line with the boy, the man picked up his easy stride. He crackled through the hulls and stepped up through the ropes and into the ring, on full display. He danced, but barely, in superb leather boxing shoes as the boy, looking on, retreated into the foreground of the moneyed men. The man's mask pronounced the jut of ears even more.

"Let's go!" the appliance-store owner yelled. "Cream them cauliflowers for 'im, Brahma!"

Buck Little went scrambling for attention off to Kelly's left. He hauled in his buddies, and Kelly heard him say: "The masked guy's got nigger in 'im. Joo see them splayed feet?"

, , ,

The match began, the two men circling. The Brahman hit the masked man with a fist not quite doubled, turning the masked man so that, as he held his face, he bent his backside to The Brahman. The Brahman dug with his feet like a bull and butted the ass before him with his head, sending the masked man into the ropes.

The crowd loved it, booed the referee, who obligingly that time gave the warning. The Brahman shook his head who-me?-I-didn't-do-it, and the mob gave approval.

The masked man recovered, circled, not fighting back but now approaching. The Brahman moved in quickly to the other's ankles, up-ending him, then pounced for a pin. The masked man wriggled to the ropes, and the referee was compelled to coax The Brahman from his opponent's chest. Again, the crowd booed.

As the masked man rose with the help of the ropes and began to turn, The Brahman was waiting with a full fist this time. Mouth juices spattered the boy at ringside, where he watched beneath the blow.

The mustachioed man now had the other against the ropes, the great ears seeming to droop, liquid oozing from beneath the dangling mask. The Brahman quickly locked the top ropes into a twist-knot around the masked man's neck and arms and left him there, dancing to center-ring, his arms raised for approval.

The referee waved his hands in a pantomime of protest. The men with money began pelting the masked man with peanuts.

The boy gazed at the hand dangling from the limber arm of the masked man, the fingers loose and apparently pointing.

Then, as if God had reached out to Adam, he took it as a sign. He saw himself circling to the corner post, waiting for The Brahman to approach for the finish. Gauging the distance to the platform, he jumped, climbed the ropes like a ladder, and perched atop the knob as The Brahman presented his back. He leaped like Roy Rogers springing onto the back of Trigger and landed square on the hump. Grabbing hold of the thick throat, the billy-goat beard, the mustaches—anything he could get—he wriggled his haunches up to clear the hump and came to rest within the pocket formed by the bulge and neck, like a saddle. He locked his legs around the neck and grabbed firmly to the ear-handles.

The men with money sprung to their feet in unison.

The Brahman spun, trying to unlock what held him. The man in the ropes disentangled himself with help from the referee and Jake, threw off the mask, and badgered The Brahman just enough to keep him from the boy.

The boy rode high, turning his head in advance of each spin, and he spotted Buck Little, dwarfed in the crowd. He saw Jake and tried, like reining, to maneuver the head to him. But when he did, he could not let go, or reach out if he could have let go, to tag his brother. He rode wild with what was beneath him and caught sight of the Collins boys, lurking like buzzards.

He was weakening. He yelled to the unmasked man: "Hit! Hit! Defend us!" But he could not be heard. In his final, desperate act, with one hand he pulled the apron, like a skirt, over The Brahman's head. Blinded, the bull could now be manipulated. The crowd was wild with the show.

The boy motioned frantically with one hand for the man in black to come on with a hit, now. And finally the man obeyed, gathering a blow from the canvas that sent The Brahman reeling like a dervish, so that the boy had to set his hand grips and legs into full lock.

The Brahman gathered speed with the spinning and, when he hit the corner post knob solar-plexus high, he spit the boy off like something lodged in his throat.

The boy flew through the air—peanut bags, shells, and nuts raining out over the crowd, silver coins sprinkling the men below with refund—and he cringed, shivered really, as he looked on at the limp hand before him, at the cheering arms, raised and animated, setting themselves strongly for the catch.

OF THE CLOTH

FOR A WHILE THERE, EVERY TIME I PICKED UP THE PAPER, it seemed, a story about another bad priest appeared on the front page. Some of their violations were recent, and some went back a long way. Last January, I had read about the first of them to come to light in recent times, an old priest whose monstrous face alone made the respected newspaper seem like the gaudiest tabloid, and the story about him like yellow journalism. Having questioned a boy about masturbation in the confessional, he had requested a demonstration. After counseling a young boy about his First Communion, he invited him to take a shower with him. I could not finish reading the account of what was called a "sampling of the offenses he has been charged with."

And now, here he is on television news, ordinary-looking, banal. The announcer says he has a choirboy's face. He is being led into the courtroom in handcuffs, wearing a black suit (but no Roman collar). As he is questioned, he includes several offenses in his casual testimony as if they have been a part of his priestly duties. Yes, he says, he has taken boys camping and to baseball games and on picnics; and, yes, he has called them to his tent and fondled them. He has helped a number of poor, single mothers eager and grateful to have a man influencing their sons. He says politely that he has deliberately identified the wounded as his prey. There have been over a hundred. He appears humbly assured, without any trace of recognition of or regret for his abominations. They are not even admissions, just a simple recounting. Surely, he is mad.

Just before that part of the news ends, the priest reacts to something—maybe a fly or a moth—by flipping his fingers in front of his face. It is, somehow, a familiar gesture to me. Long after the news is over and I have turned off the television and am in bed, it is as if I am waking up instead of trying to go to sleep. As if it is time for me and my brother to get up and go serve morning Mass. And then there I am, taken back to a particular morning in my old hometown when I was a boy in the late forties....

After Mass, as my brother and I were kneeling in the sacristy receiving the priest's blessing, a shadow darkened the small doorway leading in directly from the outside. The door had been left open—it was not so cold in the mornings yet—and as we knelt with Father's hands on our heads, receiving the double blessing, I could feel the darkness descend, and *enter*, even with my eyes closed. (I always closed my eyes when I was blessed back then.) The blessing finished, but with sounds of Latin still in my mind, I screwed my head around from my kneeling position on the floor and looked up to see what had come to darken us that morning.

Except for the clerical collar he wore and his round, pink face beneath the hat, everything about the man in the doorway was black and accented by the little crooked cigar in the side of his mouth. He was not much taller than I was when I was standing; with his girth, he resembled the snowmen we had made in winter, the black cigar a fitter mouth ornament than the sticks we'd jammed between the icy lips of our creations.

He looked at me and smiled, and everything about him changed. Morning light replaced the darkness behind him, and his face became an invitation to boyish fun.

The sacristy was hardly large enough for the three of us already there. So as he entered, Kyle and I started to get to our feet and move out of the way for our elder. But as I rose, I stepped on my too-long cassock and stumbled into him as he advanced toward Father. To catch myself, I had to push against his belly, and was embarrassed that I had to touch him so intimately. I just stood there, looking up into his large, downturned face, the dead cigar in his mouth, the ripples of neck flesh crushed under the weight of his black-hatted head. He must have been embarrassed, too, for he grabbed my arms very quickly, then gently steadied me on my feet. Kyle had retreated to a corner, and I joined him there while Father shook the man's hand. "Welcome, Brother...Vito, is it?" Father said. "I was told you wouldn't be here until evening."

"I drive better at night," Brother Vito said, taking the stubby cigar from his mouth and removing his hat with the same hand as he kneeled to receive Father's blessing.

His shoes barely touched my long cassock, and I studied him over from foot to head as he knelt there. His hair was thin at the top, I could see now that he raised his head after the blessing, but the rest of it was thick and black. Before he put his feet under him to rise, I caught sight of a small hole in the middle of his shoe sole. And when he was fully risen, he put the cigar back into his mouth and turned to look at me and Kyle, as if to check to see if we were still there.

Father introduced us, looking to Brother Vito for confirmation of his last name. Brother Vito did not give it; he merely grabbed Kyle and me by the top of the head and squeezed an almost hurtful greeting.

We were told to wait outside after we finished up, so that we could show Brother Vito where the hotel was, and Father and Brother went into the rectory and closed the door. We extinguished the altar candles as solemnly as we could in an empty church; then we disrobed and hung our cassocks and surplices in the closet just outside the little sacristy in the short hallway leading to the rectory. I turned off the light, but instead of leaving we stood near the door to listen.

Father was saying that an assistant priest was moving in tomorrow and there would not be enough room in the rectory for Brother Vito. He would have to stay in the hotel for some time, but the hotel manager was donating the cost of the room to the church. Brother Vito said that was fine with him, that he could "operate" better from a central location in town.

Kyle and I looked at each other when we heard that word. Operate. Sounded exciting.

"There's no legal authority," Father said. He sounded incredulous and a bit cross. "Besides, these Appalachian Missions have more immediate problems." Father went on to tell Brother what his true mission—another thrilling word— would be: recreational activities, helping the altar boys along on our Latin, and counseling us about what Father called "their special time in life."

"Ah, the burden," Brother said.

Father's voice became firm. "You must approach it in its ultimate sacramental purity, holy matrimony, Brother."

As they continued their discussion, Kyle made his trademark sound of disgust and turned to go outside. In the extra moment I remained by the door I heard Father mention two names, Robert and Lloyd, nobody I knew, and so I went outside with Kyle to wait for Brother Vito in the gravel driveway.

He had his hat on and the little cigar in his mouth by the time he came through the outside doorway, playfully catching each of us by the back of the neck. We took up the play and wrenched free, running through the leaves across the yard to the big, shiny DeSoto parked in front of the church. Younger and smaller than Kyle, I started to get into the back seat, but Brother Vito told me to get up front, which of course meant the middle.

I tried to lean away from the man, but there was no getting away from him in a crowded space, and already everything seemed more crowded since he had come to town. As we drove along and I bounced against him, his belly seemed even bigger round where his short, thick thighs merged into his paunch. He smelled of tobacco and talcum. His large cheeks and chin and layers of neck were an intricate mesh of black dots. If he used a straight razor (and I had a hunch that he did), the morning scraping must have been something to hear.

Suddenly his right hand shot out in front of him, and I looked for a bee. But he snapped his fingers oddly, and a flame shot from a shiny Zippo in his hand. As he smoked the cigar, his cheeks deflating like balloons, he snapped the Zippo closed by jerking it down and away with one hand, and he put it into his coat pocket, then took it out and repeated the trick, and put it back. From then on, the flame from the scratch of a match would be a puny miracle in comparison.

His labored breathing accompanied his lighting and puffing like drum brushes. The smoke from the little cigar made all other smoke—cigarette and pipe, leaf-burning and even forest-fire—seem commonplace. Coming from the black stub by way of his mouth, the smoke circled and held me.

After a great draw on the cigar he clamped it between his teeth and said, "What you boys do around here for play?"

I looked over at Kyle, who put his brow into wrinkles. "Shoot marbles and play football," I said.

"No," he said, and squeezed my leg with his thick right hand. "I mean what do you do for entertainment?" He leaned forward the few inches he was able and turned his head. "Kyle?"

"We go to a party ever once in a while," Kyle said. "There was a birthday party up at the Legion Cabin just last week." Then, before Brother had time to pursue the questioning, Kyle added, cordially, "What you doing here, Bro?" He used the shortened title with ease, or so it seemed to me. I would not have risked it so soon. But we had known other Church brothers who came to town for a number of "missions"—teaching us catechism and Latin and how to serve Mass, taking us along on visits to poor mountain people—and eventually we had called all of them "Bro."

This brother shot a glance at Kyle over my head, but then immediately recovered. With a little smile and the full confidence he'd shown since we had met him, he said: "Church business, Sonny." Then while he was relighting the cigar, he said again: "Church business."

No place was exactly far from any other place in town, but it was taking us awhile to get to the hotel because, Brother said, he wanted to see "this burg."

And so, riding through our familiar streets, I looked for little eddies of swirling leaves which blew up every now and then like a dance of leaf-fairies. The mountains were dying slowly that year, but already there seemed enough leaves to keep the smell of their burning suffused throughout the town from afternoon until late evening and all day on weekends. But along with the sad, intoxicating smell of the burning leaves, smoke rose from the coke ovens at the edge of town, so that a haze hovered like dirty gauze above our heads.

Finally, Brother Vito asked where the hotel was, we told him, and he parked the car in front of it. We tried to help him unload his bags; even he had trouble with them. As he checked in, we helped the old red cap-elevator operator struggle the bags onto a cart; then all of us and the cart boarded the elevator to the sixth floor, where the operator announced our arrival and then wheeled the bags into the room and left.

Bro set one of the bags on a table and, motioning us to sit on the bed, settled himself deep into the one big easy chair. He munched and drew on the cigar as he lighted it again, looking at me through the smoke while he was drawing in and his cheeks were collapsing. He snapped the lighter closed, down and away, and threw it in my lap. As I began trying to snap open the cover of the slippery lighter, he threw a small box to Kyle.

Kyle caught it with one hand and looked at it.

"Go ahead," Bro said.

Kyle read from the box—"Parodi"—and took one.

"Best there is," Bro said.

I took one, and we lit them several times but could not keep them going. They were short, black, and crooked, and one end was smaller than the other. What little smoke I managed to inhale spun my head, but I kept lighting and drawing.

Finally, Kyle said, "What's so good about them if you can't keep them going?"

"A man too lazy to keep up the finest, shouldn't have the finest." Bro was lighting again. "Know what I mean?" Then he reached into a nearby leather suitcase and pulled out a gun. He turned it over and showed both sides of it.

"Luger?" Kyle said, as if he'd known from the moment Brother Vito had appeared in the outside doorway to the sacristy that he'd brought a Nazi gun to town.

Bro pulled a part of the gun back and let it snap into place. "Nope. Forty-five," he said without looking at us. Then pointing the gun upward, he eased the trigger in and released the hammer, tossed the gun back into the bag, and said, "Now, what did you guys hear when you were listening at the door to the sacristy?"

⸢ ⸢ ⸢

Over the rest of that school year we saw Bro at church, in his hotel room, and when he took us out. Every now and then he'd come into the Lazy Grill, where we went with our friends for soft drinks and pinball. He'd either come in or already be sitting in a booth waiting for us when we got there after school. If we had friends with us, we abandoned them for his company, but over time a few older boys came to know him and say hello. I had the notion that they were talking about Bro and us. I suppose he scared them. To be Italian and Catholic in those mountains was bad enough, but to be "of the cloth" (an expression I'd heard in a movie) on top of that must have been more than their imaginations could take. And if that wasn't enough, there was Bro's physical appearance.

Kyle and I and two other guys were the only Catholic boys in town; the others—the Protestants—were always putting questions to us about the Church whose answers we had not yet learned in catechism. But those questions often led to all sorts of other, crazy, things for us to defend. Some boys wanted to know if priests and nuns really did have babies they buried alive under convent cellars; others, with knowing looks on their faces, said they knew damn well that that Pope did all kinds of weird things and why didn't we just come out and let them in on a few.

So Bro added to the other mysteries of the Church in that way. It was never more than a couple of minutes after he left us in the Lazy Grill (sometimes with instructions to go to his room to see him later on) that the boys with us at the time would want to know who he was and what he was doing in town. Well, we played it up pretty big for them. We told them he was a special agent, and we described to them all the guns and knives he had. He had them, too: the forty-five, a Japanese derringer, a German Luger, an Italian pistol and stiletto, even a Burmese sword which, when broken down for concealment, became a piece no longer than a letter opener.

When spring came around, he took us into the mountains for target practice. He showed us how to load and unload several of the guns and how to fire without jerking so that we became fairly good at hitting a beer can or a bottle a fair distance away. But the way he shot was something to behold. His thick hand gripped the Luger, as glistening black hairs peeked around the silver wrist watch worn on that same right hand, the face of it, with three circles of numbers, on his inner wrist. Then he clamped down on his Parodi and put a neat group of holes into a piece of paper pinned to a tree three first downs away.

One day, after we had finished target practice and were back in the hotel room, the highest manmade vantage point in town (not counting the water tower, of course), we began cleaning and oiling the guns and listening to Bro's story about when he was in the South Pacific and was sent with several other marine commandos on a secret mission. They had left a man behind as a guard for their camp, and when they returned they found the man hanging upside-down from a low tree, his skin stripped off and his flesh baking in the sun. The skin was turned inside-out and was still attached to the fingers as if, according to Bro, the man had simply bent over and pulled a long night shirt over his head and had stopped just before it fell from his hands. The wrinkled-up skin was stacked on the ground. The man was still alive.

I was getting ready to clean a Winchester .22 caliber rifle, and Kyle was sitting on the window sill working on the Luger. He had it broken down and was cleaning the bore with a rod. Bro was drinking from a glass of whiskey, facing away from me. I was sighting around the room with the rifle, aiming in on the back of Bro's head when it was turned away from me and on the top of Kyle's head as he was bent over, intent on pushing the rod into the bore and pulling it out.

Suddenly, there was an explosion. Kyle's head jerked up, and I thought sure to God I had shot him. At the last minute, I had turned my aim to a milk bottle sitting on the window sill beside him. And now he looked up at me, his eyes slits of scorn. "Just what in the hell do you think you're doing?" he said.

Bro took the gun from me and began examining it, I thought, for any other bullets. By that time Kyle was white-faced and I was running around the room in desperation. Bro took hold of me and slapped me on the face, and I stopped. I knew he'd had to do it, the way men in the movies had to slug a buddy who was losing his mind, and for a moment I forgot what had almost happened.

A loud, repeated knock at the door stopped us all. A man's voice yelled: "What's going on in there? Is anyone hurt?"

Bro opened the door a few inches and told the manager that "the boys accidentally lighted a cherry bomb," but that everything was okay, he was terribly sorry, it wouldn't happen again.

"Well, okay, Father," the voice said. "Be sure it doesn't."

All the time Kyle was looking around at the scattered shards that had been the milk bottle. Simultaneous thoughts of fear—that I had almost killed my real brother—and gratitude that I had not, assailed me and have stayed with me to this day; but at the time it put a good bit of shame into me as well, for I had shown myself to be a greenhorn with guns. Bro calmed me down, though, and after a while everything was all right again and Kyle I were even laughing, if nervously, about the incident. But I didn't shoot the guns anymore, even though Bro told me I should, to get over my fear.

The next time we went to his room, we found several gadgets and pieces of equipment. He had one of those long metal flashlights, the kind that famous sleuths used. And what he called a humidor, for his cigars. His small, mechanical pinball machine was the first we had ever seen. But what we liked most, of all the stuff, was his portable record player. With a long extension cord, we could move it to the table, the floor, or the bed and listen to the records kept in jackets mounted together between picture covers, like books.

By then the other two Catholic boys in town were pretty much a part of our sessions with and without Bro. We wouldn't have risked taking non-Catholics up there. Who knows what rumors they might have added to those already churning around about the Church and Bro? We sat around and sang along with the vocal records until we had them memorized. One of our favorites— "I'm Sittin' on Top o' the World"—had a double effect for me: From that vantage point I felt I was on top of the world with Al Jolson, but that at any moment we could be blown up like Cagney at the end of *White Heat*. Hadn't it already almost happened?

When Bro was ready to take us to the show, he'd say, "Saddle up!" and we knew what he meant. We all preferred war movies, and there were still plenty showing even four years after Japan surrendered. *Bataan, China's Little Devils, Back to Bataan*—there seemed no end of war at the movies. And being there with Bro, an experienced commando with real guns and knives, we felt closer to the actual thing as we ran the movies over and over in our talks in the big DeSoto.

Occasionally we went to technicolor movies, with beautiful girls singing and dancing so attractively that there was no way to talk about them. We drove back in silence or talked about other things. I had the feeling that Bro was waiting for one of us to try to say something about what we were thinking, but no one ever did. I wondered if he was feeling what I was.

During one of those movies, just as everyone was laughing at the main handsome man's sidekick, Bro reached over and squeezed my leg. (I was sitting between him and Kyle, where I seemed to have been spending a good deal of time lately). He let his hand rest on my knee. I wanted to push it away and change seats, but I was too scared to even look at him. I began to turn my head toward Kyle, when the hand removed and began clapping with the other one when there was not much funny stuff going on on the screen.

Bro was supposed to counsel Catholic boys at the church rectory, but by late spring he was having even non-Catholic boys meet him in his hotel room, one at a time. The boys had begun laughingly referring to the sessions as The Talk, but they wouldn't reveal precisely what they were about. When they told jokes about girls and wet dreams, they managed to get Brother Vito in on it.

A big boy everybody called Gabby said, "That Bro said nine out of ten boys beat their meat—." While he was finishing it, the others all joined in:

"And the tenth one's a liar!"

So Kyle and the others had all had identical sessions. All but me. I was still too young, Bro had been saying, but my turn would come.

"Not if the tenth one's Babs Lloyd," Gabby said, and they all laughed.

The two names I had heard in the fall while listening in on Brother and Father from the sacristy were not the first names of two boys or men but the full name of one man, Robert Lloyd, a businessman some called Bob and others called Babs. That is, he was a businessman by day; at night, if I was to believe it, he was what was called, back then, a homo. I might have been seeing him every day, but I would not have known him if I had. Gabby and some of the others had gone out with him in his convertible and had let him do things with them. They did not say openly what those things were, but they did not have to. They seemed to have it both ways: indulging themselves and making fun of Babs Lloyd.

"Maybe that Bro was sent here to nab that queer," one of the big boys said.

"Yeah," Gabby said, "and maybe he ought to nab his own self."

By the time I put together my near-killing of my brother, Bro squeezing my knee at the show, and the big boys making Bro and Babs Lloyd and themselves into after-hours figures in a dark world, I didn't want any private session with Bro.

But my turn did come.

On the day school was let out for the summer after a token morning of "assembly" and passing out report cards, as I went into the Lazy Grill with dozens of other kids milling around, talking and laughing about all the days of idleness we had before us, I saw a black hat hanging on the hook above the booth Bro usually sat in, near the back. But he wasn't in it, so I turned and was searching for Kyle, to tell him to let's get out of there, I didn't want to sit with Bro with all the regular boys and girls around, when I walked into Bro himself, right at the center of things.

He was not talking with anyone; he was just there. Kids moved around him like river water around a large rock. I searched their faces to see if they took notice of him, and they did, each one glancing at what must now have been to them the mysterious stranger even I had taken him to be last fall. He was of course in his black suit and church collar and with the Parodi, mercifully dead in his mouth.

I had been talking to a girl I had wanted to get friendly with all year. She had just told me that she was going across the street to the swimming pool that was being filled that day. It was a special time of year for all of us, a sort of welcome to summer as we would lie outstretched on the pool's concrete bottom, waiting for the rivulets of cool water to reach us, and I had just told her that I was going, too.

Only now Bro had snagged me.

"Come on over here," he said, taking me to his booth, where the Zippo and his coffee cup reserved it for us, and where, before he sat down, he snapped open the lighter that shot a flame at the cold cigar and he began exhaling smoke scenes. By the time he flipped the lighter down and away and we were sitting, I was mortified that two girls had seen and were reacting with wrinkled brows and incredulous mouths.

"I've got to go, Bro," I said.

But he told me he had something to talk to me about and that I should go to his room in an hour and let the other boys know we were going to a movie tonight.

"I don't think me and Kyle can go," I said. "We might be doing something." When he asked me what, I said, "Camping out in the mountains."

I knew he didn't camp. He'd told us before that he'd had enough of that in his commando days.

It made no difference. He insisted that I be at his room, "at noon."

The swimming pool was just beginning to rise to swimming level when I had to leave. Since I'd lain with the others until the first of the water ran around us, under us, on its way to the sloped bottom, I had to wring out my dungarees and polo shirt the best I could in the bathhouse, then put them back on and go to the hotel. (I'd walked all the way home like that many times, and would do it many more times that summer and in summers to come.)

Going through the large door and into the lobby of the hotel put a chill deep into my bones. It seemed for the first time festooned with old brocade that must have been dusty. The small newsstand in the corner was stuffed with newspapers and magazines, candy and cigarettes and cigars; but no one was tending it, and the lobby was empty. The two-seater shine stand stood by the far wall like a small stage with no players.

I entered the elevator and waited there. When I looked out, the operator appeared as if from nowhere and, strangely, asked me what I wanted. The old grump limped, and he chewed tobacco whenever he wasn't on duty. I thought he must have wanted a chew and that that's what made him so offensive. When he didn't get into the elevator with me to take me up, it was clear that he was just being that way to me. He was never that way when I was with Bro.

"Six, please," I said, looking up at the little mirror on a side wall. I'd never seen it before.

"Why don't you get on home where you belong?" he said.

I was so surprised at the remark—it was more like a plea—that I raised my head a bit haughtily. "Vito Telassi is expecting me in his room," I told him.

And that did it, or so I thought. He limped into the elevator and half-sat on the stool and started to turn the lever. But he looked at me instead, and sighed, and now I knew his meaning didn't have to do with his bad nature but with the idea that I, a young boy, was going to a stranger's room. But he closed the metal gate and the door, turned the brass lever, and as we seemed to lift off earth in that stomach-sinking rise and float upward, he studied the bottom of the door until finally he turned the lever back and stopped our ascent, opened the cage door as he gave the lever quick little jerks, making the elevator floor even with the sixth-storey's, and let me out.

"Somebody going to tell your daddy," he said as the door closed.

"That'd be a good trick," I said, looking down at the falling coach.

I went to 613 and rapped at the door. The single word *"Entrate"* sounded from within, and I turned the knob and entered, as much from the visceral urgency of the word as its meaning.

Bro was in a playful mood, but when he saw my damp clothes and that I was shivering by then he guided me into the bathroom and told me to undress and put on his bathrobe. I stood there until he left, and then did as he'd said. The bathroom was gleaming with small, white tiles and nickel-plated spigots and soap holder, the kind you don't see much anymore. On the shelf above the sink was a black-handled straight razor. I opened and closed it a few times, but I was afraid to put it near my face, and I put it back precisely where it had been. Hugging the huge robe around me, I went back into the room, where he had me sit in the deep upholstered chair while he reclined in his undershirt on the bed.

He went through the cigar-lighting routine, then began saying something. But I wasn't listening. I was thinking: He doesn't do the cigar-lighting for me or anybody else. He does it for himself! That meant something, but I wasn't sure what. But now he was looking at me, as if I was expected to respond or affirm something. "I'm sorry, Brother." I shook my head as if it had been called upon to hold too much lately. "What did you say?"

"I said, 'There are some things we need to talk about.' Where's your head, up your fanny?"

It's what he told us when we were too slow. "I guess so," I said.

"Well," he said, sounding mock-tough, or tough, "pull it out and listen up."

Back when I'd found out that Bro had talked to Kyle and the other boys about jacking off and stuff like that, I hadn't wanted a personal session with him. But before that, I remembered, now that I was sitting in front of him, I had felt left out because he had *not* called me in for a discussion. And now, as I made my face go serious, I realized how wrong I had been ever to be disappointed.

"When a boy gets to be your age—well, it'll be another year or so for you yet, I guess—but certain things start happening to him, to his body and mind, I mean. Know what I mean?" He raised his head and let some smoke sneak out of his mouth on its own.

"Sure, it's growing up," I said. I was mulling over "*it'll be another year or so.*" That I was not yet an apt subject for The Talk suited me fine. I wouldn't let on that I knew anything about what he had been talking to the others about. And I knew that my "innocence" would be convincing; Bro had always treated me more gently than the others. After that first time, I wouldn't even smoke in front of him.

"Growing up and becoming aware of his body parts," he said, "and their attraction to girls." He sucked on the Parodi, then took it out and looked at it, as if he wanted to confirm its being cold. "Son, every boy eventually plays with his body. It's what you guys call, in the confessional, doing impure things with yourselves. Nine out ten do it." He smiled. "The other guy's a liar."

What if the tenth one's Bro? a voice within me said. Or the Pope!

He quickly assured me that he was not talking to me like this was Confession; he was just telling me these things for my own good. I needed his guidance more than the others did, more than even Kyle, he told me, because I did not live with my father and Kyle would soon grow up and leave. "You must be on your guard against men who want to do things to you." He stopped, as if to gauge the effect of what he'd said, then added: "Has a man ever asked you to do something, son?"

I didn't like men calling me "son," and I didn't want to talk about my old man or hear anybody else talk about him. He was nothing to me. I told Bro I had to go home, as I got up and started into the bathroom. He turned, sitting on the bed, and said kindly that he wasn't finished. And that's when something not so innocent within me came forward; forcing firmness through a quavering voice, I told him: "I'm going home, Brother Vito."

Then he didn't object, but when I came from the bathroom in the cold, damp clothes again and was going for the door, he was standing, lighting his cigar, telling me about all the things we were going to do during the summer, reminding me not to forget what all we had done, what he had taught me. I had the feeling that I would do some terrible things in my life and that somehow I had confessed them, ahead of time, but without benefit of forgiveness.

As summer sprouted full bloom into our town ringed with mountains, Bro and the Church receded from our lives. We played football and climbed rocks, explored caves and camped out in dark hollows. We even went looking for the lonesome pine that a writer from a town near our own had written a story about many years ago. We found a big pine and called it "lonesome" and vowed that we would keep its location a secret throughout the ages. Which was not hard to live up to: When we went again to try to find it, we couldn't.

We saw Bro occasionally, but we did not ride in his car with him or go to his room. He was out of town a good part of the summer, and by the time school started in the fall we had pretty much forgotten about him.

Kyle and I returned to our larger group of friends and were even invited to a couple of parties, where we danced with girls and, when the party was outdoors, sang with them around a campfire. But we had not gone over into that sort of thing so completely that we had let go of our old ways, and so the night before Halloween several of us had decided to get an early start. I had even taken my turn by shooting out a street light with a BB gun, breaking my self-imposed abstinence of guns. Watching the street lights sizzle and puff themselves out after a BB had hit its mark was simply more than I could abstain from; and I conJerryd myself, quite easily, that BBs weren't the same as the real thing.

We had bombed a porch with rotten eggs, soaped up a few windows, and generally swaggered up and down the hills of our town as if we owned its common ground after dark. There were six of us, smoking cigarettes and using every cuss word we knew, and after some close calls (one man started chasing us, but we easily outran him) we ended up, as we always did back then, outside the gate to the graveyard on Laurel Hill. Just inside the gate was an old shack, where the caretaker kept his implements which, judging from what the graveyard looked like in full sun, must have been old beyond use, like him, or else still brand new.

It was about ten o'clock; except for the few house lights we could see from the hill, the town was done for the day. Kyle and one of the more pugnacious Blevins boys were our tacit co-leaders, and they decided that it was time to go inside the graveyard. I was told to stand guard.

"Stay put," Kyle said. I let him know I wasn't too happy about it, and he said they'd send somebody to replace me in a while. As they left me there, he said over his shoulder, with an eerie chuckle, "And keep your skin on," sending cold chills through me.

I was to stand behind the right stone pillar of the gate, or what was left of it, and to keep watch for the police. We had been stopped by them last Halloween, and only our friendship with the driver of the patrol car saved us from serious trouble. But of course a lot of the precaution was theatrical. It was unlikely that the police were out looking for us a night early. But just in case, if I saw a cop car, I was to run to the top of the hill by the statue of Mary holding a pug-faced infant and give out with the whistle our old man used to call us from blocks away when he came to town.

I took up my post while the others went through the gate; as soon as they did, they disappeared. It was so dark the pillars were merely dark shapes, the shack like a dark hole in the side of the hill. I wondered if the old caretaker was inside the shack, asleep or watching.

After about fifteen minutes, as I was wishing back one of the street lights I had shot out, the kind of footsteps made by men's dress shoes sounded close behind me, and, going rigid, I turned. I didn't want to give whoever it was the impression that I was doing anything wrong, so I began to whistle softly and to look around at the ground and over my shoulder. I was making myself think that Kyle would be back any minute now to check on me, that all his orders had been given to impress Blevins and show everybody he was capable of commanding his younger brother to such forlorn duty. But for now, I was alone with the man who had come up to me by then, unless he was going to see the old caretaker in the shack.

"Hello, sir," I said to what I could make out as a short, broad man in a suit and hat. His dress shirt and parts of his necktie glowed in the dark.

"You out playing pranks already?" His voice was scratchy, as if he was at the end of a cold.

"No," I said, loud enough for the caretaker to hear me, if he was in there. "I haven't done anything wrong, mister."

"I don't mean that you have," he said, kindly. "Have you seen two boys around here?"

"No, sir."

"Older boys," he said, as if that would alter my answer.

"I haven't seen any boys," I said.

"What are you doing here?"

I didn't answer, and so we stood silent for some time before he struck a match to look at his watch, and I saw his face. I thought I'd seen him in town from time to time.

After another minute or so, he said, "Why don't you come along with me?"

"I haven't done anything wrong, mister," I said, giving the last word a soft deference so he would recognize my innocence.

"No, no," he said. "I'll take you home. My car's just down the hill."

He sounded official, like a man with a *mission*. If he wasn't a man I might have seen in town, he could have been an undercover agent trying to break up the dope ring Bro had told us was operating around there, but which nobody else seemed to know anything about. Maybe he was working with Bro to help him catch Babs Lloyd. Whoever he was, I figured to keep him busy until my replacement arrived. If Kyle and the others came with him, all the better. Everybody would talk at once. The thrilling questions would come one after the other, about what we knew and didn't know.

"I don't have to go home yet," I said.

He seemed to take that as an acceptance of some kind, that I would go with him to some other place, and he circled my arm with his small, hard hand, so damp I could feel it through my shirt, and moved me down the hill. I jerked, but his hand moved like a clamp, and then we were there and he was putting me inside, beneath the steering wheel and across, into the aroma of smooth leather. He held on, his voice going soft and pleading. I reached with my right hand and found the handle, pulling up until it released the door, but it fell away only inches, striking an embankment or tree I could not push it against. I tried to rise, but his other hand gripped across me, holding me down. He continued to talk, but I could not perceive all the words, only what he repeated several times: "Don't try to get out and nothing will happen to you. I just want to talk to you. Will you let me talk to you?"

Something familiar—a smell—came into the car.

He was in the middle of the seat, crowding me to the right; the door was blocked but somehow fully open as well. Sobs began to punctuate his words, so that with the commotion and the sounds I couldn't be sure I felt or heard the other door open, but if it had it did not close and I dismissed it as a hope, until I felt the car depress on the far side and a strange light invade the darkness. A heaviness descended over the figure beside me, a hand prized off the one holding my arm and a loud snap! was followed by a cry of pain. A voice said something that registered clear at the time, a big hand urged me up and over the backrest, and I was fully standing on the rear seat, free to jump out and go off into the night.

As I hopped over the back and slid down the car's trunk, I saw two big boys running down the hill under a street light. I started to run after them but they were moving fast away, so I took off up the hill, through the graveyard gate, over graves, around statues and gravestones, yelling as I ran for Kyle and the others. When I reached the place where the statue of the Madonna and Child should have been standing, I saw that it had been turned over. I tried to whistle, but not a sound would come from my lips. I yelled again and again, but no one came, and so I kept on going down the other side until I came to the road. I kept running until I reached the place where I lived.

Our aunt, who had lived alone, was taking care of Kyle and me and our mother, who had been sick and often in bed for a year. As long as we went to school and church and did our duties, they didn't worry much about us being out. I was glad the women went to bed early, because I might have been crying.

A few minutes after I got in bed, wondering about Kyle, he came in, asking questions I pretended to be too sleepy to answer. He probably knew I was faking, and he chewed me out for leaving without him. "We came back and looked for you for an hour. Where the hell you been?"

Finally, I sat up. "I was waiting for somebody to relieve me," I said. "Nobody ever did." I told him that I had done what I was told to do and that when I couldn't find him and the others, I came on home. "If you looked at all, it sure as hell wasn't no hour, or else you'd of found me. That graveyard ain't so big that you couldn't." I threw the covers over me and turned to the wall.

He got in bed on his side, sighed his disgust at me, and proceeded to tell me in a tone meant to convey that logic and reason were foreign concepts to me, that they'd gone off to steal some doughnuts from a bakery truck Blevins had staked out earlier, but then that he'd come back for me himself.

First, they'd all come back for me; now only he had. If he kept going, I'd probably get the truth: nobody had.

But by then, I was not listening. Anger must have driven out the barrier to my ability to reconstruct what had happened in the crow-blackness in that car…that I had stood up in! No wonder the door had seemed open. It was a convertible. Gabby had said Babs Lloyd had a convertible and took them out in it. I almost turned to tell Kyle that I had been wrestling with Babs Lloyd while he'd been eating stolen doughnuts with Blevins. I was burning to know if he had brought any to the graveyard for me.

But there was still more to recall about my time in that car with that man—with those men. I knew now what seemed to have happened, but it was so much like a movie's nighttime scene that I had kept rejecting it as more of my fantasy. My sidesight had picked up a small, red glow coming at the side of the car, but I'd had no time then to ponder it. I had smelled the smoke and, when he had got inside, the talcum. The big light shining in like a stage spot on all our hands, one with black hairs glistening in the glow, the silver watch with the round face worn on the inner wrist, and a Luger in it touching the sobbing head beside me. "Get out, son," was what the voice had said through teeth. "You haven't been in any danger."

Had Bro somehow appeared at just that moment to save me? At the time I thought of course that he had. At the time I did not know what to think about those two big boys running so fast under the street light.

That time in my life has not existed for me for many years. A man like me who goes to war across the world and sees atrocities at close range—like the commando guard Bro and his men had found so untreatably flayed—doesn't dwell on a single night in his boyhood. And then something comes up like this priest who just sits there agreeing to all the abominable things he's accused of, like it's made no difference in anyone's life, not even his own. I suppose I've had the same attitude about my own near brush with such a man: that it's had no effect one way or the other. That's how I've been able to close it off. But there's a long way between this smug priest admitting to everything he's done and even a near brush to a boy on the other side of things. Robert Lloyd was pitiable and sad; the boy I was, was terrified and could have been hurt in the way all those altar boys were by the matter-of-fact priest whose public confession has started me thinking about these things. And now that I have, it's like everything back there is a part of what's now, too.

I have never talked with anyone about what happened in the car that night—not with Kyle and not with a priest, though I have never had reason to mistrust any of the many priests I've known. Those of my boyhood were far more to me even than what I felt whenever I called them Father. And nobody ever mentioned the events of that night to me. But now that I have been set to thinking about it—I don't know, something is not right.

It has to do with those two big boys I saw running so fast down the hill under the street light as I was sliding down the trunk of the convertible. It's strange how details can be observed but just left in your head, then come out long afterward, clear as the minute they happened. Like that dead moss that can be brought back with water years after it's turned flaky. It's like something I am listening for from a long time ago.

One of those boys was Gabby. I'm sure of it now, because—and here's what has just come to me—one of those boys ran funny. Like Gabby. (Some boys called him Crazylegs.) Gabby knew more about Babs Lloyd than anybody else; he'd been out with him in his car before, and he had met and talked with Bro.

Bro could not have come to Laurel Hill by coincidence at that precise moment to rescue me. He had said, "You haven't been in any danger." He'd had me covered all the time. Gabby and Bro had set it all up. And I was the bait. Why not Gabby? Bro needed a lamb to be able to bait the wolf, break his hand, maybe pistol whip him so he'd never bother anybody again. Besides, Gabby was friends with Babs. Some friend. He'd watched the whole thing.

They'd probably all had me covered in one way or another. Hadn't Father talked about Robert Lloyd with Bro on that first morning in the sacristy? Was this the mission with "no legal authority"? Robert Lloyd had come looking for two "older boys" by the graveyard gate, and found only me.

How had Gabby and the other boy and Bro all known I would be there, standing lone guard?

Another clump of flaky moss begins with my tears to spring into little spikes of blazing clarity.

"And keep your skin on."

Alone at the gate and without light.

And who had put me there and never come back?

Maybe Kyle set me up without any thought that I might be in danger. He might have figured that since Bro had been a Marine and had guns and knives I would be safe. Or maybe he was still mad that I'd almost shot him and he wanted me to get a taste of how it felt to be scared as hell. I don't know. He's been dead for thirty years, and I'll never know. I wish I had asked him about it, but we fell away from each other before he died and I wasn't able to even go to his funeral. I was fighting in a jungle I didn't think I'd ever get out of. Scared as hell, all right. But I had remained a devout communicant and felt protected.

Family for Kyle and me as boys was Holy Mother Church: Sisters, Brothers, and, above all, Fathers. That is why, when that priest said softly that, yes, he had "helped a number of poor, single mothers eager and grateful to have a man influencing their sons," some remote nerve within me had tingled, sending me back in time to solve the riddle that has been my life.

The men and boys I've tried to tell about here did not set me up that night, and neither did Kyle. The one who set me up—and set Kyle up, too, as now I see—was our own father, his and mine, who wasn't there at all.

CUMBERLAND
SPRING

H E HAD ESCAPED THE TOWN'S DRUNKEN STREETS WITH A FRIEND, and now he followed the older boy by several yards. They had made the woods. Kentucky and worm-eating warblers announced their coming. Somewhere from its domed ground nest an ovenbird passed itself off as a thrush, crying: teacher, teacher, teacher! A spring-peeping tree frog, X-marked as if to say, I am the One, moved to show himself, then blended away.

They moved through the broad-leaved forest of oak and sycamore and, the older boy pointing out the tulips on an occasional yellow poplar, crossed the spruce-hemlock line. Here in the land of conifers the forest floor was softer, springier to his step. Passing delicately through the gossamer of fronds, he saw down the trail to his right a pink bed of azaleas; shale slopes and orchid bogs lay beyond. It was like a large open-roofed house, an endless room. Water ran and, though he could not see the stream, he knew by the line of wildflowers— Dutchman's breeches like many spread hands above leaves that could have been mistaken for ferns, blue dwarf irises with here and there an albino patch, clumps of blue bells, small beds of yellow adder's tongue—he knew that the streambank was defined by the line of color.

It was his first time fully in, and he did not know the names of these things. He turned and caught the sun trying to hide behind a giant pine, sending its rays in a jagged burst to dapple the hemlocks. A small dome of moss, like a dropped muff in the woods, glistened at the tip of an emerald spear. He bent to see a single water drop, found out by a maverick ray, shine out like a little star, then fall in a silent shattering.

They were skirting ground pine and other clubmoss and came upon a cluster of chanterelle, more like coral than the meaty fungi they were. Earlier, they had crossed the stream through one of the shale beds, using footholds in the crevices that sprouted spleenworts and other ferns. His companion had pointed out the signs of good fossil-hunting there. And when he had been shown the trail to the limestone cave in Lester Cove, he had wanted to go there as well.

"We can't take it all in in a day," his friend told him. "Today it'll be the ridge. Next time, maybe we'll climb Vulture's Roost or go on up to the cave. Too much at a time'll ruin it." The older boy crushed a sweet shrub and let him sniff. "Ain't that something?" he said.

"Sure is." He saw some small empty bottles. "What's them?"

"Lemon extract," the older boy said. "Cheapest drunk there is, next to canned heat. We'd take them out with us, but we'd be all day. Let's go on."

He saw a flash of color in the wingbars and sides of a bay-breasted warbler perched in a run of Virginia creeper. Looking up at a pine tall as a building, he lost his balance, but righted himself before going over. He asked his friend: "How'd you like to climb that there?"

"Maybe we will some day. C'mon."

They emerged into a glade ringed with dogwood in flower. From here he could see across to a ridge of rocky balds of the highlands where Vulture's Roost was said to be. The prolific rhododendron, interlaced with fading redbud, adorned the base of the balds, offering the summit like hands elevating an oblation. Below, whatever green could struggle to light, had fought to get there, and stayed. But mingled with the creeper and other vines was a patch of color as yet unnamed to him. He had heard the word heather, and secretly called it that.

"That's moss phlox. Probably where a cabin was."

Upon the bank where the stream touched the glade's curve, white boneset, dazzling cardinal flowers, and purple Joe-pyeweed were sunning.

The forest below looked like a mass of green clouds. He saw a shadow pass, looked up, and said: "Eagle!"

"Huh-uh," his friend said, smiling, "but I wished it was. That there's just a buzzard. But there's plenty of 'em over in the next county."

Always the next county over.

Then the friend told of the legends of hawks, of golden and bald eagles, of falcons, and what they had been reputed to carry off.

He heard all of this with few questions as they went in again at the high side and climbed another hour until they reached the peak. He had anticipated a picture in the sky, revealed at first look; he had thought that he was going to see from the top something beyond telling, something only guessed at before: a long range so high, so blue and stretching lazily out and up that it would bring mountain-earth and sky together, a new heaven.

"See there," his friend said.

"Huh-uh."

"There. Yonder."

"Oh. Uh-huh."

He said he saw it; he thought he did. But his anticipation of seeing had been too great. Or maybe it was because he wanted it to be so much more.

"You still ain't looking in the right place, or else you're looking too hard. Look up. It ain't across. It's high."

He did, and saw only sky. He shook his head.

His friend took his neck in his left hand and turned it, pointing with his right finger, crouching behind him to align what was to be seen.

"Now, not the near ridge," he said, "nor the one after that. See?"

The boy squinted. He counted ridges, and ran out of them.

Then he looked up, just beyond the layers of them, beyond the last he could see. And he found a ragged line, barely traced out above the lesser ridge, beyond where ridges ought to go. It was a secret then! But there it was. Bumps rose on his thin arms. His scalp quivered. His eyes misted. "You mean...you mean...there?"

His companion nodded and swallowed audibly. "You ever see such a thing?"

It was blue, a scar of a line that split the sky, blue beyond the last green, and hidden just right. The longer he looked, the more distinct it became, so that he could find it even after he looked away. Now that it was so easy, he wondered why he had not found it the first time.

, , ,

They started down another way, to see as much as they could. Descending an escarpment, they went back into full cover, springing on the humus of conifers, going down. At first, he thought he mis-heard the sound, but then his friend stopped. They listened together. Yes, it was the unmistakable, though faint, sound of bleating. They moved on, alert, but they heard another sound, much more distinct, like a flute. Then the bleating again.

They followed the sounds or, rather, they came closer to them as they progressed by the course of the stream. Going by, he grabbed at a clump of laurel, and it broke, draping his head and shoulder. He whirled, laughing, to free himself of the garland, then was shushed by his friend. They had turned into the open camp of two men, or a man and a large boy, only half-heartedly trying to conceal themselves behind trees partly ringed with moss thick and spongy as a down comforter. The boy had a tin whistle in his hand.

The man was holding a pistol.

He swallowed, not daring to reach the laurel bough hiding an eye. A goat dashed across the clearing, its wattles swinging. And in the middle of the camp, flat, black rocks were stacked.

"What you boys a-wantin'?" said the man, putting the pistol in his front overall pocket as he came from behind the tree.

"We was just walkin' on home," the boy's friend said.

"Yeah," he added feebly. "We was only just goin' on home."

The man cocked his head to the side. "Where you two been?"

"Come up the other side, just for lookin'."

"Yeah."

The man now spoke coaxingly: "Well, come on over here then."

"What's them?" the boy said, pointing. "Looks like coal."

"Now you boys listen to me. I'm goin' to show you somethin', now that you're here anyways. But if I ever hear a you sayin' anything about it to anybody, I'll fix you good. Hear? Now what's you boys's names?"

They told him, and where they lived. He wanted to know street names, names of relatives, said he knew some of them. They answered his questions with exaggerated humility, for boys.

"We ain't goin' to say nothin', mister," he said, shaking his head, now free of the laurel.

"Well, I druther you hadn't a seen it, but now that you have I'm a-goin' to show you the full thing."

He took them to a large piece of downed bush and moved it aside. There was a hole in the bank, pick and ax handles protruding. The man explained about the coal. It was cannel, he said, and bird's-eye at that, so rich it fairly oozed oil. There was a full vein of it, as he'd guess, with no parting other than a two-inch facing of mother-of-coal. It might well change further on back, he said, but here it had star-shaped radiations—he called them starry eyes—all over the face of it. It was the richest there was in Virginia, next to hard coal, which never grew here anyway.

And he meant to get him some.

The boy had heard that this was what was called national forest, but he did not understand about land ownership. To him it was all just land.

"How you goin' to get it out?" his companion asked.

"Got me a pony and sled. I'll get it out okay. You boys thirsty?"

The mountain man handed round a naked canteen, first to the large boy, who drank around his tobacco quid. The guide shook off the offer, then raised his eyebrows when the younger boy reached. His mouth was crying for a draft of coolness, and he took the proffered liquid eagerly, not fully divining his friend's gesture. He let the canteen pour itself into him in the way a boy will try to get all the cola he can if allowed only one swallow. It burnt—Sweet Jesus, it burnt—all the way down, so bad his throat was going to catch fire, and he ran to the stream and dunked his head, letting the water and whatever was in it run freely into his mouth. He swallowed as much of it as he could till at last his throat cooled.

Then he was standing by with the three of them, hearing the tin whistle, looking into a cage of some kind, and he had no fear.

"Catched 'em myself," the mountain man was saying. "Real beauts, ain't they?"

He focused in on the head of the one, open-mouthed, in hour-glass-figured coils, its eyes yellow as amber.

"That there's a copperhead. Meanest sumbitch there ever was."

Then he heard the rattle, saw the beads quake at the end of the other one, saw its pupil-slits cut vertical the hate of its eyes, saw even the heat pits dilating below.

"That? Just a timber rattler. Common as worms 'round here."

He felt the friendly hand urge his back onward, away. Heard his friend's voice apologize for whatever they had done, heard it promise that, no, sir, they wouldn't ever tell a soul about nothing.

And then they were going down again, the stream hiding the sounds they were making, and he was dizzy. His stomach burned, and he wanted more of the stream. But the friend took him strongly onward, and they came to what the friend told him was the reservoir.

"You can drink all a that you want to."

He stretched himself across the spillway, the hand holding him by the pants' seat. He let his arm dangle into the pool before him and, when the ripples subsided, he saw about his own face in the water-mirror several red-spotted newts.

When the salamanders came, he took one by the tail. "This here one a those without any lungs?" he asked.

His friend's quiet shrug distorted in the ripples.

He held it up. "Look at that silly smile and those big eyes. Like marbles. Dare me to eat it?"

"Th'ow that thing back and let's go." His friend pulled him up, splashed water in his face while he held him, and guided him back to the descent.

But for the strong, steady hand that reached out to him from time to time, he would surely have fallen. His legs were moving on their own, for his mind could not direct them. Yet it registered there that he heard the sound of a fiddle, and it occurred to him that they were passing near the cabin of some family the town did not know.

As they broke through the last cover of the lower treeline, the heat and damp hit him in the eyes. He thought that he might be suffocating, and he retched, without slowing. He tried to clear his head, taking his temples between his hands, rubbing. He saw black swirls of dust at the tipple they were nearing, trucks growling with their loads, men black-faced and angered, yelling in pantomime. And at the leveling of the creek a large rock held fast a washing machine along with winter's accumulation clinging in turn to that, the mud from the thaw having plastered the weeds flat and dry.

He was now crossing to behind the tipple, on dry land, crushing thistle-milk, catching to his clothes the burrs and nettles from the parched growth just beyond the creekbank. He could not hear behind him at the treeline the song of the rain frogs, waiting to descend, to breed in water they were trying to cause by their music. And, had he looked, he could not have seen them either, for they were colored into the ridged bark patterns of what they waited in.

The two boy-shapes circled the tipple, the men, the trucks. And they walked on, one holding the other, into the grim spring.

OFF TO WAR

IT WAS ONE OF THOSE SUMMER SUNDAYS, when it seemed that the sparse trees on the ridge had leaved out just enough to cover over the road scars to the tipple. Flush had worked the midnight shift and would have been lying dust-caked on the cot, but this morning he had washed from the pail on the porch and was dressed in a pair of gabardine pants and white dress shirt he'd got at the Salvation Army.

His mother, Jewel, was outside, waiting for his sister, Nellie, when he came from the house. She hadn't said anything much yet, except to ask him when he'd first come in from washing if he wanted anything to eat. He told her no, but he'd taken some coffee from her pot to be sociable. When he saw that she was looking him over and was likely ready to say something about his voluntary dressing, he told her that Frank Pisa was going to church with him.

"Ever since that cave-in, you been thicker'n thieves with that dago boy. Just 'cause he he'ped you don't mean you got to go and ast him to go to meetin'."

"I went to his church with him, and he wants to go with me to mine."

"You been to one of them Cathlick"—she gave out a little cackle—"messes"?

"Nah." He said it as if to dispel such a notion. "Just a little one. Called Benediction."

"What was hit like?" She spoke with that emphasis she could place just right, that lazy indifference she used when she most wanted to catch him up.

But he didn't care this morning. "Smelled something awful." He wrinkled his nose, giving her some of what he knew she wanted.

"That's that incense, they call it." She said it as if whoever could even so much as think of using anything so vile in a church could never be saved.

"Like sweet carbide," he said, but figured he'd better stop being so nice—she might suspect something. Still, he added, moving away from her, "They ought to use it in the mines."

"They got 'em a real churchhouse over there?"

"Nah. Just get together in a store."

"Well, what time's he a-coming? We got to get going. Eleanor!"

Nellie came outside in a flowered jersey dress and flat shoes and stood beside Jewel, in black. She'd married a boy from over on Jessup's Branch when he came home on furlough before being sent overseas. He'd never worked in the mines.

And there came Frank down the hill in a suit and white shirt, whistling, swinging his long arms.

"You'd think that boy come from a rich family instead of just them hunks and dagos over by Dant, wouldn't you?"

Flush thought, No, only you would. "He's just really got to dress up on Sundays. They're kind of finicky about them things."

"You looking pretty good your own self this morning." Her tone was almost complimentary till she added: "You sick?"

Flush anticipated the follow-on question by saying, "He's already been to one church this morning."

"I'd think ours'd be pretty tame for him. Come on now, Eleanor. Dry up and let's go. They ain't no man worth crying over for six months. Anyways," she added, with her natural blend of concern and disdain, "he'll be back. His kind never git kilt."

Flush delayed, even though Frank was getting too close. Finally, he hurried over to head him off. Frank, a head taller than Flush, waved over Flush's head at the females, his full white shirt cuff showing beneath his tight tweed coat. Flush turned him around and got him walking. "Don't let them hear you. And don't move your hands so much when you talk. You all set?" Flush had to walk two steps to his one.

"Damn right, I'm set. You?"

"Unbutton that top button, Pisa. You look like a country jake."

"You set?" Frank said skeptically, undoing the top button.

"And when'd you get that coat, when you was four?"

"Said: How about you?" Frank's tone insinuated that he knew Flush wasn't so set.

"All but the money."

Frank stopped. "I goddamn knowed it."

Flush urged him on.

"What you mean, 'All but the money'?"

"They ain't any. I went through every pocketbook and wallet in the house."

"Damn game last night." Frank spoke through his teeth. "I told you to get the hell out of there, but huh-uh. Now what we going to do?"

"Don't worry about it. I'll get some."

"We taking off in a hour, and you're going to get some!"

"Keep them durn mitts down, will you? They see you excited back there, they going to know something's up."

"You think I got enough for both of us? The old man give me all he had, which wadn't all that much."

"You won't need to, I'm telling you." Flush spoke mock solemnly as he looked at the little church they were approaching.

"Well, I'm a son-of-a—"

"Yep. And you're the one going to do it. Floyd waiting? Got your paper signed?"

"Floyd's been ready since Wednesday. What else that old ramp got to do? And, yeah, got my paper right here." Frank tapped his jacket pocket. "What about yours?"

"She wouldn't sign. Hell, I didn't even ask her."

Frank stopped with a loud sigh. "You little—. You ain't done one thing you said you was. And what you mean I'm 'the one going to do it'?"

"Keep walking." Flush looked back and sort of nodded at the females, far enough behind. "I'll get it signed okay. Now here's what you do after church, when the preacher comes out front to get congratulated...."

, , ,

They sat on the front bench, sanctimonious-looking as a pair of Latter Day Saints who'd wandered into Bellum a few weeks ago, and hurried out of town after their first stop. Frank was rigid, his hands on his knees, except that he kept brushing at his dark hair. Every time he laid his hand back on his knee, he put a spot of oil on his britches. He nodded his head with every sentence the preacher uttered, and when the preacher said, "Now, let's bow down and pray," Frank let his head drop down so suddenly and with his chin making a little thud onto his chest, it seemed he'd just had heart failure and died sitting straight up on the bench.

With the congregation muttering and generally responding to the preacher's warm-up, Flush whispered out of the side of his mouth, "Don't overdo it."

Frank whispered back, still smiling, without moving his mouth, "Go fuck yourself."

And then Preacher Renfro got going. His face squinched in like a ferret's, he said he had "graaaave things to talk about concerning that war. Hit ain't no accidint it's a-bleeding our land of all our young men. It's them three—Hitler, Tojo, and Mussolini—got together and figgered out what to do to tear this country apart, and all them in power just a-falling fer it hook, line, and sinker. I tell you—."

Frank nudged Flush, but Flush didn't dare look at him.

In a while the preacher was hollering about how "Jaasus-a come out of the wilderness and preached-a the gospel-a." He yelled out the "root causes of war, which is sinning, fornicating, Roosevelt, Japs, Germans, Eye-tayuns, Jews—all of 'em a-rotating like spokes round the same axle. That's why they call 'em that. They're all mixed up together, I tell you."

Flush whispered, his hand over his mouth: "Notice he left out drinking."

But Frank's smile had faded. His shoulders slumped.

"Take it easy. He didn't mean you."

When the preacher finished, he called for those who were ready to repent and be saved to come up and testify.

Frank rose—all six feet of him—before Flush could stop him. He walked up to the preacher, who had come off his box behind the pulpit, and intoned, as mournfully and near tears as if he meant it: "Save me, sir. I'm a sinner."

The preacher hesitated, scrutinizing. Then he looked around and smirked. "I can see that you are. On your knees, boy."

The congregation came alive with this new soul—in a darker skin than theirs—to save from damnation. From every corner coal miners and women, even children, called on the Lord to give Brother Renfro the power to do what needed doing. "Amen, Brother!" "Yessir, Lordy!" "Show 'im the way, Brother Renfro!"

Frank was aslant before the preacher. It looked as if he might just topple, and Flush had to laugh in the commotion. Then Frank kneeled, still off-center, and folded his hands. The preacher touched Frank's head, yelled out to lighten this boy's load (but his face was saying to lighten his complexion), and Frank swung out his arms.

"I'm saved! Glory be. I'm saved!" Frank stood, still askew, and walked that way back to the bench, crossing himself and muttering, "Thank you, Father." He put his hands on his knees and the asinine smile back on his face and watched while two miners led Dummy Bledsoe, a mute and hunchbacked dwarf, to the preacher, who had advertised all week that he was going to make Dummy speak at long last.

Everybody was yelling now, witnessing and praying. Dummy looked at the preacher; the preacher looked around and hushed them all with his hands. "They's a dark presence in here today. I can feel it. Now take this man"—the preacher told two miners, motioning toward Dummy with his outstretched palms—"on back to his seat and I'll pray over him next week. Sister Nancy John!"

A skinny, ribbon-bedecked woman in her thirties or fifties stood at the end of the front bench.

"Pass the plate, child," the preacher said as if he was about to cry, "while I go outside and pray in the garden."

"Where he keeps a jug," Flush whispered.

Frank let out the beginning of a horse laugh but turned it into a cough so colossal everybody looked at him. Then Sister Nancy John was before them, looking angelically over their heads and handing a pie plate to Flush. Flush flipped his thumb on the underside of the plate, at the same time pretending to drop in a coin, and passed it to Frank, who looked at it as if he'd never seen one before in his life, and Sister Nancy John took it back. All the time Frank's eyes bore through her dress like invisible augers until, finally, he removed his jacket and draped it over his lap in a futile attempt to conceal what had sprung up there.

After the service Flush stood by with Nellie while Jewel wondered out loud: "That sister of yours and them younguns: a-livin' like heathens, I expect."

"Her husband ain't the church-going type. You know that."

"Last time she was here, she said he'd let her and the younguns go."

Flush broke in: "Agreeing to that man means about as much as a oath to make Dummy talk."

"Hush up," Jewel said. "The preacher's a-comin'. Good thing that other'n high-tailed it outen here. Now you got to apologize fer him."

"Sure is good-looking."

Flush understood that Nellie meant Frank, not the preacher. He looked at his mother, and for the first time in his memory he felt something for her. Her eyes glinted in the sun; her head went up, proud. He wanted to say good-bye. She was getting older, around the eyes, and he would not see her again for a long time, maybe never. As she and Nellie began to walk to the preacher, Flush patted Nellie on the arm. At least it was something. "I'm going up the street," he said, and moved away, fast.

⸝ ⸝ ⸝

Frank was waiting at Pod's with their bags and a pocket of change. He gave the coins to Flush.

"Any trouble?"

"You kidding? I left my Saint Christopher medal and scapular in the plate. That preacher'll think the dark presence is haunting that church from now on." His voice went mean: "That little white-trash prick'll know better than try to fuck with olive trash again!"

As Flush knocked at Pod's door (the pool room was "closed" on Sundays), he was laughing, shaking his head over that holy medal supposed to stave off car wrecks and that dirty, little worn-out rag Frank had kept around his neck on a string. "Be careful who you let into the white-trash category. I come from these people!"

"Well, you can have 'em," Frank said. "My old man's moving the family over into Kentucky tomorrow. I ain't *never* coming back here."

Buford, a forty-year-old boy who always wore a railroad cap, let them in, and they walked through the empty pool room towards the back as Buford made his whistle sound—*whoo-whoo*—behind them. Floyd Gilliam was sitting in an old movie seat by the wall. Flush gave him a respectful nod. "We'll be ready shortly, Mister Gilliam."

Floyd adjusted his cap, and spat near a spittoon.

"What you mean, 'shortly'?" Frank said. "We only got about two minutes till the preacher figures it out. You want to go to France or jail?"

"Keep your shirt on." Flush went through the doorway into Pod's back room, as Frank asked Mister Gilliam if he'd go start the truck.

"We'll be right out." He turned to Flush. "What the hell you doing? They ain't no time for gambling, for Chrissake."

"Nah, it ain't that. C'mon."

Pod was dealing blackjack. He looked up with tired, bulbous eyes and gave a barely perceptible nod for the others to make room.

"I ain't playing."

"How about you, guinea?"

The others laughed.

"Say, Pod, do me a little favor here." Flush pulled out the paper.

"What you got there," one of the men said, "marriage license? I been legal-like daddy to a bunch of boys."

"Hurry up," Frank told Flush.

"What's your rush, dago?" another man said.

"Hell, we got to go to war."

"You're already there," another man said.

"That man knows his Latin," another man said.

"What we got here?"

"I'm enlisting, Pod. Sign for me. The old lady wouldn't."

"Why don't you just sign it yourself?"

"Because I got to be able to say I didn't." Flush looked around, at the color-defying walls, the slick wood floor, the burlap sack hanging in the back doorway leading to the famous, reputedly ceramic trough back there. No sense to waste a door because, once you'd seen it, once you'd used it, nothing could have hidden it from the eyes in your head, let alone from your nose. But sitting at the poker table you smelled only cards and money, cigarette smoke and men. Something like an ache assailed him. He'd had the time of his life back here in this hole in the wall.

"Worried about lying? It'd still be that."

"Sort of. They might could trace my handwriting."

"How about the dago there?" Pod smiled seriously.

"Pisa? Hell, he can't write his own name." Flush hit Frank on the arm, to be doing something while he waited, to dispel the odd feeling building in him. "Nah, he's going to be right there with me. They'd catch us sure'n hell. Think that face could hide anything?"

"That why you don't play cards?" Pod asked Frank.

"Yes, sir." He gave a head motion to Flush to get on with it.

"It's got to be you." Flush looked Pod in the eye with the same stinging urgency, beyond the present request, as when he'd said, "*Flush beats*," those years ago.

Pod took a pencil from his pocket and signed "Arthur Ramey."

The name startled Flush. "It ought to be hers." He looked at the big chair that had been his father's before it became his own after the cave-in of '35.

"I ain't a-signing your mother's."

"But I got to tell them my old man's dead."

"Why?" Pod's voice became almost soothing. "Just tell them he ain't."

"We got it," Frank said. "Let's get."

"By the way," Flush said, "if Preacher Renfro comes snooping around, tell him you ain't seen us."

"What the hell'd that wino be doing in here?" one of the men said. "He don't gamble, but that's about all he don't do."

They all laughed. When they stopped, one of the men said, "You two knock off the collection plate?"

"Yes, sir," Frank said. "How'd you know?"

"Wouldn't be the first time," another man said. "That preacher's hollered and called it praying for more than one stake in a game he don't know nothing about. How you getting out? Coal train over at Dant?"

"Mister Gilliam," Frank said—"if we ever *get* out."

"Old Floyd," one said: "Gooder'n ary angel."

"Give them a quick tower," Flush said.

"You crazy!"

"Ah, go on. Like a good-bye."

"Yeah," one of the men said, "I ain't seen you do that since one day in the mine last year."

Frank rolled his eyes, then stiffened to full height and leaned twenty degrees off vertical.

"Tilt, tally. Tilt." It was one of the men.

Frank went another couple of degrees then righted himself. "Now, let's get going or I'm leaving without you." He grabbed Flush by the arm.

"Just a minute." Pod got up slow as something stuck, went to a box and pulled out a Mason jar half full of clear liquid. "You might could use this on your way to France."

Frank took the jar. "Thanks, Pod. Be seeing you." He sort of nodded to the others.

One of them said: "Boy, if you could take you a gallon jug of that over to France, you'd be wore out before you got there."

"Hey, guinea, bring us back a couple a hairs from ol' Hitler's mustache," one of the men said.

"Yeah," another one said, "or one of Tojo's little nuts."

Flush said "So long" to everybody, but he meant it for Pod, who with something like a sad smile on his face spoke up as they left the room: "You two peckerheads don't go off now and get your own balls blowed off."

, , ,

In the coal truck making its way through the mountains, Flush sat in the middle, the eightball-topped gearshift curving up from the floor between his legs. Floyd's cigarette ash was as long as the original Camel, not a speck of paper showing. Floyd bounced with each bump like a part of the truck and the ash a part of him.

Frank put his left arm across the top of the seat and propped his right in the open window. "Ever been to war, Mister Gilliam?"

"Bellum or the action?"

The two boys mock-laughed.

"That's a good one," Flush said.

Frank said, "The action."

"Damn right."

"What's it like?"

"Put weight on a man."

"What you mean, 'weight'?"

"Picked me up a perm'nent half of a pound back in nineteen and seb'mteen."

Frank showed Flush by his look that they should humor him, he had the truck. "How's that, Mister Gilliam?"

"Shrapnel. Leg and shoulders."

"Damn," Flush said. "Hurt?"

"Only when it rains, or's getting ready to."

Frank took a drink from the Mason jar and passed it to Flush. Flush took a pull and passed it to Floyd. They all lit cigarettes, Floyd's having disappeared without visibly being touched.

The truck had slowed to creeping on the sixty-degree serpentine road. Floyd shifted gears, grunted, shifted again, his elbow catching Flush in the stomach. The truck almost stalled.

"Good thing this truck ain't loaded." Frank seemed to hate a silence. "It'd take us till the armistice to get there, and this here war ain't even started yet for us. How many gears you got in this durn thing anyway, Mister Gilliam?"

"'Nough." Floyd shifted again, double-clutching as fast as single-. "I'll get you there." He spat out the window. His mouth sort of smiled, showing crooked teeth like little yellow tombstones. His eyes almost closed. He held the gear-shift knob in his right hand, just above Flush's lap.

Frank laughed. "If Mister Gilliam here finds him any more gears, they ain't going to be no need for you to go to no France, good buddy. You might just as well stay at home with Nancy John Kincaid." He pulled a Moon Pie out of his pocket. "Anybody want some?" Nobody did. Frank took two bites and it was gone. He washed it down with moonshine and passed the jar.

"What you going to do over there in France for Moon Pies?" Flush looked at Floyd. "Sumbitch loves them better'n spaghetti."

"*Pizza Luna*: That's what my old man calls them. Got me a case in my bag." He propped his knees on what was left of the truck's dashboard and let his head fall onto the top of the backrest, hitting the rear window. "The hell with clothes. I don't plan to be wearing none but about half the time anyway, and Uncle Sam'll provide them."

"Them Moon Pies ain't going to last forever." Floyd made that little sound that came out somewhere between a scoff and a laugh: "Heh. Might have to get the sweet tooth for sumpn else."

"Like what?" Frank said.

"Well." Floyd lowered his head but looked off somewhere. "Like pussy."

Frank sat up like a jack-in-the-box and punched Flush with his elbow. "See?" He shook him. "They *grow* it over there—right, Mister Gilliam?"

"That's the truth. Whole durn country just loaded with women and wine, and both of 'em just a-waitin' on you two to get there." Floyd looked out the window and said in his flattest whine: "All we got here's coal."

"Don't forget moonshine." Flush held the jar up and shook it. "And Nancy John Kinkaid."

Frank pushed his feet on the floorboard and leaned out the window until he hung on the door frame by his waist.

Flush grabbed him by the belt. "What the hell you trying to do, fly to France?"

"This is my last trip up this snake-ass road to nowheres." Frank yelled, and continued yelling, to the ridges and hollows: "Ah rezzervore, coal! French ginch, here we come!"

"Get in here." Flush pulled him back in.

"But now, you boys watch yourselves." Floyd shook his head and peered over at Flush. "They's women out there make that cave-in you boys come th'ough look like a frolic. The dago here's maybe been around some, but Bellum, Virginia, ain't

France, now. I mean, joking around about pussy with the colored guys pulling coke over in Hawthorne's one thing; getting in with a Frenchie dame who's maybe got a few Frogs already hanging around is something you don't want to mess with."

Flush and Frank looked at him, then at each other.

"I know what I'm a-talkin' about. One time, I was a-layin' into this little old farm gal when somebody commenced pounding below us on the ceiling. I stopped and was ready to grab my clothes and lam it out the window, but she got aholt of me good and laughed and someway got it across to me that it was just her mother a-wantin' her turn."

Frank went solemn as a statue, and finally spoke: "Go-od-da-umn."

But you never knew when a miner was putting you on. They must have made real mistakes all the time, but often they faked them just to get a laugh. So a boy didn't always know when he was being kidded. The dirt on their faces and clothes most of the time was like a part of them, permanent make-up in their roles as laborers and clowns. And the colored guys: You couldn't see the dirt, but they didn't need any make-up. A few minutes on a corner with four or five of them going non-stop and a boy'd piss in his pants laughing.

But Floyd wasn't laughing. "Looky, I never had no boys of my own, and my daddy never give me the advice I'm trying to give you. Just don't go a-thinking them French women's anything like Nancy John Kinkaid or even Darcy Sturgill. You're all just alike to them two, but a French woeman can handle all kinds, and you're only just one of 'em.

"So just remember, now: A Frenchie'll turn you ever' which way but aloose." He gave his little grin. "And a straight don't beat a flush even in mule stud no-where but here."

"It don't?" Flush said.

"Sure don't. That's just the mountain twist on the game."

"So any place else in the world and I'd've won that pot."

"You might've. But you maybe wouldn't've won that day, except it being that day in Bellum."

"If they played like the rest of the world I would've. I had the flush."

"Oh, I was there. Knowed ever' card on the table, 'cept Pod's hole. They was just three players left the last round, so it was easier to follow."

"But Pod folded."

"Yeah, he folded—after he checked, called your bet and Maggard's raise, and raised seven hisself. Then called Maggard's last raise."

"A measly quarter."

"Yeah. By that time you was out of money. Hit never was between Maggard and Pod."

"Pod still folded, so it come down to me and Maggard."

"Pod maybe had you both beat."

Even Frank was giving it his attention. Since that day, everybody, card player or not, had heard about that game.

"After the last card, he checked."

"I know he did. But think about it. If he's got his full house and's called, he's got to show. He's got to win it all." Floyd looked off someplace, leaving the truck to drive itself for a while. "They wasn't no suckerin' go on."

"And if he don't have his filly?"

"If he don't, then what's he doing calling and raising? He sure knowed you had your flush." Floyd pursed his lips into a smile. "Hell, everybody there knowed that. Whatever Pod had, he went as far as he could take you—and that pot, too."

Flush fastened hard onto what he was being told.

Floyd lit a cigarette and now drew long and hard on it. "Tell me: You ever play for stakes that high again after that day?"

"No, never did. Nobody but Pod could afford to."

"You think any of 'em could afford it any better when they first let you sit in and you just a boy? You think Goff and Dye could?"

Flush did not answer. He'd seen what was left of the two men after the cave-in, and he was sent immediately outside, to the bed of the same truck they now rode in as had taken them off the mountain that day, to how he felt then, about the hills, and home, and coal. He took a drink from the jar, seeing over the rim the tree branches lift in the wind, like waving.

"You thought you had 'em both beat that day? Is that what you thought, boy?"

"Yessir, I sure did." Flush saw the card table, ran that last hand—all of it, fast—back through his head.

"Well, you might think on this: Nobody knowed Pod's hole card. Not even Pod. He never looked." Floyd wrinkled his brow as he glanced at Flush. "That pot had to be built up, and it just worked out you last three looked good on top. That's the hand they'd been waiting for."

"Why didn't they just let me win the goddamn thing?"

"Well, for one thing, what would Maggard do for his family, losing that much? Most of it was Pod's money you two split or Maggard won clean."

"And for another?"

"For another, you needed to be give a lesson to, not just money. What would you of learned elsewise?" Impatience had come into his tone. "Seems you maybe still do. Anyways, you get in a poker game in the army, you better get the rules straight."

"Well, just tell me this: How did they know I'd think a flush beat a straight in the first place? I didn't hear all the rules, but how did they know that either?"

"You forgettin' you all three sat there with the cards coming one at a time? All you could've had was a flush, or a pair. It was clear to everybody but you, and you bettin' the light money."

So. He had become a regular, namesake to the hand he held that first day he had ascended, a boy of nine, to his dead daddy's chair at the table. In the intervening years he had laughed about the time of his knowledge, and no one had ever let on. It would not have come to him that there were such coarse men who would sweeten a pot, then throw it in such a way. But that was the way of them. They would never have sent wasteful flowers or gifts to survivors; but they might, in a back room, when coal dust was heavy in the fading light and no one could really tell for sure and those who could would not dare speak of it—they might drop a game to a boy bereft and send him on his way so that others would never know the truth and suspect charity and come running at every little calamity.

"I be damn if I can understand it," Frank said. "You been running that card game over in your head for six years, remembering ever' card played. How 'bout concentrating a little bit on just where we're a-heading now?"

"Well, now, listen here," Floyd said, changing tones, "you two don't go over there and get yourselves kilt."

"Them French women that mean?" Frank patted his thighs several times, loud and quick.

"Don't go joking. I'm talking 'bout war now."

"Yessir."

They were all quiet for a moment, as if each one were contemplating the truck's sounds and rhythms. Boys knew trucks as well as men did, some better. This one, long past any prime it might once have had, was just at the stall point. Frank began to rock forward and backward, his legs stiff, his feet on the floorboard, as if he was pushing the truck along. A big, surly grin appeared on his face. "Women! War! That little preacher said two of the root causes of war was fornicating and Eye-tayuns, didn't he?" He put his arm around Flush, shaking him, pounding his feet on the floorboard. "Well, th'ow this sumbitch in bulldog, Mister Gilliam. Me and Flush here gonna go make ourselves some war!"

WHEN CASSIE FREEMONT WALKED BY

THEY SAID TOMMY FLEMING COULD FIX IT. They said he could fix anything on a car, as long as it wasn't foreign or too new. So I left the two old men at the gas station—men I'd known when I was a boy—and I drove the streets until I found what they'd said was Tommy's house, so small and plain I couldn't believe it was the one. But I parked my ailing car, turned the key off, kept it in gear while I pushed in the brake and let the clutch out to stop the motor, and got out. Another motor sounded behind the house, and I went to see if it was Tommy back there.

A man on the far side at the back was tinkering with a lawn mower. He had his back to me, and I felt uneasy coming up on him like that. But the mower roared, and I would not be heard if I spoke. Then the motor stopped and the man said something tight and hard, as he grabbed the pullrope and jerked then turned a screw on the carburetor. The motor caught; smoke rose around the man's legs.

The legs sheathed in jeans were Scat Fleming's all right—slightly bowed, lean. The rest was Scat, too: muscly shoulders not so broad, a barely thickened waist; the neck now more sinewy; the thin hair that had made Scat look like an older man at 19. And now? If I was coming up on 45 myself, Scat would be over 50. Seven, eight years difference back then meant a lot.

From the angle I had on him there were all the markings of Tommy "Scat" Fleming—All-County Tailback '46, '47, '48, '49. And would have been back in '50 but was declared ineligible because of his age, and then sent off to Korea. It was a bleak day in town. I had seen in the faces of the two old men at the service station that they maybe still begrudged it. They hadn't said anything to me; they didn't know who I was. But as I turned to go they began to talk. There wasn't ever anybody in a football uniform like that boy. Never was and never would be.

The motor stopped.

"Hello, Scat," I said.

Fleming turned, a questioning look on the same face I'd known, though now grayed with stubble, the hairline recessed, so that I felt that I gazed at an awful future from 35 years ago. Because I felt at that moment all that younger, like a boy who had seen the future back then and, knowing what it was, would somehow be safe from it. But of course it was only passing silliness. When Fleming spoke some greeting, not specific or even strong as he ought, being Tommy Fleming, I just said, "They said you could maybe fix my car."

"They did?" He spoke without any particular conviction; he didn't really care who "they" were. It was like he'd heard everything that might be said about him and cars and the Bill Bledsoes of the world—those below him and above him too who had admired what he could do on a football field. It was something like regret that I sensed Fleming feel in that moment.

"Do you think you can?" I spoke vaguely on purpose.

"Wellsir, that depends on what the trouble is."

That little *sir* didn't set well. The past year I'd lost my job and family. Words like that reversed things, and I didn't feel up to it. "Guys down at the ESSO… EXXON said it sounded like it was dieselin'." I'd fallen into my old voice.

"What year?"

"Seventy-nine."

"American make?"

He rubbed one hand against the other, with sound, and I saw them as the rough mitts they'd been even when he was a boy.

"Plymouth." I clenched my own hands, now even bigger than his.

"Pull it on back around here and let's take a look."

Going to the car, I understood that Tommy didn't remember me. It had been so long since I had lived as an inferior to almost everyone in town, but I had come back a couple of times: once to bury my mother, once to show my family where I grew up.

On the second trip I had gone to the pool room for a little poker game and had seen Fleming (the one time in all those years), drunk and weaving, shooting pool and still blasting on the break like a cannon. I'd said, "Hi, Scat," on his way by, but there was no answer to be heard.

During the poker game I'd heard one of the men say how sorry Fleming was, and I thought it meant how filled with regret he was, that he'd reacted to some-body's, or his own, family tragedy. As talk continued I realized what I should have known already and would have if it hadn't been for other things on my mind: What was meant was that Tommy Fleming, over-the-hill football star, was "a sorry, no-'count bastard," as one of the men finally put it.

Not long after that, I heard how Tommy was thrown out of the pool room for fighting. Then he sank low, lower yet because of his once high standing in the town. Through the years "Scat" might just as well have been changed to "Trouble."

But he seemed steady now as he directed me to stop the car where he wanted it. I turned the ignition off, figuring to show him the problem, but it worked all right now, of course. He had me pop the hood latch and looked over the carburetor. "Pretty dirty," he pronounced. "I'd have to clean it up and adjust it. Probably tune it up. Can you leave it awhile?"

I told him I could but not for long. "I might ought to get me a car with that new fuel injection," I said.

He kind of smiled, and then I flat out said, "Don't you remember me, Scat?"

"Sure." He coughed. "You one of them Bledsoe boys?"

I hadn't heard "one of them Bledsoe boys" since my high-school days, when Bledsoe seemed to be the same as "white trash." And then I remembered: One of Fleming's family branches was attached to a prominent family. He didn't have the name—what was it?—but his mother had been a...yes, a Whittaker. Tommy Fleming had lived for some time in one of the town's two biggest houses, as close to a mansion as that town had ever known. And here he was now, calling me white trash in so many words. Some things just never changed, no matter how long you were away.

When I was coming along in that town, if something was different, especially bad or strange, about anybody, everybody called him that. Boytime had been peopled with the likes of Polecat, Silver Dick, and Puny. They'd called me Slick, a jab at me always hustling a game of poker when I could, and—. Well, I had to admit now as I stood before the great Tommy Fleming, they'd maybe been right.

I had found my way into a business college, and after that with a few months of study on my own I took a test and got a job as a stock broker with a small company in Richmond. What it amounted to was that I got to sit and smoke and, when computers came along, to play with them. I was a legitimate bookie for anybody with enough money to lay a bet on some corporation, and I couldn't ever beat that. There were always suckers loaded with dough and not idea one of what to do with it.

I'd been lucky at first, made a small bundle on the market myself, and enough later on to get a wife and buy a house and let Alice have all the babies she wanted, which turned out to be three. I could even keep playing poker but be respectable. Nobody knew I was still just the same Bill Bledsoe, least of all me.

Then the big award came: Broker of the Year. Airline tickets to Vegas for two, put up in The Dunes, and all the trimmings. I talked Alice into going along with me and taking the kids. It would be like a family vacation, I told her, but I really wanted to show her what I could do in the big time. She could get a sitter and fool around with the slots for a while, and the kids would keep her busy the rest of the time.

Only as soon as I saw the green felt tables, with nothing else deep-rooted enough in me to keep it down, Chance sprung up inside like jimson weed. My mistress, Risk, sprawled in all the glitter, and I dived into her. That company I worked for might just as well have given whiskey to a drunk.

After three days Alice was crazy with worry. She'd got hooked herself and was out of money, too. The motel manager put a stop to her charging meals at the restaurant. I had become a round-the-clock haunter of the tables. Alice had been unable to even talk to me, she told me later. She'd finally come to her senses and returned home with the kids. Good thing they had round-trip tickets.

So those who'd called me Slick all those years had been right, but they'd been wrong too. I wasn't all that slick. Who else could lose at the green felt tables not just all his money but wired loans and credit-card advances and his family to boot? (I'd heard that Alice was already seeing a man and might be getting married again.) All that malarkey from shrinks about gamblers wanting to lose—maybe they had something. Seems like after my climb I pretty much did everything I could just to be once more what I always was and had just heard: one of them Bledsoe boys.

I nodded slightly.

Fleming gave a little movement in that carved face of his, and I had the feeling that at his age he could run back punts for the pros. At the same time resentment rose in me like nausea, and I choked it back. In that flash of time I had before the calm Fleming, who seemed to have all the time he'd ever need for anything, I knew that I must connect at last to my old hero, even now that I hated him. Maybe I always had.

"I used to lace your shoes in the dressing room and help you off with your jersey," I said. "I bet you don't remember."

Fleming gave a little laugh-cough. "Yeah, there were always a bunch of little guys hanging around down there."

I was thinking how I'd helped him for a full year in '48, then was water boy in '49. How he'd called me Billy Boy, and the other guys sometimes took it up, too, not always Bledsoe or Slick.

Billy Boy. Just like in the song.

"Remember how it smelled down there?" I wanted to take him back with me, to reach him on a level of memory surely any boy who'd ever been in the basement dressing room of the old high school would be able to recall.

"How's that?" he said. "You mean the tape and stuff?"

I could smell in my mind that mixture of liniment, sweat, piss, leather, and that other something of boys on the verge of being men. It was—I looked at Fleming's face looking over the carburetor—all mingled with the sound of cleats, the tightening of strings gripping leather pads, the serious talk by the coach before the game. I could now see myself back there, privileged: Carrying their water and running errands, I was allowed to listen to the pep talk, to slap a rump on their way out to do battle. I'd felt like part of the team.

"Yeah, you know," I said. "Don't you ever think of that, Scat?"

A screen door squeaked open and slammed. Fleming stepped away from the car, wiping his hands on his jeans. He seemed almost to blush, as the woman glanced at us and sort of winked at him, came down the small porch and went to some nearby flowers.

By her walk, I knew her.

She bounced—no, that wasn't it. She sashayed or flounced—whatever it was, her fuller hips swayed, but it was not just the fetching movement kept in my head all these years. It was some relaxed quality, a way about her that made me recall in a flashing moment the day she came to town.

It was so sunny the town seemed the center of all creation. I was running the streets with a couple of ramps, rifling pockets at the swimming pool, swiping empties at the Pepsi plant. The older boys and girls were gathered across the street from the pool, and I left the ramps I was with and went over to the edge of the crowd, then slipped through. The new grade-school teacher was talking to the high-school kids just like she was one of them. She was not much older than the oldest of them, but she had a presence beyond all the others. She was dressed in clothes the oldest girl there would not have been able to wear. She was so new and lively and had been so absent in my usual world, but I had not missed her until just then, when I first saw her.

She didn't talk like anybody else in town, except maybe for Miss Carlson, the new music teacher. The older kids called her Cassie, and she called them by their first names like she'd known them all their lives. Standing there on the sunny street that day, she was already a recognized member of the town. She didn't have to do anything or even be anything; she just was, like that.

Then somebody must have thought it was time for a little fun. "Hey, Bledsoe," one of the big boys called. "Come on over here."

And I went, right into the center where all the attention was being paid, right before the new woman the others were calling Cassie. I looked up at her through my prided dirty blond forelock. Her voice was so relaxing I could have gone away with her and just grown old listening to her talk. She reached over and cleared away my hair, and then I saw her full. A breeze blew her short hair up so that it fringed her head, and the sun caught it there as if in the moment she was being made to blaze for me. My forehead burned from the touch of her cool hand, and I felt for the first time something like regret for all the dirty little things I had done.

"Do a trick for the lady, Bledsoe," one of the boys said.

"Yeah, show her a card trick, Slick," another added, then said to Cassie: "He carries a little deck of cards every place he goes."

"Don't have 'em with me," I said.

"Yeah? What's these?" Somebody took out the little playing cards from my back pocket.

"Give me those, you son-of-a-bitch," I said between my teeth, and I felt the blood rush to my scalp.

The woman turned from me and began to talk to the others.

I walked off after the cards were given back to me and stood watching as they broke up, going off in all directions and not paying me any mind, like I was a part of the streets again where I stayed most of the time. But then I watched that Cassie Freemont walk down the block. When she was near the corner, I took off through the back alley and came out as she was crossing and watched her walk down the next block until she went into a store.

After that day, whenever I saw her coming—and I could spot her three blocks away—I'd go to a parking meter and when she was passing I'd hold myself out horizontally on the pole, a trick I'd learned from one of the big boys. It was maybe even Scat. She never looked, but everything about her said *follow me*.

And I did begin to follow her, at some distance, to the house where she was staying, to dry-goods and grocery stores, wherever she led me.

One early morning, after I had passed the coke ovens and come to the edge of town, I cut to the back streets and saw her up the way. Only the two of us were out yet, and I was careful not to drag my feet. When she reached the school block, she crossed the street and went to the Catholic church that looked like a big log cabin. She stopped at the door, took a scarf out of her pocketbook and put it on her head, and went inside.

I went on to the schoolyard and practiced shooting marbles till the boys came and the games began. But I watched the door of the church, and after a half hour or so it opened and a few people came out and went their way. After a few minutes Miss Freemont came out with the priest and, taking the scarf off her head, walked in that way she had across the street and into the school building.

I saw her just about every morning, and when winter came and the school-yard froze and snow covered it, I went early anyway. At first, after she'd go into the church, I'd take off for a cafe to warm up. I timed my return to school so I could see her again. But I got tired of that, and one morning I went into the church and sat in the back pew.

I'd heard about the Catholics. When my mother was alive and took me to the Primitive Baptist Church, she told me many times, "Don't you ever get your-self mixed up with them Catholics." The preacher even told us from the pulpit that now that the Catholic church and all those nuns and priests were coming into the area, it wouldn't be long till they'd be trying to snag us all. He gave a mean laugh and said, "Hit's the only only church they ever was."

While I sat back there by myself, the six or seven people scattered around and about as many hospital nuns on the front row kneeled and sat, stood and kneeled again, like exercise. The priest was dressed up like men in old Bible mov-ies and speaking in that Latin that everybody knew was dead. Miss Freemont had the scarf on her head and was exercising like everybody else, so I stood when they did, once, but I felt like a little fool imitating what my mother said to stay away from.

After a while, all the people in there went up to the railing and kneeled and took the white cloth hanging across the railing and put it like one long napkin under their chins. The priest came down from the altar to the railing with a golden goblet and took out something small and white for everybody, and they ate it.

I looked at each face as they got up and returned to their seats. They had their hands together the long way under their chins. Their faces—especially the nuns'—were so peaceful, I wondered what it was they were eating so carefully. If a bad man had wandered in there, the sight of the dozen of them would have made him ashamed. And added to it all were the flickering flames of many can-dles in little red and blue glasses.

When the priest started up again, I fixed onto a colored statue of a man with a beard wearing a robe and holding a baby I took to be little Jesus. The big cross above the altar was hard to look at after I recognized the baby. It made the time from being little to getting killed like that seem so short. Besides, Jesus on the cross was bloody and almost naked. They should have covered him up.

I left early and watched Miss Freemont come out of the church. She was talking to the nuns. She was the prettiest woman I had ever seen, but standing outside after church she was so beautiful I couldn't look at her without turning away every now and then.

After that, I didn't go early anymore until spring, when the marble games began again. By then, when I saw her a block or two ahead of me, I wondered how she could walk the way she did when she was going to pray.

And now, after all this time, here she was, just across the yard, and I spoke her name at last: "Hello, Cassie."

Fleming didn't look too happy at me being so familiar, but he told her that I used to live in town when I was a boy and she said, "Oh."

"Bill Bledsoe," I said.

She squinted against the sun, the same as she had that first day in town when I had faced her in the middle of the crowd. "I'm getting old," she said, "but I don't believe I'm old enough to have taught you in fifth grade."

I wanted to tell her how ashamed I'd felt after I'd cussed in front of her and how I'd thought about it all the time since. Even though I had a reputation for trouble before that, it had been because she was there that had fixed itself in my mind so that everything I did afterwards seemed to compare to it. Not that I actually learned enough from it to change my ways and turn the family name around.

There came a time when I was still young that I resented the hold the woman held over me, and I tried to stop watching for her. Somehow her power over me had seemed to add to the humiliation I felt being a Bledsoe.

And now I felt it all over again, the good and the bad, with Tommy Fleming's words still sounding in my head like the effects of a hangover. How she'd come out the screen door and gone directly to the flowers. If it had been somebody else with her husband, she would have come over with the idea of being introduced, or at least with a little curiosity. They didn't really know or even care who I was.

"I met you when you first came to town," was all I said.

"That's been some time now," she said.

Fleming seemed a little impatient. "If you want to leave it, you can come back in a couple of hours. It ought to be ready by then."

The house I'd called home when I was a boy and had left for good as soon as I could, had fallen down. The paint, beyond even flaking, left a ghost-like hue to the boards.

I went to my old aunt's house. She opened the door and stood behind the screen door, and I tried to smile into her set face as I opened the screen door and put my hand on her shoulder. The must and body odors of age and its doomed maintenance filled the room like a haze. The old woman went to sit in her worn spot on the couch and spit snuff juice into the fireplace burning in May. Near the corner off a side of the hearth, in a wooden wheelchair, my daddy sat like a mannequin.

"What happened?" I said, casually.

"Stroke. 'Bout six weeks back. Ain't got the strenth to keep baccer in his jaw, let alone spit."

"Why didn't you let me know?" I was just saying words, not meaning them.

"Didn't know where you was. You couldn't of done nothing noways. You want I should get up and get you something?"

I thought of what "something" might be, and I told her no.

We stared for long minutes at the fireplace coals, like blackened biscuits with glowing rings.

"You watch him awhile," she said. "I got to go down to the corner store and get me some snuff and things." She got up and stood at the door until I gave her a few dollars from what little I had. "He'p him to the slop jar while I'm gone," she said in a tone to let me know how many times she had done so. "His bottom part works okay." She raised a dark-spotted handkerchief to her mouth and closed the door behind her.

The screen door slammed shut, and I turned to the wheelchair and began pacing like those movie lawyers when they got a dumb bunny on the stand and know it.

"Well, Mastiff—that's what they call you, ain't it?—how you doing now, good buddy?" I made it sound cordial, so he'd know it wasn't.

He was just a blueprint of the brute he'd been. The creases in his face were mortared with coal dust. I picked up a corner of the blanket on his lap and pulled it back. Underneath, the same calloused hands with seven fingers between them were crossed like a stack of thick twigs. The nails were yellow and gnarly like corns with black crowns.

"That little finger went to market. That little finger went, too," I said, pointing at two missing ones. When one of the sausage-thick stubs twitched, I dropped the blanket and went to the fire.

There, I picked up the poker and turned to him. "Hey, you," I said. "Yes, you. Bledsoe boy. Get your skinny little ass over there to that slop jar and do your business." I pointed the poker to the covered pot beyond him. "And look at me when I'm talking to you. Sit up straight there, goddamnit, before I give you something to slump about.

"Don't have to go? Want me to beat the shit out of you, Mastiff?"

I held the poker at an angle in front of me, like a marine with his piece. "Why, you ain't hardly no mastiff a-tall. I bet you ain't much more than a puppy-dog. I bet you ain't but just a runt down where it counts."

I made what I said next sound reasonable to a boy: "Now just get yourself on over there, and don't you go a-dribblin' on the floor or I'll have to cut off whatever you got left."

I thought I heard a sound from him, but it could have been the fire.

"Warm enough?" I said. "Want me to perk up the flames for you?" I touched the poker to the coals, thinking how shrinks don't know a thing about it, there ain't a man alive wants to lose, not even the wretch sitting over there across the room.

And I knew, by God, I didn't.

"If you ain't going to that pot just on the other side of you, where you going to be able to go to?" I looked at his empty eyes. "I tell you where you going, you mean old bastard. You going to the fiery furnace, and I don't mean back to the coke ovens."

Suddenly, there came into my head like a picture before my eyes my frail mother settling under the big man with singed eyebrows and coke streaks all over him. I shook it away.

"And you going to drag me with you if I let you."

I was crying, and I wanted him to see my goddamn tears, to remind him of hers. The two of us had grown crooked in the shade of this man and his brothers and cousins—all of a kind—and now I was so near some act of defilement I had to leave the house to thwart it.

I walked the back streets for what must have been an hour. When the rage went down and I could see, I was near enough to Cassie Freemont's church that I went to it and walked inside. I sat in the same spot I'd sat in that morning so long ago. Colored-glass windows with curved tops had been added, and plaques hung around the walls with scenes of Jesus carrying the cross. A few candles flickered in the red and blue glasses under a statue of Mary, and I sensed that peace I had seen on the faces of those people who had taken communion that morning.

But something was wrong with the statue of the bearded saint. When I was there before, he was holding baby Jesus in his other arm. It couldn't be, but I was sure of it. As sure as my name—.

As sure as Bledsoe.

I left the church and walked around to pass the time till the car was ready. I began to look around at the efforts people had made in trying to improve a yard or a tiny house: flowers in a painted wooden box; a path of stones to a door; flowering bushes with names that leaped into my mind—azalea, forsythia, dogwood. And all around bees hovering, robins hopping and pecking at the ground for their brood.

By the time I turned the last corner onto the Flemings' block, I felt like I lived in this pleasant little town born from coal and trying to cover its scars. I felt like an adult man with a real home, the very house I was coming up on, where Cassie and Tommy Fleming sat on the top step of the front porch just like they'd been waiting for me to come back.

Walking up to them, I saw myself as Tommy Fleming (and how I'd wished I was so often when I was a boy), sitting beside Cassie, and more than that.

I needed something to say, so I said, "What was wrong with it?"

"Mainly the timing was off," Fleming said. "I cleaned her up a little, too."

I glanced at Cassie, hoping she'd say something so I wouldn't have to go back to that motel room. But she didn't, though I had the feeling that they'd been talking about me while I was gone and that now they knew who I was.

"How much I owe you?" I said, remembering now that I'd given my aunt what might be crucial dollars.

"Forget it," Fleming said, and Cassie seemed to stiffen against the charity they likely could not afford.

Fleming being so off-handed now made me uneasy. "What you mean?" I said. "Man does a job, he ought to get paid." Yet if he took my bluff and came up high, it'd be like I'd called a sucker bet.

"All that time you carried water and laced football shoes—nobody paid you anything for that," he said. "Let's just say I'm returning the favor."

It might have been all right if Cassie had smiled her agreement or just said something in support—sure or go ahead, anything—but she was quiet, sitting there peaceful as if she didn't live with a sorry no-'count. While I'd gone to my old man's house, they'd sat out here on the steps, thinking, talking. They'd placed me, all right.

"I don't want to be paid back for any of that." When I leave here, I thought, it's back to the dark room for a night, and then—. "Listen—"

But Fleming was on his feet. "Just take it easy. Maybe you'd better just go on now." He added in a voice a real daddy would use to coax: "Take your car and go on, okay?"

Getting the shit beat out of me by Tommy Fleming was better than nothing at all and a damn sight better than charity. I shouted at him, and he started up.

"Come on," I said.

But Cassie held him by the waist and said, softly, "No, Thomas."

"What's the matter with you?" Fleming said without raising his voice. He rubbed Cassie's shoulder, clearly letting her know he was calmed by her.

He was so relaxed, so without fear that anything could happen to him. I could have hit him easily.

Then I broke. I let it all spill out, how I'd felt like a ramp when I was a boy and going to school in torn, dirty clothes and looked down on by the Whittakers and others like them. Sure, I'd crawled after the likes of Tommy Fleming and craved even the shadow of those above him. So my people were no-'count. I looked Scat Fleming right in his face and said, "You haven't always been on top of the world either." Almost crying by now, I turned to go.

"Boy, don't I know it." There was regret in his voice. "Don't go like that. Come on back and let's cool off. Maybe we can talk about it if we just settle down."

And then Cassie had me by the hand and led me back to the porch. Remembered shame brought more shame, so there was no getting it out. Fleming said very little while I lit a cigarette. Cassie brought lemonade, and I asked if they had anything stronger. She avoided giving an answer, but her face said it would come in due time.

"We don't use it," Fleming said.

I sort of laughed, then checked myself and said, "I mean, I thought you did."

"Oh, I did, all right. Used up my share and maybe yours, too."

"You mean you quit cold?"

Now he laughed briefly. "I don't know about that. Took a while just to want to."

Cassie had no knowing smile on her lips, nothing like that at all. She was as calm as if a simple fact had just been stated. But how, for God's sake? Everybody knew how rotten Scat had been all those years, how after his glory days and quick hitch in Korea with just enough time to get himself a ribbon or two for bravery he'd come back spoiled as a kid. Only it was all over for him and he didn't know it. Everybody else in town knew he was a has-been, even if he was a legend.

Everybody except Cassie, who was everybody that counted.

"Yeah?" I said. "But how'd you do it? Go to Cassie's church?" I was afraid I'd gone too far, and added, "Old Hardshell like you?" I was overstepping, I knew, but something crucial seemed to be resting on me being able to be familiar with them.

"Not quite," he said. "Just once a year."

"How's that?" I said.

"Once a year, when I go to the priest and swear off drinking," he said, just like it was cleaning the windows and putting on the summer screens.

"And it works?" I said.

"Seems to," he said, and laughed. "I figure, each time, I can do it for just a year."

"How long's it been?" I said.

"Oh, right smart," he said.

I could see he didn't want to keep getting questions like this from me, so I stopped. "Listen," I said, before knowing what I was going to say next. It must have sounded like I was asking them to listen for something from the past, something in the wind, something strange because, now that we had come together, we had to take care of whatever it was. "Don't you ever think about how it was, Scat?" Back those years ago, it was said that all Scat Fleming ever thought about was how it was and that's why he drank and would destroy himself. But he hadn't. Now, I had to know that if the past was not so clear to Scat Fleming, who had been great there, it would be dead to me, who had been nothing much.

"Wellsir, it's a pretty good place when you're there," Fleming said. "By the time you get wherever you go, it can be a mighty heavy load to carry if you take it with you. Know what I mean?"

"I sure do," I said.

I told them of the magic the two of them had made for me. I told them about my jobs and how well I'd done in the financial world. And I told them about Alice and the kids, just like we were still together.

Then I told Cassie how humiliated I was that day that the older kids had goaded me in front of her, how they were always trying to get me to do bad things so they could laugh at me, which wasn't hard at all. I finally just came out and told her how bad I'd felt when she had turned away from me because of what I'd said, and how many times I'd wished it back.

But I stopped short of telling her the unearthly pleasure I had taken all those years from watching her walk by and how I followed her inside the church and watched her there. But what I wanted to tell her most of all was not about the past years but what had come to me in the church just some minutes ago about how I might have saved myself from where I went afterwards. Right that very minute, I felt a shiver go through me, like I was trying to follow after the image of Cassie Freemont Fleming walking down the street, and it was my first walk, ever.

"I'm sorry I failed you so soon after we met," she said. "I was so young and got too much attention, I'm afraid."

"I shouldn't have cussed in front of you," I said. "I'm sorry, too."

She offered her hand for shaking, and as I took it I was mindful how rough my own was. The peaceful look on her face made me quiver, as when I was a boy letting water or told by my daddy to do something or what he'd do to me.

"Can you forgive me?" she said. "Let's all three forgive and forget. And whenever you're back with your family, stop by." She kissed the air at Tommy and went into the house.

"I will," I called after her, like I could just go get my family and come back for a visit.

"You be sure to do that," Scat said, as we shook hands.

"Thanks for fixing the car, Scat," I said.

"Don't mention it, Billy Boy," he said, and smiled, and turned to go to the house.

Scat. Still winning after all these years. And why not? It was Scat Fleming who, when thrills were hard to come by, had given plenty of them to Bledsoe boys of all kinds. Some had mined coal and pulled coke; some had married. Some had gone to war and died alone; some had grown old sitting at service stations. It was Tommy Fleming who had made memories for those who might not have had any of their own. Scat Fleming who had performed week after week when maybe he too was troubled or sad, when everybody was looking to him to come through, and he did. He never threw the ball, much. Didn't have to. Just ran. And punted every now and then when he couldn't. But mainly just ran.

I turned toward the car, thinking, I will. I will undo what I have done to cause my recent loss, not try to undo something I did so long ago that caused me shame when I was just a boy. I will swear off, like Scat, and get Cassie to tell Alice how I've changed before she marries again. Then I'll come back with my own family, and me and Alice will be just the way Scat and Cassie are now.

DEATH OF AN ELDER

I will fix him like a peg in a sure spot, to be a place of honor for his family.

— Isaiah 22:23

THE THREE OF US, ON THE MORNING OF THE FUNERAL, descended the twenty-six wooden steps from the one house and stepped into full sun already heating the sidewalk of Mason Avenue, and, before the spring of the screen door could snap the mechanism to full closing, we had opened my other grandmother's door and were stepping onto the blue carpeted staircase of the other house, ascending those twenty-six stairsteps with Nick leading the way and mother holding my twelve-year old hand. Her grip was at the same time both encouraging and restraining. I had the feeling that she was pulling me back and urging me on alternate steps.

I looked up into our ascension, fascinated beyond the moment by the new bright soles of Nick's shoes before my face and the odd little squeaks their new leather was making. I tried to turn to see if mine, too, flashed backward, but Mother's handgrip wrenched me aright and I had to content myself with what was before me and with only imagined sounds that I hoped I was making with my own new shoes.

Nick reached the top, and I could hear the voice, unmistakable, of Aunt Flora. She was embracing Nick, patting him on the shoulder, and barking, "HOW YOU'VE GROWN!"

I had expected something else. The voice of the woman had no remorse in it, and I wanted my first family funeral to be sad, at least solemn. I had come with a sprig from some flower from Grandmother Scarpi's wild garden, as Nick had, but already flowers seemed out of place here. From the way she was greeting us—all three of us by then—a tambourine might have been more appropriate than flowers.

I noticed, however, a strained moment as Mother moved from the last step into the other color of the upper hallway. Bright colors of every imaginable hue dazzled my sense of direction, but I caught nonetheless the edge to Aunt Flora's voice as she said, "Why, Rosie Scarpi, it's so good that you came." I watched her face as they hugged and saw the little play of smile over Mother's shoulder.

Even a whisper from the lips of this woman was racket to my ears. She was incapable of soft expression, and so when she raised her voice to be heard by those other in various parts of the house, an involuntary jerk almost sent me back down the stairs. "Hey, everybody! Looks who's here!" It was not just the level of the sound, the pitch of it, that caused my discomposure; at least to me, it was the obvious tone of the words that shrieked, extended, meant: And shouldn't be. Besides, the three of us knew already that my father was in this house somewhere. She had not led us quietly, nor even ostentatiously, to his side; nor had she singled him out in her announcement. She had merely called "everybody"—that is, nobody in particular.

The Morellis in the house, and their descendants, began to emerge, and Mother smiled uneasily as if to brace herself against a coming assault. She placed each of her hands lightly atop Nick's shoulder and mine. One by one, and in groups, they came from the back, from side rooms, from the front room, where the odor of carnations was strongest. Their faces, and accompanying names, were like a summons to the past, only recently called up in death, and we—the three of us standing mute for the moment on the lavender carpet—played the guessing game of who-might-this-be? and I'm-interested-to-know.

Aunt Rosa, who had married and divorced and borne a daughter by a local coal miner, and who had then run off, as they said back then, with a furrier from Richmond, strolled the length of the hall in fox furs like a queen to greet us. Although I had not seen her in several years, her voice, second in grating intensity to Aunt Flora's, drove deep in, like remembered ether. "And look at *this* one," she was saying as she bent to me. I grappled with her neck and the tiny button eyes and frozen claws of the little foxes that had died to keep her warm on a spring day inside a house in Virginia. Face to face with one of the taxidermied heads, inside whose small, cavelike mouth teeth shone like growths in a cavern, I winced and jerked away. She rose to her full height—six feet at least, perched as she was atop five-inch spike heels—and she said, "Why, honey...," and turned quickly behind her voice, which was going already in another direction.

Aunt Dorothy, who had come from Illinois and who alone among her sister possessed some quiet dignity, waited her turn and, when it came, gave a quick and awkward hug to Nick and me, greeting Mother with a handshake, and introduced us as if for the first time to her husband, Uncle Angelo, who seemed to marvel at the evidence before him: His wife's brother's children still survived! I half-expected him to say, Why, you're still alive (maybe even adding Thank God!); but, with an unsmiling face that showed something remembered out of resentment transmuted now to compassion, he seemed to know what the others had forgotten or else were doing an actor's job of concealing.

New and known cousins came forth, all well-behaved, finely groomed, bona fide grandchildren of the woman who had not yet shown her face and the corpse that the smell of carnation was telling me lay in the front room. Mary Charles, Aunt Rosie's only contribution to the clan, but the first of anyone's issue in the hierarchy, was now a delicious teenager who hugged so sincerely with such abandon that when I saw the healthy pink around the whiteness of her starlet's teeth and felt the full power of what a pair of breasts such as hers might command, I covered instinctively my crooked little front teeth with my tongue and said at the same time, in a voice that must have sounded as if I had a cleft palate, "Haarroo, Moarry Jaws." After which, I sneaked a dozen glances at her photograph within which, on the cherry gateleg table, she sat as a child in white rabbit fur with one leg tucked delicately beneath the other. I wanted to find the secret to her beauty, but I dared not linger over the lithe body of the living woman-girl.

She was brimming with recall. "Why, I haven't seen you two since I was a Donna Vista and you-all were at...What was the name of that place?"

"Saint Elverno," Nick reminded her.

"Oh, yes." She was now remembering, evidently, what someone had told her. "Why, I heard that that was a school for—." She covered her mouth with her tapered fingers and laughed.

"Oh, we didn't stay long," I said. "We came home after that Christmas banquet, and we stayed home.

Two sets of cousins came in trios, themselves double-first cousin—Antolinis all—their appellations a tongue-numbing entanglement of the Italian penchant for running a name through a lineage like the longest strand of spaghetti and the Southern way of giving, and using, two to each bearer. There were Aunt Flora's and Uncle George's three: Helen Eleanor, George Angelo, and Franky; and Aunt Dorothy's and Uncle Angelo's three: Angelo Lee, Dorothy Ann and Tony. There was not a Johnny in the lot.

A set of forgotten images appeared to me as I renewed acquaintances with these, my first cousins. The youngest of the two sets were, for all I knew or could remember, strangers already on firm ground. But the others had been (though I could not tell exactly when), for a little while, playmates; and the oldest of each trio had even been my schoolmates. Now I had it! In Illinois, in West Virginia, wherever they had lived then, stopping by with my father staying on for a few weeks, or was it months, or even a year? Why, I had been in school plays with them, had ridden the bus with them! And on their visitations to Arno, had caught lightning bugs and torn off the glow for rings, had tied June bugs to thread, had…They related the details to Nick and me with what seemed perfect recall.

These renewals were not animated nor overly loud, but rather decorous, even refined. It was all like a conversation with little adults. I would not have thought to throw my arms around any one of them, even if they had been less formally dressed; and, while the absence of such ostentatious affection in the corridor beyond the wall to my right would have been unthinkable, here it brought ambivalent relief. I missed the show, yes. I suppose I even wanted it, but at the same time I was thankful not to be obligated to return it.

I saw Mother's dark head of hair nodding in conversation with someone on the far side of her. She turned briefly, searching, and when she located Nick, and then me, she pointed us out to her listener and smiled back into her dialogue. I waved that I was having a grand time now that I remembered who everybody was.

Or almost everybody. There were more in the kitchen, and we were being taken by the group back there to enter and be recognized.

A man who could have passed for Gary Cooper sat at the kitchen table with the woman I was constrained to call Grandmother. He was lean and angular, like

Cooper, and I fancied as he rose in slow-motion to greet us that he would nod and say, Yup. Instead, he bent down between Nick and me and put a hand to my head, the other to Nick's waist.

Then it came to me, even before Nick began addressing him as Uncle Frank, that this man was my father's half-brother, the son of the woman sitting across the kitchen table and an unknown man somewhere back in the old country. And now I remembered *his* house somewhere in West Virginia, I remembered some of *his* children as playmates, classmates, babysitters, cousins. I remembered a couple of his wives and, now, especially, his oldest son, called Nicholas. Nick and I had had some good times with him on a river bank and in his father's dance hall.

Uncle Frank had come alone, though, and after he greeted my mother with a fatherly embrace and revealed by the sympathy in his look that he was sorry for something that passed between them unspoken, he stood aside so that all attention was focused across the table.

She looked like a buddha in mourning. "Ay-yi-yi," she sighed, stretching her flabby arms in such a way that I felt that Nick and I were expected to kneel, or at least genuflect, in supplication before her. Nick had no choice: He went immediately into the arms and was kissed by the mouth of the face between the arms with repeated fishlike suckings so feignedly arduous that I thought she meant to eat his cheek as I had seen her devour a chicken's foot from one of her admittedly delicious stews. Though I tired to dredge up some other feeling a grandson should have at such a moment, it was all that would come to me: Her cooking was good, if you didn't ask what was in it.

When my turn came, I resisted as best I could by moving in with my hand outstretched before me and immediately patting her upper arm in a show of sympathy so exaggerated that I must have looked as if I were beating a tattoo on her just to see her flesh swing. But she grabbed me by the face and sucked at me until the sounds commingled with her sobbing, unrestrained, interrupted by her mixture of Slavic, English, and Cumberland Mountain so dramatic I couldn't make out what she was saying.

"A-a-a-a-a-a oom necka mah chiddysbah, mah Tonee. Mah Tonee. Ay-yi-yi."

As Uncle Frank moved in for comfort, saying, "Now, Mom. Now, Mom," she thrust me from her so that my teeth smashed together.

Aunt Rosa, at full power, piped in from the doorway with her sweetest smile, "HedoeslooksomuchlikeTonydon'the?" She talked like a machine gun.

"Yes, he does," whispered Aunt Flora.

All the time Mother stood by, waiting to make an overture, looking on as the others were remembering Uncle tony through me. The Antolinis, I could see through the window, were playing a proper game on the adjoining back porch, beyond which a formal garden bloomed to perfection. Mother moved toward the woman as if seeking an audience with a dignitary and, when Mother addressed her, there was sympathy in her whisperings, though awkward movements to console. Those at the doorway strained to hear and, as I looked their way, they moved in to the stove, the sink, the cabinets. By then, Mother had completed her actions and voicings and was drying her eyes and giving a gentle awkward pat to the shoulder of the woman looking blankly at the floor, uttering still, "Ay-yi-yi."

Finally, Uncle Angelo came to the door and motioned to the three of us. Mother seemed relieved at the chance to exit. Nick and I clutched our little sprigs and wanted to unload them. So we moved away with gratitude, but with awkwardness, leaving behind the dolorous woman—the woman who had, early one morning, some years ago, ambushed and beaten to unconsciousness my mother on her way to work.

"Do you want to see Johnny?" Uncle Angelo whispered to Mother as he led us from the kitchen. "If you do, he's in the front room." Then he bent to Nick and me, as if preparing us. "You're two fine young men—*due buoni giovanotti.*"

And then we were alone at the far end of the long, strange hallway. I could see into the bathroom across from the kitchen a full array of bric-a-brac, lace, decorative soaplets and hand towels no bigger than wash cloths, pastels of all shades. As we began the walk forward, I glanced back at the toilet bowl, so laced and ribboned and camouflaged against what it was that, though I had to pee in the worst way, I would sooner have thought to belch at the communion rail than to desecrate that little shine with my water.

We began to walk to my father, to the front chamber toward the odor of carnations.

Nick, at thirteen, was already as tall as Mother—no compliment to his size since she was a scant five feet. Nonetheless, he again led the way, as if he were husband and father to the two of us, the one who would somehow break ground, take us forward into the future by way of the past, if by no other means than that I sensed he garnered of confidence with the new soles flashing backward. But now he was muffled, as we were, the semi-stifled squeaks of his new leather barely audible as his shoes sank, then rose, sank, and rose again, in this part of the hallway's thick lavender covering.

I savored the child in white rabbit fur then turned to my left where, on the wall, half a dozen Antolinis stole a glance, then followed with twelve glittering eyes as we passed. Ceramic cats and dogs and geese and ducks slept and wagged in silently frozen little scenes on tiny glass shelves. Through the first door to the right I spied an ironing board, a curtain stretcher, and several wicker baskets neatly placed. In a corner, mercifully scaled to size, though still dominant, sat a plaster giraffe, as silent as if it were alive

Flowered ottomans blocked our path so that Mother and I were made to form a single line behind Nick. She slipped behind me. Now I could only feel her presence and glance back to see that she followed still. There were both resignation and a determined look of anticipation on her face. The latter seemed for my benefit. Caught in the middle, I could neither dash ahead no retreat. And just beyond the wall to my left was the other hallway, the familiar one, where I longed to be and where, I was sure, Aunt Carm and others had their ears to the crack on their side.

The gaiety of the flowered walls and sky-blue woodwork framed the corridor, urging us on. The second room to the right was stunned to what I imagined was elegance. As flowers darted about in dark idyls on the walls and a chandelier's prisms waited above for the light, a long dining table stood on legs with daintily-curled feet so life-like that at any moment it might pick up its crocheted table-dress and begin the minuet. A deep, rich sideboard dazzled the far wall, and everywhere on complementary tables and stands were doilies, doilies, doilies. The fuchsin rug that held all this seemed to have soaked its color from the scarlet wines, or blood.

, , ,

I disarranged an antimacassar on a chair in the hall's sitting area as I brushed it with my hand and, when I stopped and turned back to set it straight, Mother bumped me, gave the thing a final touch, and guided me forward.

There was no mistaking the man in the outsized photograph on the next table. He was caught in the air, slim, arrayed like Astair, arms outstretched in dance. Hair slicked back, a narrow mustache between his thin, set lips and tailored nose, he was gaunt with comeliness, forever with his feet off the ground in patent leather. The healthy hollows of his cheeks, with accompanying angularity of bones, must have won a wife or more for him. Somewhere, I knew, was a boy with my name—son of this man whose name I had—but he was not in this house. And this man was no more than a shadow to me, had caused me, moments ago, to be wept over. For whatever reason, he was something like a legend in my memory, my Uncle Tony. And he was dead.

We were now passing a bedroom by the part of the hallway just before the top of the stairs. It occurred to me that Nick could simply veer left and we could be out of there forever, silently down and away. But he didn't. And when I passed the stair top, I felt compelled to accept its cool invitation, but I didn't. Then I thought that perhaps Mother had changed her mind and that, when she passed *she* would descend and that we would turn and follow. But she was behind me still, and moving forward. I wanted to shout, It's not too late!

A window in the inner wall separating this bedroom from the hall was curtained so heavily that it served no purpose. Through the door's opening the four-poster showed itself, satin-covered, pillow rolled, a fall of rectangular light illuminating the bed from the skylight. There was a nightgown, or housecoat, placed idly across the arm of a stuffed chair in a corner—the only mistake so far.

This, I knew, was the master bedroom, where Grandmother Morelli had slept alone for years.

Adjoining this room—there was a door in the separating wall within—was another bedroom. Each had its own entrance off the hallway. I glanced into this one with only passing regard.

The front room was beyond.

As we neared the front of the hall with its own little sitting area arranged around a glossy upright piano laden with more photographs on the top pane and a hand-crank cherry Victrola, I looked out the window, around Nick, directly ahead. Except for the various skylights and the window suggesting itself from the front room, this was the only opening to direct light. I could see mountains and, below them, the tops of two building across the street.

One final photograph, inescapable, held me in that last, long moment before we were to turn in to the funeral chamber. I was certain Nick and Mother must as well have been arrested by it. The man in the picture was smoking—that is, he held a cigarette raised easily, casually, at a point between his missing lower part and his face. The cigarette, caught between the index and middle fingers of his right hand, curled its still smoke, somehow swirled it up and out the top of the photographs's upper end. While an eddy of it played about the nostrils of a fairly bulbous nose (beneath which the mustache seemed modeled after Clark Gable's), the face was implacable, as if it were accustomed to such little nuisances. The mouth was set as if the jaw muscles were tensed ever so slightly. It was apparent, though, that the invisible teeth were clamping down, which highlighted the jaw's tenseness in the lower cheekbone. It was not a smile that played; the eyes made this apparent. They were protruding eyes, pushing out of their sockets in a strain so marked that blinking must have been painful. An ophthalmologist might have diagnosed Graves' disease. Yet, there was nothing sickly, nothing even unpleasing, about the aggregation of features. They combined to a strength—no, a power—somehow incongruous with and, at the same time, in consonance with the dress: dark jacket with faint pin stripes and sharp lapels of a 1940's vintage; white dress shirt whose collar ends disappeared beneath the coat's lapels so smoothly that one could not see the junctures clearly; necktie of slightly less darkness than the jacket, the tie knotted cleanly and symmetrically aligned below an adam's apple swallowed invisible by a neck so powerful that one could not discern if the shirt's top were spaced by a tailor's design and a necktie or held apart by the rigid neck muscles; small pearl stickpin retaining the necktie after having given it just enough slack to lift the knot and allow for an arc of clearance from the upper buttons; larger pearl cuff link caught by the photographer's light so that it gleamed just perceptibly at the space of white cuff below the hand that held the cigarette; fedora set at the brow's top crease, suggesting a wide forehead or a thinning hairline.

We turned into the doorway, Mother and I stacking up behind Nick so that I could not see. I was looking at Nick's nape, wondering why he was so sternly stopped. When he lifted his right arm to scratch somewhere around his head, I ducked quickly and peered through his armpit. The darkly shiny box was visible to me, its front brass carrying arm lowered like a bar's rail for leaning, a velvet-covered kneeler placed before it. Nick lowered his arm, blocking me, so I lifted it myself this time, for another look. And I spotted the man in the photograph I had just seen. He was sitting in a corner chair.

Nick moved to the left of the inner door; I moved to the right. Except for the hat and cigarette, he was dressed the same as in the picture, though now, of course, I could see the matching trousers, the brown, perforated shoes. He was gazing at the casket in the room's center, and I felt that we had violated his privacy.

He looked directly at Mother and rose in an easy, graceful motion. Standing by the chair, be buttoned his jacked effortlessly with his left hand without look-ing down. It was clear that this was an adult moment and, yet, when he strode quietly across the fuchsia rug, looking still at Mother, he went to Nick.

He was not a tall man but, compared to the three of us, and with his boxer's body moving in tailored cloth, he seemed to fill up the room above us. Passing to Nick, he blocked the window's light, sending his shadow my way. Within the last step of Nick he unbuttoned his jacket as easily as he had buttoned it before and slid its front panel in a smooth move to the side. At the same time he spread the other coat half with his right hand, then grasped his trousers' creases with respective sets of forefingers and thumbs, lifting as he squatted in front of Nick. His shoes, I could see, took the strain with ease, in the way that calfskin molded over a last to perfection is broken in already without the period of bothersome squeaks to the wearer a lesser leather might require. This squared-off padding of his jacket's left shoulder was set firm on his tensed shoulder as I watched him re-acquainting himself with Nick.

He placed his hands on Nick's shoulders, and I could see the thickness of the left one, the calluses thick as corn kernels, the dress ring pinched onto his third finger. What must his right one have looked like by now—the one so ac-customed to wielding his cobbler's knives and hammer? Words from somewhere, wherever they come from at such odd moments, were pushing out of me.... words like *fasten* and *peg*...yes, I had it now. We had learned it at Bible school: *I will fix him like a peg in a sure spot, to be a place of honor for his family.*

Mother moved toward me and put her hands on my shoulders. We were to watch together. When he took Nick gently to him, moving his arms around Nick's back into a full embrace, Mother squeezed me nervously. She was, I could feel, preparing herself, or me, for a turn.

I looked at the casket. From my position, I could not see all of what was inside it, only the outline of a barely-haired head. To my right, though surrounded by the walls's myriad paper-entrapped leaves, I saw a familiar framed photograph of the man I knew was in the casket. The features were hard, tough, the jaws thick and strong. No teeth were showing through the vise-like mouth set against a picture-taker's antics. But then, as if a boy had taken up a crayon in mischief, a sweeping, black hand-bar mustache seemed colored, or pasted, on the upper lip. Without the smile, the similarity to Jerry Colonna was inescapable. The curling symmetry of the mustache's blackness gave a caricature to the stern, even grim, face held up by no discernible neck, but squatting on the black suit's coat in an old-world elegance, the top of the watch chain visible at the bottom, swinging into the suggestion of a vest's pocket.

As the man across the room rose from Nick, I expected him to re-button his jacket. He did not, and I was mildly disappointed. It was only footsteps to me and, as he passed easily over, looking kindly at Mother, he did take the creases into this fingers and squat before me in the same way as he had before Nick. Then he took me to his chest and kissed me with dozens of prickles to my cheek so that I marveled at the delicacy of the lips' cool touch, the cruelty of the hairs above them. Such an admixture of affection and roughness, I decided, was a welcomed oddity to my smooth cheek which had, for too many years, been accustomed to the wetness of an aunt's excitations, the awkwardness of an uncle's hand.

Like his mother in the kitchen only minutes before, he wept over me, into me—or, rather, I had the notion that he wept as he clutched me to him. I put my arms around his shoulders and back as far as they would reach, and I began to try to comfort him. But I was really trying to comfort myself, to stall for time so that I would not have to hear words about what he might be thinking. Why was *I* the cause of such grief? Was I marked, cast forever like a picture in their eyes into not me but the image of someone else dead?

Then he retrieved himself, and I could see that there were no tears. I looked above the eyes to avoid them and was struck instead by the scalp that showed itself through thinning hairs at the frontal lobe of the skull.

In a liquid movement, he rose from me, catching Mother's hand in his own. Nick and I moved away, to the casket. I could hear their embrace as we walked in fuchsia, in light, to death.

I took hold of the brass rail as we stood on either side of the kneeler. "Look at the diamonds," I whispered, pointing with a nod of my head to the rosary laced between the fingers of the crossed hands that seemed somehow flat, as if they had been deflated.

"SSSssshhh. They're not *diamonds*. Just cut glass, rhinestones."

To me they were diamonds, as the watch chain was pure gold, tucked as it was into the little cut of the vest pocket.

I had not looked at the face, and thought for a moment that I would not. But Nick by now was evidently gazing at it, his hands crossed before him in solemnity, or its semblance.

So I looked.

There was no handle-bar mustache, no hair whatsoever on the upper lip. This was not Uncle Tony, not my father, not Nick, not I, certainly not Jerry Colonna. This was a bald-headed man, shaved to cleanness, a manikin really, who had sat out his last years on a wooden box on the sidewalk in front of his shoe shop directly below us; who had, from time to time, thrown silver dollars to two boys after we had passed him in silence and fear, and who then turned away as we scurried after his silver on the concrete.

We remembered then our crumpled flowers, like weeds now, and we placed them dutifully near the blanket that spelled out FATHER in roses over the casket's lower half.

THE LEGEND OF THE HAPPY SWIMMING POOL

from J. D.

H IS WORLD WAS ONCE YOUNG AND JOYOUS, was all he could ever have hoped it to be. He had carried his memories of it in just that way for a good many years. It had lived in his boyish dreams as the one great truth—the world itself—something to be known, though never completely, something to be endured, though never with malice. His thoughts of that world (he had finally come to call it that "other" world, the one that had ceased to be, just as, after a click, clear and real, a motor would cease to whir, a light would cease to shine)—his thoughts had somehow gotten buried in the muddle of daily chores as student and teacher, as father and husband, as body and spirit.

But those other thoughts had run in his fancy long before the click, longer than the time that had passed since the click. And since, he had spent a great deal of time wondering, figuring, just when the click had come.

So he had divided his life in his mind—not cunningly—into the pre-click and post-click eras. The one he had equated with a kind of unwished-for adulthood with all of its responsibilities, its joys (different from those of the other world), its defeats; the other, he had equated with boyhood and young manhood. Lately, it seemed, the defeats had dominated in the post-click era. Their dominance was no result of any particular failures on his part (not that he had not failed at times). They simply were not that kind.

They were the little ones. The ones that come to one born into the world of romance, nurtured on the spells and dreams of another time, jolted by the stop-whir reality of the click. The little ones that shut out the special shaft of light that he had seen only seldom *then*, now not at all. The ones that change the smells of the other world into vile and gaseously vitriolic, strange aromas. Gone were the whiffs of wondrous things even more scintillating by the sounds of their names than by the inhalations of their sweetness: the barley, the rye, the thyme and rosemary, alfalfa and sassafras, sorghum and simple hay. And where were the other *sounds* now? (It seemed that everything of the other world, the other time, was becoming "the other.") The hollow clop of an occasional horse down the little main street, between the cars, where drivers gave way as if obeying, from respect—even a kind of homage—, an unwritten first rule of the road for car and horse as for ship and sail. A rail car coupling with a bump that could be heard throughout the five blocks of his town. The amateurish band that practiced more than it ever hoped to play, but which had the gall to do both (the single old tuba player swaying and rocking as if he were blowing the swing of Dorsey rather than "The Thunderer" of Sousa). Silenced now was the popping machine (the real click might have done it in) that popped out silos of corn for boys hungry for anything but healthy food.

Oh, how many times he had thought of these things, or things like them. It was as if everything worth hearing, seeing, and smelling belonged to the other time and that no amount of wishing could bring it back. Because, even if one were able to find an item or two that worked the spell (an occasional whittling knife from boyhood, a handful of cat's-eye marbles), the item could never exist whole because it could never again be surrounded by its true element. What did one whittle? There was wood to be had, sure, but living in an apartment complex did one not have to purchase it, and then buy at least a board-foot or two? Wooded areas around Tara Rental Homes were so clean there was nothing to be found of any use. And he could just see himself going to The World's Most Unusual Lumber Store and asking for a scrap piece of cedar. But even, even if the wood problem did not exist, *where* did one whittle? He imagined himself at times sitting on the metal bench (couldn't even carve on that) in the tot-lot of Tara Rental Homes, or else in the recreation area, while the mothers watched the kids and the fathers played basketball, he whittling away, going at it, while his messy shavings piled up below him. Or off in some corner at an evening party by the pool, with a quid of Brown Mule in his jaw, honing his Robeson on a small emery stone, waiting deliciously to sink it into an old piece of white cedar he had uncovered on a trip back home and brought back like a treasure from the Far East. Like the cat's-eyes he had returned with, like jewels.

For one thing, his wife would never brook such useless indulgence in public. For another, he could never permit *himself* such indulgence because he—like the things out of their element—would be as archaic as an old grizzled knight come riding up on his steed one day at the Tara Shopping Center. Why, they'd stone him, mock him out of his mail and armor. And if they did him no physical harm, they would do worse: ignore him. Nothing, nothing could be sadder than for a quixote to go unnoticed.

So, yes, it was all vanity, all *time* and vanity, to be precise, that had worked their rust into his armor. And he had been so careful to groom himself against such a possibility. Had watched long and hard as a boy the great romantic figures, from afar and at close range. Sometimes the distance was so great, he had not actually observed; had, rather, gotten them into his bones through scattered snatches of talk he had heard and overheard, through tapestry-covered radio speakers filled with static, through old movies, through scratchy recording discs. All the shabby, tinseled ghosts of sport and screen, of song and sight. Who were they? And did they really matter all that much now, in the "real world," as the current phrase would have it? Mostly, they were names, personalities. voices, batting stances, dancing styles, numbers on jerseys; they were classy clothes, pretty faces, overstuffed chairs and anti-macassars, shined shoes and graceful strides; they were razzmatazz, dixieland, soft shoe, stage shows, coaches, and titles. They were, in short, the other.

These and other voices and shapes had worked their ways upon him, into him, so that room, office, car, home, mind—they all haunted and were haunting, came back at odd times, those spectral personages—flesh, stone, cloth, image—that would not let him be.

Nor would she. She alone the queen of all the shades who ruled the graveyard in his head.

,   ,   ,

Now, as if some treacherous, delicious irony had worked itself for twenty years, he has been brought back to the town of specters, to the movie theater of ghosts, in the town where the haunts were born. Somehow he has managed to "make it," as they say when somebody writes a novel that gets noticed. One book, and here he is in the wings of the most haunting building of his life. Strange, after all the remarkable ones. Not one mossy hall of college has remained vivid. Not one "Fine Arts" structure of his teaching career. Not the new high-school building nor the sparkling gymnasium. Nor a commercial behemoth, nor a conference hall, nor a true theatre, in the British tradition. None. Just this old wreck of a movie house called simply the show. Where ghosts and all were born. Where his imagination was conceived, gestated, and hatched— that persistent, stalking old friendly enemy of his that would not let go nor, now, die.

Some aggressive PR man has had the notion—and courage—to do the booking, to hold the "world premiere" of the movie made from his book. (It has all come upon him so fast and kept him so busy that he hasn't had the time to use some of the first money to get out of Tara.) On the marquee outside, the boy who has unwittingly succeeded the author standing now in the wings of his own imagination has botched with even more pitiful maroon plastic letters (could they be the same ones?) of twenty years ago the billing

ARNO'S OWN

GABE REMINI IN PERSON

BEFORE THIER OL$_D$

Everything has been arranged by the PR staffs of the publishing company and the filming studio. A top magazine will cover. A near-local and—it is hoped—a national television spot. Radio (certainly Country Jim will do it on his show, as a favor to Gabe). A newspaper columnist has promised to be on hand. Everything, it seems to him, but *Field and Stream*, though they are not, of course, all on hand, what with the intricacies of electronic syndication and the art of guessing.

It is the biggest thing the other world has ever seen, except perhaps for the time when Francis Lane, All-American and now professional, exhibited his trophies at The Jewel Box.

He waits, in the wings, with book in hand, where twenty years before he lurked as usher guarding the rear exit door (and let in more boys than the number of paid customers already in their seats); where he as assistant manager at thirteen stood with Lash Larue and his whip just before The Lash was to go on stage and crack cigarettes out of the hands of volunteer kids from the front row; where, after the show, he and his brother and the boys who had slipped in shot craps with the janitor, projectionist, and other ushers and lost a week's pay of eight dollars. And the time he had waited all morning in the back alley by the exit door (before he was assistant manager) just to *see* Don "Red' Barry before his stage appearance. And the time he had his pictur taken with Sunset Carson, holding one of Sunset's guns. Ed Taylor and his horse Bob White. The dancing Hawaiian girls. Chet Davis with his dirty jokes (run out of town on the third joke). The minstrel shows put on by the Lions and the Kiwanians. When he had emceed the Sunmaid bread contest where thirty or so young girls had competed to see who looked most like the five-year-old on the package, and then the judges had given the five-dollar gift certificate and six-months' supply of bread to the only thirteen-year-old on stage (and the bread given all in one lump award). His pantomime imitation of Johnny Ray doing "Cry." And of (was it Bob Eberly's?) "Easter Parade." But, most of all, the time he had imitated Al Jolson at the height of the Jazz Singer's resurgence after *The Jolson Story*—had mimed him in oversized bow-tie, and had won first place in the amateur contest, the other contestant coming in a close second—billed that time as Gabie "Jolson" Rimini. (He had seen someone just today, on the street, who had been in that audience and who said that she *still* thought he had actually sung that song.)

Now, he hears his name announced by someone who has walked past him, who has gone to stage center behind the drawn tattered maroon curtain that used to run by motor from a switch in the projection booth *click* and has parted it and walked through. Now he hears the full house in half-applause, and he wonders fleetingly if the PR man has paid admissions to fill it.

He walks past the screen and has a flash of memory more vivid than even the others. He goes to the lower right corner behind the curtain and places his finger into the hole made by Peg Leg Collins, who shot at the screen when Ed

Taylor, in a stage show, was on his horse Bob White showing the kids how rearing was done.

He steps through the crack in the dusty curtain, taking over from the one who has done the introduction. He faces the people squarely. Hardly a Nobel audience, and he hardly the laureate. For all the cowboys, dancers. acrobats, horses—and all that they left on this stage—never a person to read. But just a preliminary to the picture. Just a token appearance.

Only it all comes rushing back at him in the rusty pool of light that floods him from the portable spot off stage left in the aisle. The spot confuses him momentarily. Used to be a regular one up there that came from out of one of the holes above the balcony where the blacks sat. *click*

Then, when the other lights from the camera crews find him, he becomes unsettled even more. Such brightness seems out of place here. Virtually the entire theater bursts into light, so that the pitiful little spot becomes redundant. A PR man has had the foresight to bring a lectern, a slender stand that allows him a place to rest his book without concealing him completely from the audience.

He sets the book on the support and walks out of the immediate glare to extreme upper left. He squints toward the wall by the lower right seats. The audience wonders, stiff in their seats. Only eyes and necks turn. He walks back to the podium, smiles furtively, as if he is not going to share the secret.

But he does. "I just wanted to see if the tobacco juice stains were still on the wall."

They like it. It shows that he remembers, knows, that things between them are not so different. They roar approval.

"WELL, ARE THEY GABE?" one yells.

"And *then* some," he says.

They like this even more.

There is a settling down period. Squirming and fixing.

Arranging. They've *now* come to hear what he has to say.

"Hello, friends," he begins, and with fear of sounding pompous or political—or both—he rushes on, "Now-I-didn't-come-here-to-give-you-a-speech-so-rest-easy."

To which they do. He sees through the glare an old man in a suit too tight for him, his choking white collar curling at the ends. The man looks at the woman next to him and smiles with great pleasure. His big hands are crossed on his belly, and he wriggles back slightly to attention.

Then he takes a handful of popcorn from the woman who is herself testing it kernel by kernel, her gaze on the stage.

"I've just come to introduce the film—uh—the show to you and to read a little passage from the book I've written."

They have no popcorn for the third showing of The Mummy *this Saturday so his brother goes scrounging. Loads up two empty boxes with leftovers found in boxes here and there and comes back like a Magus with a bag of myrrh. They feast for another showing, jump up again at the serial, and go to the Men's Room before Nyoka has to deal with getting herself out of the quicksand from last week.*

"What I'm going to read doesn't appear in the fi—, in the movie you're going to see in a few minutes which, by the way, is called, the same as the book, *Before We're Old.* Maybe the marquee boy ran out of Ws, but I can understand that. We only had one when I was setting marquee. I might suggest, if you're out there in the audience, that you try an M upside down if you get stuck again. The hooks won't fit right, but there use to be some black plumber's tape in the right-hand drawer of Buddy's desk." *click*

As before, they're delighted, and he can't help thinking how much more lively it is to speak to simple folks than to write for book people whose reactions to his words he'll never know, and that, while he has managed a small hand in the screenplay, to try to save it, it has been a butcher's job.

When they laid out of school to go to the show, they'd have to crawl under the right-hand seats by the wall after being let in the rear iron exit door behind the stage by another friendly usher. Because every day at one o'clock their grandmother would go, sometimes with an aunt, mostly alone. Coming through the iron door, they'd crouch to the floor, for effect and for actual stealth, then come crawling through to the theater floor where, first off, they'd look for the faint glint of two eyeglass lenses that sat just to their left of dead center. The other guys already there would have to move over to make room for them by the wall, and more than once the tobacco stream had reached such heights that there was just no fording it. And more than once she got wise, began listening for his brother's deeper voice, even on days when the gang of boys had already seen the show and weren't there. But that didn't stop her, just having seen it already. Said later, when she told him about it all, that she went as much to get out of the house as to see a picture show. But that then, when television. . . . click More than once she jerked them up by the scruff and ran them out. More often, though, she just let them be, even when she knew, and that was clear because you didn't get by with much from her. And even on one occasion, after the other guys had heard her coming, had already scattered (had scattered or hit the floor, stream and all), leaving only him frozen in his seat, she surprised the lot of them with a number ten poke of home popped corn and a mayonnaise jar full of RC. But you never could tell. You couldn't push it too far. She was sly. Dropping hints about the current Frankenstein show, to goad you into a talk with her about it, then ramshaking you for knowing the answers. click

"I'm going to read a passage from the book that appears in the f—, in the movie as only a smile on the face of the main character. It's when he—his name's Dominick in the book, changed to Sonny in the movie—when he has met his old girlfriend at a high school reunion and hasn't seen her for twenty years. I just call the passage 'The Legend of the Happy Swimming Pool,' and I want to acknowledge here and now that I owe a debt of thanks to the man I've dedicated the book to for the title and for a few words about what it means, as Dominick explains it in the story. I'll take up from the place where they're alone after the class picnic.

" ' "How have you been?" asked Donna, brushing at her face, which had certainly aged, as his own had, but which housed still the same lips, the same mouth, from which came the same voice unheard for twenty years.

" ' "Oh, I've managed. Not too well, I suppose, but I've etched out a life or two."

" ' "Sonny, let's not kid one another. We're too old for that."

" ' "O.K. Let's *not* kid each other," and he thought to soften his tone. "Let's start out with calling things the way they are. My name, for instance. Donna, my name is Dominick. Some of the guys around here used to call me Nick or Dom and other variations, but you would never call me anything but Sonny." He turned away briefly because, still, after the years, it was hard for him to speak directly to her. This was the best he had managed, ever, though her spell over him was not broken by any means.

" ' "Well, I—"

" ' "No. Let me finish. Please. I used to like the name you gave me, just because it came from you. It was something at least. And I used to think it was your own special name for me, something between only us. Because you're the only one who ever called me that. But don't you see? It's the very symbol of the thing that kept us apart. I was Catholic, you were Protestant. I was Italian-American, you were English-American—I guess. The same old shibboleths that have kept the world apart since the beginning—and especially the ones that keep people apart in *this* country, just because there are so many different *kinds* here—they kept *us* apart, too. And now, *you've* been through a marriage, and *I've* made a career out of getting myself engaged, and you're still calling me Sonny. If there's any hope for us now, you must look at me and call me by my name, my God-given name, even if you don't *like* it."

" ' "Oh, but I do, I do like it. I always have. It wasn't me who sent you away from the house that day after we'd decided to get engaged. It was Mother. If—"

" ' "Let's stop right there. Mother. You're a mother now yourself, Donna. You're a mature woman. I think I've loved you ever since before I met you, and I don't even know if I ever told you so, even after we'd decided to get engaged."

" ' "Hush," she said. And she smiled the old way that brought back most of the years, made them live again as if they had been something other than wasted. Then she kissed him as she was whispering something he could not make out. It was a simple kiss, an almost friendly kiss, a kiss without heat or compassion in it that made him want to weep with relief.

" 'As he drew her gently back from him, letting his eyes tell her what his soul already knew, he said, "Yes. Yes. But you *still* haven't said it."

" ' "Dominick. Dominick." She let the word linger in the air between them. "Maybe," she said, "I thought your name sounded too much like mine," and she laughed up at the trees.

" 'Later, as they sat on the bridge at River Road, after his mind had raced ahead, making plans, testing himself against the time when he would have to try, not just to live again the life he had missed, but to live again with a major alteration to his ego, he looked wistfully up the creek.

" ' "What is it?" she said. "Happy?"

" ' "Oh, I was just thinking about this dream I've had a number of times. It's the kind of happy dream that is worse than any nightmare."

" ' "What do you mean? How can it be a nightmare if it's happy?"

" ' "Because it's a dream."

" ' "I don't understand."

" ' "Well, every time, I've just come home after having been away a long time. I'm a complete stranger, even in my own old home. There's nobody there who knows me. Nobody on the streets. I always end up walking through the entire town, every street, every alley, every nook and cranny that has ever haunted me. I'm dressed in a suit that I shouldn't be dressed in, because I'm not the man who has been away, but the boy who seems in the dream never to have left. I'm just walking, going to houses of old friends who are not at home, dropping in at pool rooms, the theater, restaurants, service stations, drug stores. And what I'm looking for is always clear to me, though in the dream—it's hard to explain—in the dream I know it as a *dreamer* but not as the boy walking and looking. What I'm looking for is a friend, a person who knew me as I was before I left. And it isn't you. Sorry. It is *sometimes* you, but mostly it's just a friend I'm looking for. And by the time I've run out of places to search, I hear—again, as a dreamer, not as the wanderer—I hear voices, sounds from a group of people talking and laughing, shouting and playing, and I'm going through the gate of the swimming pool. The sound reaches me—this is, finally, as the boy in the dream—after I'm inside the gate. And when I *get* inside, you're all there, all the friends I've ever known as a boy. You're there, too, but again, sorry—it's not *just* you I'm glad to see, not at first anyway. All of you are tanned and happy, running and splashing. When I get to the side of the pool, I have on trunks like the rest of you. Then someone waves from the top of the old stone bathhouse, waves and laughs clear as clean water, then calls out above the other voices like a booming god from heaven, 'Where You Been? We Been Waiting For You.' That's when I wake up."

" ' She rubbed his arm gently. "But that's a *happy* dream," she said, putting her head on his shoulder. "How could that ever be a nightmare?"

" ' "Up until now it was a nightmare because it could never come true, in any way, not with you especially. The actual nightmare I could live with—and did—

for a long time. But the happy dream—no, that's worse than any bad dream. Waking up and finding it was only a dream—that's what's unbearable."

"'"But now you've come home, haven't you, Sonny?" And she laughed an oddly resounding echo of a laugh up the creek.'"

The audience does not know the reading is finished. Not until he drops his head in a slight bow, almost dramatically, and flicks his hands resting on either side of the lectern—a gesture of finality, almost catharsis. Then led (as he suspects briefly) by the PR men, they applaud and he has the feeling that they are doing so without full understanding but rather from some sense of obligation to be polite to the "good old boy" who is—at least has been—one of them.

There is an awkward moment following the applause when the spot has to be removed audibly, when Gabriel is asked by the promoter to hand down the lectern. Several pictures are taken, and footage of film is rolled. Some newsmen and their equipment merely remain where they are until after Gabriel walks back through the wing and appears through the door by the right front seats. As he goes through, he has the urge to hit the floor on all fours, to search out the twin glints up the aisle.

There is a light or two on him, several more flashes, and as he walks alone up the aisle he shakes a hand or two and sees a face here and there that he nods to without recognizing its name. It is a long walk, for he feels the same as he has felt in the classroom after having given what he has considered to be a particularly stimulating lecture, just to find out that most of the class hadn't read the story. But there is goodness here in this building. He can feel it. He senses it in the aisle and hopes they will enjoy the film that has been all but pushed upon them as an act of patriotism.

In the lobby he smiles, nods at the old woman taking up tickets who used to be the girl who served beer at the tavern on the outskirts of town. He talks to a few PR men who offer congratulations and tell him it was a smashing success. Then he sees the manager, who comes at him with his hand outstretched for shaking.

"Gabe! Hot damn! Enjoyed it. You done real good. Great for business. Come on up to the office, or are you going to watch the show? If you ain't let's go up to the office and have a little snort."

"No, I don't think I'll see it again." He has had so much of lurking behind sets, trying to get his bid in for a change here and there, so much of watching the cutting room scuffles, and the rushes and the criticism and the comments from guests and old actors and consulting directors and producers that, now, he is full of it, wishes almost that it was all just still in his head. "Yeah, I'll take a snort, Buddy."

The manager smiles, puts his arm around Gabriel's shoulder, and leads him up the frayed carpet of the stairs. But midway, they are interrupted by the sound of a voice, a feminine voice, that stops Gabriel cold. "Mr. Reemin-eye. Mr. Reemin-eye. Could I get your autograph?"

As he turns, the girl is already behind him, and he knows before he looks that there is something special in the voice. It isn't just the sound of the mountains, the mispronunciation of the name. It is the intake of breath just before the "Could," the almost—there is no other word for it—cute sound of the voice as if it came from an actress trained to effect eternal youth. "You go on up, Buddy. I'll be there after a while."

He finishes his turn and stares down at the face that is now one step below, down to twenty years back. "Ellie! My God!" he half screams, and his hands go involuntarily over the book he has been carrying as if he means to wipe out thing he has created.

The girl's smiling anticipation dwindles to near fear. Then it changes to recognition. "No. Ellie's daughter. *Janie*," she says, looking directly into his eyes.

But he still stares, still clutches at his creation. Then, his fixation subsides. He becomes self-conscious. "Please come up stairs," he says, and uses the moment to steer her around him without looking again at her face. He walks behind her while he collects himself, settles his blood with a deliberate sigh that must sound to the girl like hot air let out of a balloon.

The legs before him are those he knew, tanned, taut, slim. The dress is much shorter, and with pain and pleasure he allows himself the revelation of what he knows already is there: the almost swayed back that accentuates the hips that swell almost horizontally backward but do not flare to the sides. She bounces up before him, oblivious.

In the upper hallway she proffers a piece of paper, and as he looks at it dumbly she says, "Your autograph, please."

"Oh, yes. That." He opens the book to the title page ans scrawls something "to Janie" and hands it over.

"For *me*? Well, thanks."

"Have you read it? Do you know the story?

"Just what you said about it tonight." But she looks more knowledgeable than she is letting on, he thinks. "I pieced together a lot of the story from what you said, and from what I'd heard about you from other people." Then, without changing expression. "You know my mother. You called me by her name." It is not a question; it is a challenge. She wants to talk about it, to hear bout it, but she does not want to ask about it.

Just then there is a man's voice at the top of the stairs. "Janie. Janie. Come on now. Your mother's waiting in the car. You were supposed tomeet us outside.

"Oh, Daddy, this is Mr. Reemin-eye, the man who wrote *Before They're Old*."

As he shakes the rough hand and says without knowing it that he is pleased to meet him, he does not correct the error. It is too weel established here. And as the girls smiles with what has to be pleasure at the confrontation, he does not even scrutinize this unknown and, apparently, unknowing "rival."

"Your mother says if you're going to the lake tomorrow you'd better get home and get your things ready. She'll be fuming in the car."

But that does not seem to ruffle her. She stands between the two men with something akin to pleasure and mischief. "Well, I just *had* to see him. He's only going to be here tonight, aren't you, Mr. Reemin-eye? Did you and Mother win at bridge? Thanks for the book, Mr. Reemin-eye. I'll try to read it real soon."

The man nods to Gabriel, and he and the girl go off down the stairs. Gabriel stands looking after them, long after they have vanished. Then he slips into the manager's office like somebody who has just been dismissed and is looking for a drinking buddy. But before he speaks a word to Buddy he goes to the window to catch sight of a woman's hand setting itself on the car door where the window is rolled down, just as the hand drives off.

➤ ➤ ➤

The theater is closed. He stands in the outside lobby, two blocks from his old home, and thinks how little he seems to have moved, in terms of mental distance, in twenty years. Buddy has staggered up the street to the one hotel. No cars are left on the roads except those driven by boys making late rounds.

He has drunk a lot, but he is not drunk. Just heightened, tensed, ready for talk and thought—good talk and deep thought—but even the people who can't give them are gone.

He walks under the marquee, stations himself precisely for the dramatic turn. Then, slowly, he pivots to face the pitiful letters, the D having finally dropped.

Arno's Own

Gabe Remini In Person

Before Thier Ol

No better nor any worse than others had done to his name, he thinks. And the THIER, spelling and usage aside, a nice little error. They. Yes, THEY. Not WE. Not he. And he had come back to find it out.

The diesel engine at the rail yard is warming up, begins to move slowly across town. And where will it go? he thinks.

He, too, has a trip to make, tomorrow. A plane to catch.

He looks back to the marquee. Arno, he thinks. What it wants is a subdued mediocrity, a mediocrity so subdued that even its attempts to subdue it are mediocre. It wants some cheap little thrills which have been discarded, perhaps, in another time. A little bastion of vulgarity ready to squash anything that is not vulgar, machine-made, suitable to the crowd. Discarded in another *time*? And isn't that what he has thought he wanted?

And yet…yet…he loves it still. Without Arno there wouldn't be even the question. And as for the legends—the legends be hanged. They are best when their truths remain unknown. *click*

He picks up the cracked D and starts the two blocks to his bed for the night. But it will be only a bed. His own true resting place is now miles away, where he will be tomorrow.

He hurries now, out of his element, wondering what Sara and the kids will think when they see the news. He is running now, a slow, lazy lope, parallel to the more sluggish diesel across town which seems to be getting nowhere and doing a good job of it. He sails the D far out across the road and loses sight of it in the darkness. It will be good to get home to his own people.

SUMMERTIME
AT THE BREEZY

I CANNOT RECALL HOW LONG IT HAD BEEN SINCE our father had left us, but there must have been adequate time for me and my older brother, Jerry, to have become used to the habits of freedom we had taken up when he had left us the other times, long enough even for me to have ceased wondering when he would show up and reclaim us under his authority. From Grandmother's house we were free to come and go after school until supper and, beginning that day, during the daylight hours of summer. I had finished fourth grade that year, as Jerry had fifth, and it seemed to me then, as it does now, that when the good work is done the liberty should follow. Grandmother and Mother must have agreed, for we found ourselves not just free but with Grandmother's permission that if we should get hungry while we were swimming we should go across the street to The Breezy and get something to eat on credit.

It was the last day of school. The swimming pool was going to be filled today.

The swimming pool's walls were of tan stone block, mortared jaggedly. Two large pillars, crowned with small pyramids of mortar, marked the entrance, above which was chiseled what we laughed at for its odd name: MUNICIPAL. Lesser pillars were set at the corners and at intervals between, with horizontal iron railings making a fence. On the far side of the long dimension the bathhouse stood like a battlement, its enclosed top deck a place for sunning. On the street side a long, low wall of the tan blocks ran past the swimming pool in both directions.

Beyond the far side, through a train yard, several sets of tracks stretched to the ends of town; beyond the tracks was that part of town known as the Southside. Beyond the Southside rose the mountains. The town was ringed by mountains. It was as if we lived high up, but still within a huge bowl, at the center of which a swimming pool had been made to look like a small, open castle.

Although I hadn't been in town at the ending of my other school years, it still seemed that it had always been the same: On the day before filling the swimming pool, dozens of boys and girls came with brooms to scrub the changing rooms of the bathhouse and the bottom of the pool and, as far as we could reach, the walls of the pool, while Coach Carson, pool manager, rinsed our work (and us) with a spray he created from a many sectioned hose by forcing his thumb partly in the sheared end. As school was let out the last day, after a mere hour of assembly and handing out of report cards, we grade-schoolers ran the few blocks to the swimming pool and laid our books (which we would later sell to buy books for the next grade) on the grassy stretch between the pool and the outer wall. Some changed in the bathhouse; most of us boys and a few girls had our swimming suits on under our clothes; older boys stripped down to their dungarees, removed their belts, and rolled up their pantlegs.

I went with the others, by way of the steps at the shallow end, into the empty swimming pool where the newly painted aquamarine walls, dazzling in the sun, seemed already to contain the waters of a lagoon. Coach Carson, carrying a wrench as big as his arm, came from the bathhouse office and headed to the shallow end and the twin giant spigots freshly painted silver. We avoided the blistering seams of tar-caulked cracks, recently filled in by the town's rickety, devilish machine, as we made our way down the slope. The two ladders at the deep end were only four steps long, leaving a good six feet to the bottom. As Jimbo Blevins, in ragged, dirty dungarees, descended one of the ladders, Coach Carson hollered, as only he could holler, "Out! Get out!" Jimbo retreated the way he had come, up the ladder and over the wall, as Coach's words bounced around the walls and we jockeyed for places on the coveted slope to the deep end, lying on our stomachs, waiting with our arms out.

My bare chest, legs, and arms were hot on the pebbly concrete crunching my bones when I moved, but I had my place and it was a good one. I could no longer see Coach Carson, but I did see Jerry with his older friend Jim Collier. I put my cheek to the hot concrete and made myself stand it until I could stand it. Below me and to my right, when I made the effort, I could see the face of a girl. She was looking up at me, and now she seemed to smile. It seemed to me then the most beautiful but the saddest face I had ever looked upon. As she lowered her head and I saw the pigtails and ribbons, she became Patricia Little, who sat in front of me in school.

Yelling and squealing sounded above, and I stretched my arms out and set my chin on the concrete, my eyes straight ahead. I wriggled to the left to avoid looking into two feet which began to raise and lower alternately, like a good swim kick. Trickles of water oozed around and under the arms above me, then from under the legs. My shoulders were the first to feel it, warm and soft. I raised up a little, then squished my stomach back down. Coolness replaced the warmth, and along with it a wave of new sound descended from the slope: The squealing changed to *ohs* and *ahs*, and I rolled to my back as I saw others do; cool water was now in rivulets all around. We sat up, then stood and went the rest of the way down to the crease where the bottom leveled out into a cavernous ten-foot-deep section.

We were allowed to stay there until about a foot of water had risen. Then it was out of the pool and up on the sides, where we played around and waited, watching like sentinels the slow rise of water. *At the first real depth, boys begin jumping then diving from the sides; as the water rises, they take to the two-foot then five-foot diving boards. High-school girls arrive in colorful, tight swimming suits; older boys in flashy trunks. As those of us below them watch, they dive and prance and touch one another, sending their laughter above the rest of us. Finally, as a kind of official opening, Harold Duncan, greased and bronzed lifeguard, will walk the ladder to the ten-foot board, will spring up and up and, with scarcely a splash, cut the water's surface in a blaze of color. And summer will begin.*

That is the way I remembered it from the other two times we were here on the last day of school. But then something happened that would change forever the way I felt, even about the swimming pool and The Breezy.

The water had come up almost to full depth; little waves played in the slight wind and were helped along by the numbers of us. I had fallen in with my brother and Jim, who had been befriended by an older girl from out of town. While near the four-foot depth Jim swam around her like a shark, she stood near the side, a dull look on her face that occasionally changed into half a smile. Jerry caught be by the arm and pointed out the girl with his head. "Come on," he said. "We'll show you something."

I always felt privileged to be included when Jerry and Jim were together, and especially so when they had discovered something new. Jerry led me to within several feet of the girl, who continued gazing across the pool. She seemed bored. So when Jerry dived on one side of her and I followed his lead on the other and we came up at the same time, flinging our hair out of our eyes, I was startled when she looked me in the eye, and I stood on my tiptoes, then treaded water until Jim swam over and told me what to do.

I was to swim underwater toward her, keeping my eyes open (they always were). "Get a lot of air," he said, "and stay down awhile." He'd take care of the rest.

I was all set, when a commotion at the deep end sent everyone scurrying, the lifeguard blowing his whistle, and Coach Carson running out of the bathhouse office. Like everyone else, I turned to see what was going on. Jim and Jerry swam a few feet toward the action, then pulled themselves up and out and ran down the side of the pool. Jim made an urgent motion for me to stay put and, as I took it to mean, keep the girl where she was; but when I turned back, she was going up the steps at the shallow end.

I pulled myself up and out and began to walk to the gathering crowd, hearing as I went that "Patsy Little's drowned." I stopped, seeing in my head the pigtails I had sat behind, the wisps of neck hairs I had gazed at idly all spring. Was the face that had recently smiled so sweetly, so sadly, at me now blue and still?

The crowd parted, and Coach Carson came leading a very much alive but crying Patsy Little through the swimming-pool gate to his car. An older boy everybody called Toodles had gone in after her with his clothes, wrist watch, and shoes on; and now he stood there, dripping, when Harold Duncan put his arm around him, talking to him like an old friend, and led him to the bathhouse.

Suddenly, I was cold and hungry, and I told Jerry. He said he was too, and we started across the street to The Breezy. Jim Collier said he was going home because I let the out-of-town girl get away. Before I could tell him I hadn't wanted her to go, he was gone, just like that.

Jerry was doing the hot tar hop, waiting for a car to go by. I was still on the grassy plot between the swimming-pool fence and the street wall, waiting for a clear shot across, when a chubby, red-headed boy named Lowell came running— or trying to run—from Jimbo Blevins, who caught up with him nearby, turned him around, hit him an awful blow in the face with his fist, and ran on. I thought Lowell might fall over dead, but he just bled through the nose and mouth and cried without sound and hurried away as if he didn't want anybody to know, or to see him.

, , ,

The Breezy was a square, wooden structure, something like a stand except larger. Counters were attached and stools placed around three sides, the tops of which were opened and closed by horizontally hinged panels bigger than doors. It was all green and white.

The aroma from The Breezy made me hungrier, and I made my way quickly across to it and sat on a stool beside Jerry. We'd been at the pool most of the day and it was close to suppertime, but a hot dog sure would taste good. We ordered one each. Jerry added a hamburger, so I told Mickey Bonetta to bring me one, too.

Mickey yelled into the back, "Two hot dogs, two hamburgers, Pop."

"Two hotsa dog, two homboorg," came the reply.

We ordered Grapettes and ate the hot dogs steeped in chili sauce and raw onions and mustard within soft, steamed buns.

We were sitting on the right side, glancing across the street to the pool, not saying anything to each other, when the hamburgers came and Jerry took one and his Grapette and told Mickey to charge for the bottle, he'd bring it back for deposit.

"Where you going?" I said.

"Come on," he said, and took off.

I started to follow him, but was held there by the cozy moment.

Now that I have thought so deliberately about that day, I see myself, a boy sitting there, then as now, although The Breezy, one of my most loved manmade places, has long since vanished. I can hear laughter, yelling, whistling from the swimming pool which is nowhere, except when the picture of it comes into my head. A radio is playing. Mickey Bonetta gives food orders to his father, cooking in the back. Mister Bonetta always repeats what his son says to him—"One hot dog, Pop;" "One-a hotsa dog"—and while we boys have laughed at the response, I sit there now with my large, juicy hamburger and hope for more customers to come so that I can hear the Bonettas' exchanges. The radio announcer is talking about Truman and Dewey againg, and then a song begins to play.

What a melody I heard that day for the first time: a song without words. The dreamy sounds from instruments I could only guess at mingled with those from the swimming pool in a kind of fugue. High-school boys had begun running off the ten-foot board, one after the other, making sounds like large watermelons thrown into the water. The hamburger was warm and soft in my hands, and I pressed everything together—thick meat and onion, tomato, lettuce and pickle, mayonnaise—to make it fit my mouth for the first bite. My hind end was squishy warm on the stool, and I was swinging my legs alternately so that my toes softly touched the wood below the counter. Everything smelled so good. Each bite I took was a delicious mouthful, almost more than I could chew. And throughout it all The Three Sons played *Twilight Time.*

"Two hamburgers."

I had finished and was getting ready to go, but something was not right. There was no reply.

"Two hamburgers, Pop."

I lingered and, after a brief delay, heard "Two homboorg" but with something hard added to the tone of it. Then Mickey spoke to me to confirm that he was to charge 60 cents—62 including the deposit on Jerry's bottle—to our grandmother's bill. I might have shrugged or scratched my head, and that must have been good enough. So I turned and, the instrumental melody coming alive in me, went to the curb and stood looking at the swimming pool, the mountains beyond.

It was that time of day in our town when something like a veil seemed to descend from the sky. It was as if, gone over the mountains, it had left a gauzy net behind, and, as it began to settle, it changed everything below, putting glaze and shadow on the sidewalks and streets and a hazy glow over the swimming pool. Five-o'clock water was all different from noon's.

While the moodful lull at that hour often brought on an edge of sadness, I had no such feeling that day. My encounter with the out-of-town girl had not come off. Patsy Little had not drowned. While Lowell had been hurt by the vicious attack by Jimbo Blevins, he had not fallen over dead but had been able to run away. And Mickey's father had been satisfied by the little word added by his son.

What almost changed the way I felt and would feel about even the swimming pool had not yet happened.

I can see beyond the low wall that Patsy Little is still at the pool, and I am anxious to go over and try to impress her before it closes. Train car couple in big sound across the way, then begin to roll. A steam engine puffs out a large doughnut of smoke, then belches soot into the glow over the swimming pool. I have reached the middle of the street without first having checked for a clear way. Cars driving by in the far lane block my passage. The pavement burns my feet, and I begin to hop from one to the other, waiting for an opening, when I see, through the spaces of the line of cars, a man, on the other side of the low wall, standing on the grassy plot by the shallow end of the pool. He has a bloody rag around his head. He is wearing swimming trunks too tight for him, swaying as he rebukes someone below him. With each hop I make I can see him a little better. Then he turns and, with the mustache, I see who it is. I hop, move up between the two lines of traffic, and hop again, now seeing Jerry cowered and red-faced below him. Coach Carson has stopped his car and is getting out, saying, "What's the matter here? What happened to you, man?" Cars are stopped, sounding their horns. My feet are so hot I need to stay in the air, and where did all the cars from so suddenly, drivers and children looking at me and looking at the man with the bloody rag around his head, who says, "Hit my head on the bottom. Why?" Coach Carson has gone up and over the low wall, and I see him spot Jerry and soften. I turn back, for The Breezy, but it is not there, and now cars are passing on both sides of me, their occupants waving and speaking kindly but not letting me through. My feet are blistered, the soles are slick, and I leap wildly straight up, hoping to stay airborne, when I see that the swimming pool is gone, too. It is that time of day when all things go home, but everything is now gone, except the mountains, and the twilight song.

Something was set forever. A magic was fixed by the song, by the mountains, which had saved me.

➤   ➤   ➤

Every sound and smell would become a switch for a stored moment, each moment an imminent scene. From then on I would fill up with the switches and would never know when one might be turned on. The scenes would range all the way back to darkness, to the ten years before that day that seemed to begin it all, and forward for several years until they stop accumulating. Each switch, when closed, would become a sudden pathway to the swimming pool, or to The Breezy, or to any of the myriad moments when and where my self back there might try again and again to set things right.

Finally, I know why I have cared so much for what is no longer here, how I can with a simple act of will put my other self, the boy, into any spot in the swimming pool, above or below, or even without, the water, into the bathhouse or on top of it. The man's drunken appearance that day changed the way I felt about the swimming pool. It made me love it and The Breezy and summertime so much more than I would have had to. While the man had not come back that day to reclaim anyone, he had reclaimed me, forever. That is why the boy is leaping in the air back there. Until he can reconstruct the swimming pool and The Breezy, there will not be a place where he can go.

And so…he must remain with me.

ABOUT THE AUTHOR

Joseph Maiolo was born in West Virginia, was raised in the Cumberland Mountains of southwest Virginia, and has earned degrees from the University of Virginia (M.A.), the University of North Carolina at Greensboro (M.F.A.), and the United States Naval Academy (B.S.). He is presently a professor of English at the University of Minnesota Duluth, where he teaches literature and fiction writing. His short stories have been published in *The Sewanee Review, Ploughshares, Shenandoah, The Texas Review, The Greensboro Review*, other magazines, and anthologies. Several of his stories and a novella have won national awards, including citation in *The Best American Short Stories*, a Pushcart Prize, two National Endowment for the Arts Literary Fellowships, and three PEN/Syndicated Fiction Awards. Two of the PEN prize stories have been read on National Public Radio's "The Sound of Writing." Maiolo's work has also received a Bush Artist Fellowship and a Loft-McKnight Award of Distinction in Fiction. "The Girl and the Serpent," an excerpt from his memoir in progress, was published by Beacon Press (Boston) in *Resurrecting Grace: Remembering Catholic Childhoods*. Maiolo has completed two novels, assembled a collection of his short stories, and is revising an Appalachian Virginia memoir.

Maiolo has also co-written the screenplays MY TURKISH MISSILE CRISIS and MOUNTAIN, both currently seeking production, and has written an original screenplay, LEIF'S TUNE. His co-written play, *The Man Who Moved a Mountain*, has enjoyed several productions in southwest Virginia; another play, *Once on Buffalo Mountain*, was dramatically read at the Appalachian Festival of Plays and Playwrights at the Barter Theatre in Abingdon, Virginia. Maiolo has written the treatment for *Moving Mountains*, a video tribute to Robert Childress, in production at the time of this publication.

Additionally, Maiolo has written the lyrics to a suite of four songs (music by Thomas Wegren)—folk, classical, jazz, and rock—which has been performed in concert with orchestra and singers.

CPSIA information can be obtained at www.ICGtesting.com
Printed in the USA
BVOW010344201112

306010BV00004B/10/P